THE DRAGON BUSINESS

THE DRAGON BUSINESS

KEVIN J. ANDERSON

47NORTH

Originally published as a Kindle Serial, November 2013.

Published by 47North, Seattle

www.apub.com

ISBN-13: 9781477819463
ISBN-10: 1477819460

Cover design by Cyanotype Book Architects

Library of Congress Control Number: 2013954929

Printed in the United States of America

PROLOGUE

GLORY DAYS! AH, I love to relive the daring rescues, pulse-pounding adventures, and feats of bravery against towering enemies (monsters included).

I am King Cullin, renowned slayer of dragons. You might have heard of me? I've been featured in the songs of many a minstrel, plays by legendary bards, even a few ingenious puppet shows (although the queen thinks the puppets are silly).

My exploits are known far and wide. I make sure of it by spending a goodly sum from the royal treasury on image building and public relations—a necessary but often overlooked part of ruling. And it's a good economic investment: if I make myself seem intimidating enough, no foolish rival will attack my kingdom. Thus, we save the significant expense, not to mention inconvenience, of a full-scale war. Being a king isn't all about jousting and feasting; there's a lot of administrative work even for a famous dragon slayer.

Who would doubt my claims? There's demonstrable proof that my kingdom has been completely dragon-free since the start of my reign.

My long-suffering queen finds my exploits endearing, but she's heard me tell the stories so many times that they've lost their sparkle. Nevertheless, I earned my chops as a dragon slayer, even if by a roundabout way. . . .

Tonight, my anticipation builds as the sun sets. For the excitement that I've planned for myself and my son, I gather appropriate disguises for our night on the town. Since the prince is thirteen and entirely unseasoned in carousing, this should be interesting. For him, a "wild night" means that he lights an extra candle to read by. That's about to change.

He's a thin milky-skinned boy with blond hair that would be unruly if it weren't coiffed so often. His name is Maurice. I wanted to give him a heroic name, something edgy and powerful from the Great Sagas—but sometimes it is the better part of valor to lose the argument with your wife.

I always hoped for a son who could raise a little hell, earn a nickname like Giant-Killer, or Ogres' Bane—even Dragon Slayer, Junior. But Maurice it is, and I intend to raise my boy right.

A father has certain obligations. The prince has to be exposed to reality to balance out his sheltered, fairy-tale life. I want him to be a good king someday: wise, skeptical (although not necessarily jaded), and not easily conned, unlike some of the rulers my friends and I duped, back in the day.

Maurice already believes too much that he shouldn't—and I have a pathological aversion to gullibility. A year ago, I caught him reading a book of beautifully illustrated poems about fairy princes. The special limited edition was numbered and leather-bound, signed by the poet, the illustrator, and supposedly by the fairy prince himself—and my son actually believed those ridiculous stories!

The last straw, though, was last week, when a flamboyant traveler came to court wearing a purple silk shirt and the feather of some exotic bird stuck in his hat. He charmed Maurice with outrageous tales and tried to sell him a "unicorn horn with additional magical powers that were acquired when it leapt through a rainbow." The boy was so enthralled he couldn't open the doors of the royal treasury fast enough. I caught him just as he was about to hand over a sack of gold coins (an entire month's worth of his allowance) to the confidence man. I ran the traveler out of the castle and all the way out of the kingdom. Maurice sulked for days afterward.

If my son doesn't get a dose of reality soon, he'll be eaten alive when he becomes king.

So, I've decided to take him down to the tavern where he can meet real people and hear real adventures. That'll cure him of that fairy-tale nonsense before it sets in too deeply. (I'm no stranger to nonsense, having done plenty of it over the course of my own life, but at least I know the difference.)

I enter the boy's bedchamber, sighing at the pastel window coverings, tapestries, embroidered dragons, stuffed unicorns. He looks up from a piece of parchment, and I see he is scribing the answers to one of those newly invented brainteaser crossword puzzles. Maurice enjoys the puzzles, though I find them frustrating due to the lack of standardized spelling across the land.

Smiling, I hold up the two ragged cloaks I've brought with me. "Time to go, son. You'll enjoy this—I promise." He wasn't enthusiastic when I first made the suggestion, and he doesn't seem enthusiastic about it now.

"Mother says it's foolishness."

"The queen and I come from different worlds," I say. "I want you to learn new things, broaden your base of experience."

"Will it make me a better king?" He seems hopeful.

I think of Reeger and the seedy crowd at the Scabby Wench, the noise, the smells, the bawdy jokes. "Getting out among real people will make you a better leader. A prince is a prince, but you need to be a *person*, too. Besides, we'll have a good time, you and me."

"You and *I*."

I may be King Cullin the Dragon Slayer, but I fear my son will be known as King Maurice Who Speaks with Proper Grammar.

I hand him one of the cloaks, a startling contrast to the fine peach and mauve silks he wears. He runs his fingers along the fabric—mid-grade burlap, dyed with lampblack. "What's wrong with the clothes I have on?" he asks.

"They look like a prince's clothes, and that defeats the purpose. We're going incognito."

"Couldn't I go incognito as a traveling prince?"

I don my cloak. "You need to get into the spirit of this adventure." Maurice struggles into the cloak. I offer him a dried apricot from a pouch I keep with me, but he says he isn't hungry. Nervous, I think.

We leave the prince's chambers and walk past the coats of arms of local noble families. A blank spot on the stone wall shows where we recently took down the banner of Sir Vincent—now indelibly known as Sir Vincent the Ineffective, because of his habit of falling off his horse during jousting matches even before an opponent's lance struck him.

I told Vincent that he can hang his brown-on-brown coat of arms in the castle hall again as soon as he earns back his honor. When Vincent asked how he could do that, I gave him Prince Maurice's signed-and-numbered limited edition of poems and dispatched him on a quest to have the fairy prince personalize the volume. This quest serves two purposes: it will keep Sir Vincent out of my hair for months or years to come, and it will keep the silly poems away from Maurice. . . .

Now as night falls, the town stirs. People close up shoppes, light lanterns, serve meals. The queen has her own dinner delivered to her private rooms: salad, cottage cheese, and dried apricots. She likes to eat healthy, and she's watching her waistline.

When she hears us creeping past—well, *I* am creeping, while Maurice shuffles along—she calls out, "Don't let any harm come to my boy, Cullin."

"I wouldn't dream of it, dear. I'll keep him safe."

"And no more than two tankards of ale, you hear?"

"The boy's only thirteen, dear. I'll limit him to one."

"I don't like ale," Maurice says. "I'd rather have cider."

"I was talking about *you*, husband. And don't go filling the boy's head with silly tales."

"My dear, I am trying to *empty* his head of silly tales. He needs to learn how the world works."

"Oh, you and your old comrades!" the queen calls. "Tricks and confidence schemes."

I hurry the boy down the hall. "Like I said, the way the world works." As I think of her sitting alone in her tower room, I call back, "Stay safe—don't let any dragons get you."

My starry-eyed son is a prince, he lives in a castle, and he has a lot of book learning about the kingdom he will one day rule. His knowledge of the land comes from maps, however, rather than seeing the landscape firsthand. I don't want him to be a theoretical monarch.

He's been taught his letters, mathematics, astrology; he knows all seventeen medicinal uses for leeches; he can write all of the alchemical symbols from memory. He also adores silly tales about honorable knights and their quests. He sighs at the thought of armies going to war over a rose petal for some princess. Such nonsense! Maurice will be a man soon, and it's time for him to learn important lessons—like the dragon business.

As we make our way through the town streets, I reach over and mess up Maurice's golden locks, much to his dismay. I say, "We're on a secret mission now—this is part of your disguise. What if some rogue discovers that we're the king and the prince? He could kidnap us, whisk us off into the woods, tie us to a tree, and hold us hostage until your mother agrees to pay him a ransom. And you can just imagine what she'd say to *that*."

Maurice's eyes go wide. "Why would anyone kidnap us? We're nice people."

"Rogues aren't nice people, son. And if they don't get their ransom, they might snip off one of your fingers or toes as an inducement."

Maurice is horrified. He flexes his pale soft hand. "Which finger?"

"They'd start with the little one just to get warmed up. After that, it depends on how close it is to the weekend."

"What does the weekend have to do with anything?"

"For a weekend special they might cut off your whole hand."

Maurice swallows hard and yanks his hood down over his messy hair.

Reaching the tavern, the two of us stop beneath a wooden placard that hangs on chains above the door. The crude painting shows a particularly ugly and blotchy woman. *The Scabby Wench*.

My old friend Reeger is the innkeeper, bartender, cook, bouncer, and best customer. His wife, Wendria, keeps a low profile, since she's the only woman who works at the Scabby Wench. Across the land, local regulations require inns and taverns to fulfill the anticipated needs of travelers, and such needs often include prostitutional services. Reeger (and Wendria in particular) are not too keen on that, so they named their establishment the Scabby Wench as a disincentive to travelers looking for a roll in the hay. When the name of the tavern isn't enough, one look at Wendria is usually sufficient.

Reeger's wife has a pretty name, which is about the best that can be said for her. And cleavage. That's not to say cleavage isn't *enough* for some customers, especially after a few tankards of ale. Wendria has a square face, a square body, solid hips, and legs that were built for furniture—in other words, she's a perfect match for Reeger. He's no prize either, but he's been my friend since the time I was Maurice's age. Wendria makes him happy.

You don't need to marry a princess to be happy.

I open the tavern door, and the noise knocks us backward like a storm wind. Many faces turn, give us a quick once-over, and conversation starts up again. Despite our clever disguises, most of the regulars here know who I am. Because of my upbringing, I feel more at home among common people than fancy lords and ladies anyway.

The Scabby Wench is your typical tavern, with a great room, a roaring fire, a bar featuring kegs of ale from local microbreweries, and jugs of wine. A high shelf holds bottles of expensive liqueurs for those who prefer fancy drinks like appletinis. Reeger even keeps a hollowed-out coconut for the rare occasion when someone orders an expensive tropical drink, but that's not the usual clientele of the Scabby Wench.

It's payday for many of the local peasants and escaped slaves, so the tavern is bustling. Crowded around one creaking plank table are a dozen mercenaries passing through from some local war, eager to spend their spoils.

Maurice stares, wide-eyed and intimidated. I point to a raw plank table and two rickety benches not far from the fireplace. It's also close to the stage, where the minstrel will perform.

The Scabby Wench is known throughout the kingdom for its live music every Saturday night. I expect the prince will be more interested in my stories, though, because they are *true stories* about how his father gained his reputation, earned the hand of a princess, and won his kingdom. What boy wouldn't be fascinated?

Maurice squirms on the splintery bench (a far cry from the plush cushions of the throne and his lounging chairs), and he keeps scratching in his medium-grade burlap cloak. We both shrug down our hoods.

Reeger comes over with a grin wide enough to show that he isn't the least bit self-conscious about his bad teeth. He carries two chipped ceramic tankards filled with foam-topped ale. Maurice turns up his nose. "I don't like ale."

"You'll like this one, lad," Reeger says. "I watered it down just for you."

"Same price, I suppose?" I say.

Reeger lifts his stubbly chin. "Rust! Of course, Sire—I wouldn't charge you for the extra effort of diluting the brew."

Same old Reeger.

The tufts of black hair on Reeger's head have had very little acquaintance with comb, brush, or shampoo. His brown eyes are unevenly set—which would be unsettling, except that he also tilts his head at an angle, so that the eyes are in line, even if his face isn't.

His rounded nose looks as if it's been broken many times, but it's actually just nonaesthetic. Whiskers cover his chin, but not enough to be called a beard even by a chronic optimist. I call it "hedgehog pattern baldness," which Reeger thinks is witty. His laugh is the best thing about him.

He sets down the two tankards and uses his fingernail to pick at something stuck between his teeth. "About time you brought the young prince with you, Cullin."

"That's *King* Cullin, Reeger. Or 'Sire' will do in a pinch."

He rolls his eyes. "Crotchrust! Anyone who's seen you scrubbing skid marks out of your unmentionables in a stream doesn't have to call you Sire."

"I suppose there's no need to be formal," I say. "Besides, Prince Maurice and I are in disguise, invisible faces in the crowd while we watch our people."

Reeger takes a coin from another customer who is trying to pay so he can leave before the music starts. Reeger bites down on the coin to make sure it's real, then holds it toward me. "Cullin, how can you be in disguise when your face is on every coin in the realm?"

"It's not a very good likeness. How many people bother to look at their coins before they spend them?"

Reeger pockets the coin. "No argument from me . . . Sire."

Prince Maurice blows on the foam in his tankard, moving the suds around but not deigning to drink. I slurp mine, make an appreciative grimace at the sour taste. The beer at the Scabby Wench is so awful one has to drink it quickly.

I'm about to start my story for the prince when the tavern door bursts open, and a wild-eyed man stumbles in. His hair is unkempt, his mouth agape, his eyes flashing from side to side. The stranger's clothes are tattered, and I can see singe marks along the hem and sleeves of his cloak. "I barely survived!" He coughs, heaving great breaths. "Some ale, please! A full tankard before I tell my story."

"You got the coin to pay for it?" Reeger asks.

The man extends his trembling hands. "No time for that—this is an emergency, a disaster! There's been an attack!"

"Rust, there's always time to pay for your drinks."

The people in the tavern mutter. The mercenaries hunch over their table whispering to one another, no doubt discussing prices if their services should be needed in a local crisis.

Reeger fills a tankard from a keg behind the bar and comes back to the stranger. "If it turns out to be a real emergency, then the ale's half price. More often than not, emergencies are the result of poor planning."

The panicked stranger is wild-eyed. "It's a *dragon*, I tell you! Peasant huts burned, fields torched, footprints everywhere. No telling how many people the monster devoured. Somebody has to kill it—we need a great hero."

Gasps go around the tavern hall. "A dragon?"

Reeger yanks back the extended tankard before the terrified stranger can seize it. "A dragon, you say?"

"Yes—on the edge of the kingdom, sure to terrorize the whole land. We must do something!"

Reeger scratches his stubbly chin and gives me a knowing look. He winks before raising his voice to the crowd. "Did you all hear that? A dragon terrorizing the kingdom!" Then he guffaws. Everyone else starts chuckling. Even the mercenaries begin laughing.

The stranger is astonished. "But . . . but we need a dragon slayer! I know a brave knight. We must hire him to slay the beast before it murders anyone else."

"No we don't, lad—and you'd best get out of here before you cause yourself more trouble. Last person who came in with a story like that, I sank him up to his ankles in our outhouse—head first."

"But . . . the dragon." Gasping, the stranger spreads his arms. "Huge. A giant wingspan. Horrible scales. Breathing fire." He seemed to be running out of vocabulary. "It was very big."

Reeger looks at me. I shrug, giving him my tacit permission, so he strides to a large cabinet built into the tavern wall. "I'm not impressed by dragons. Bloodrust, we've already got plenty of dragon heads."

He flings open the cabinet door to reveal six monstrous reptilian trophies. Some of the teeth are yellowed and falling out; the eye sockets are empty. Suture marks show where the scaly hide was stitched back together after being stuffed. Horns stick out from improbable places.

"I know all about your business, lad," Reeger says with a warning growl. "Now run along and find a more gullible kingdom."

The mood is growing ugly in the Scabby Wench, and some of the peasants move toward the stranger with the singed and tattered cloak. His demeanor changes. He looks disappointed, then haughty as he tries to gather his dignity. Straight-backed, showing no further panic or sense of urgency, he stalks out of the tavern as if we are beneath contempt.

As the conversation begins to pick up again, a good-humored Reeger announces a round of ale for everyone "courtesy of King Cullin, the true dragon slayer!" I suppose the expense is a worthwhile investment from the royal treasury.

Maurice remains wide-eyed. "But, Father—if there's a dragon, aren't you concerned?"

I respond with a snort. "Trust me, there's no dragon, son. If I were a different kind of monarch, I'd have his tongue cut out for trying to scam all of us, but I'm a generous man."

I like telling myself that. Truth is, I've been in that desperate stranger's shoes before, and I'm glad no other king saw fit to remove *my* tongue. Now, I'm paying it forward.

The young prince shakes his head with growing dismay. "But why did that man say there was a dragon? What is Reeger doing with all those dragon heads in his cabinet? This isn't like it is in stories."

"Because those are just *stories*, son. The truth is quite different. Let me tell you what really happened, how your father became known as a dragon slayer. In fact, I wasn't much older than you . . ."

Reeger brings the boy a glass of sweet cider to replace his untouched ale. Leaning over, he says in a stage whisper, "What he's about to tell you is true, lad. Just don't let him exaggerate his own part at the expense of mine or Dalbry's."

I shoo Reeger away, glad that I finally have the prince's attention. He's intrigued. "Let me think of a good place to start telling our adventures." I shift on the bench, and a splinter digs into my buttocks, but I ignore it. I clear my throat and say, "A story begins at the beginning—unless there's a frame story."

"What's a frame story?" Maurice asks.

"It's a literary device. Nothing you need to worry about now."

I heave a wistful sigh and let my thoughts go back to the good old days. "When I was your age . . ."

CHAPTER ONE

ASHTOK'S KINGDOM SEEMED as good a place to start as any.

The land from sea to sea was a patchwork quilt of kingdoms, principalities, duchies, earldoms, baronies, and assorted ethnic neighborhoods. A person couldn't throw a stick without going over some border or other. Anybody who could afford a larger-than-normal house called it a castle and crowned himself king.

It was a land of opportunities and a land of geographical confusion; kingdoms were always in flux, and mapmakers had job security.

The kingdom ruled by Ashtok was average; the people were average; the economy was average. His castle had crenelated battlements, stone turrets, and a shallow moat that was more of a landscaping conceit than a significant defensive measure.

On his interior walls, Ashtok displayed oil paintings of stern-looking nobles dressed in clothes from bygone days. The faces in the portraits bore no resemblance to King Ashtok; when questioned about this, he would admit that he had purchased the paintings in a clearance sale from another castle that was being torn down.

Ashtok was particularly proud of the parquet floor in his throne room, polished strips of wood inlaid in beautiful patterns and waxed every morning so that the entire chamber smelled of lemon oil and beeswax.

Ashtok was a slender, middle-aged man whose left arm ended in a stump. He had lost his hand, not in any great battle, but from an infected badger bite. The king had reached into a badger hole to retrieve a button that popped loose from his cloak, and the badger took offense at the intrusion. King Ashtok did not often tell that particular story.

One day while at court, Ashtok sat on his throne, bored. As a hobby, he had decided to work on developing his psychic powers. With his one hand, he would draw a playing card from the deck in his lap and try to guess the number and suit before he turned it over. After an hour with little success, the king decided that his psychic powers were better classified as "post-predictive," because when he tried to guess the card *after* he looked at it, he was correct nearly every time.

The throne room doors were thrown open with a dramatic flourish, and the court herald scurried in ahead of two unexpected visitors. Startled, Ashtok knocked the playing cards from his lap, and when he tried to catch the pile with his left hand, he failed because he no longer had a left hand.

The herald struggled to announce the visitors, but tripped over his words because he had forgotten to ask their names. "Sire, these two strangers from far-off lands request an audience with you. A knight and his squire."

A distinguished knight strode in with perfect posture and confidence. His pointed steel-gray beard was combed and trimmed. His chain mail had obviously seen many years of use but was well mended and maintained. A long sword hung at his hip, and a bright orange sash crossed his chest. A stiff cape of scales hung heavy from his shoulders.

He was accompanied by a young squire, a loyal, useful, and talented lad named Cullin. The squire moved forward, but his feet skidded on the fine parquet floor, because of the buildup of wax and polish. Catching his balance, he stood before the throne.

The knight bowed. "I am Sir Dalbry, Majesty, and this is Squire Cullin. I have come in response to the crisis in your kingdom."

"Crisis?" Ashtok asked. "What crisis?"

Dalbry regarded him for a long moment. "Then it is a good thing I am here."

The young squire piped up, "Majesty, brave Sir Dalbry is a renowned dragon slayer. Surely you have heard of him? The minstrels sing of him across the land."

Ashtok quickly covered his ignorance. "Of course, we've heard of him. I know the songs, though I can't quite remember how the tune goes right now."

In fact, there were no songs—not yet—but that was on Cullin's list of things to do. As he bowed before the throne, he saw his reflection on the gleaming floor—his mouse-brown hair, his handsome features, his youthful optimism, and his bright sparkling eyes.

"It's strange when you tell the story like that," says Prince Maurice.

"Like what?" I ask.

"I mean, referring to yourself as Cullin. It's jarring. Ruins my suspension of disbelief."

I hope he doesn't keep interrupting, because then I'll never finish the tale before last call at the tavern. Since the boy does a lot of reading, I try to explain in terms he'll understand. "All I did was switch from first person to third person. It's a perfectly acceptable narrative technique."

Maurice finishes his sweet cider. The brownish foam on top of his untouched tankard of ale has congealed to the consistency of meringue. "Still doesn't make me believe the story really happened. When I hear you talk about how handsome and intelligent you were, it makes you an unreliable narrator."

"Not unreliable whatsoever." I realize I must be sounding defensive, but I can't deny that the queen would probably agree with him. I wish he had shown some of that skepticism with the traveler selling rainbow-impregnated unicorn horns. "Just pay attention now."

Since Dalbry's and Cullin's boots were covered with mud, they left tracks on the parquet floor. Servants rushed in behind them with rags to wipe away the dirt, then they restored the shine with elbow grease.

From his high throne, Ashtok addressed the servants. "When you're finished there, pick up my playing cards. I need them back on my lap."

The servants hurried to do so.

Sir Dalbry faced the throne with a look of modest nonchalance as young Cullin sang his praises. "See here, Sire—his sash is orange because it reminds him of flames from the throats of all the dragons he has slain." The squire ran around and held out the edge of the knight's scaled cape. "And this is a genuine dragon hide, taken from a giant monster that nearly killed my master. He skinned the dragon after he killed it."

Sir Dalbry drew his sword and pointed to the polished black gems set into its hilt. "These are made of hardened dragon's blood, droplets that fell on the ground and petrified as soon as my reptilian nemesis was dead." He turned the sword so that Ashtok could be suitably impressed.

Cullin knew the gems were simple obsidian, and the "dragonskin" cape was the hide of an alligator sold to them by a swampland trader from far in the south. But Ashtok seemed convinced, and that was what mattered.

The one-handed king leaned forward on his throne. "But what does all this talk of dragons have to do with me? And what is this crisis you mentioned? Shall I call for my treasurer? In my experience, a crisis is usually expensive."

Cullin certainly hoped that the situation would prove to be expensive, but he and Dalbry had to set up their scheme further.

"I mention dragons, Sire, in order to establish my credentials." Dalbry stroked his gray beard. "Your kingdom is currently being attacked by a bloodthirsty dragon. Are you not aware of the devastation the monster has already caused?"

Ashtok looked disturbed. "I . . . haven't read today's newspaper yet."

Although some distant lands had invested in the printing press, Ashtok's kingdom was not yet at the cutting edge of technology. His newspapers were painstakingly transcribed by a group of reporter monks, who took a week to write out the articles by hand and illuminate each edition of the daily newspaper, the *Olden Tymes*. Thus it was difficult for even a king to keep up with current events.

That worked in their favor, from Cullin's point of view.

Dalbry continued. "Peasant houses burned, livestock carried off. There are strange noises in the night, shadows across the moon."

The ladies at court looked up from their embroidery. One young lady pricked her finger with a needle, then gasped as a drop of blood stained the white cloth and ruined the pattern.

Cullin hurried over to the girl, who had a very pretty face. "Might I have that, my lady?" He looked up at the throne, explaining to Ashtok, "Virgin's blood can be very useful in attracting a dragon." Cullin lowered his voice to a stage whisper, "You *are* a virgin, aren't you?"

"Of course, sir!" The other ladies looked away, muttering, shuffling their dainty feet. The girl dabbed more blood from her finger and handed him the bloodstained cloth, looking at him defiantly. "Surely you can tell the purity of a virgin's blood just by looking at it."

Cullin folded the cloth and tucked it into his belt. "Absolutely. The purest of the pure."

The court chamberlain admitted, "I have also heard rumors in town, Sire. The people are frightened. Something needs to be done before there's a panic."

"But why would a dragon decide to prey here?" Ashtok said. "My kingdom hardly boasts enough wealth to tempt a dragon."

"Who can comprehend the larger reptiles, Sire?" Dalbry said with a shrug. "I am an accomplished dragon slayer, references available upon request. I will use my expertise to rid your kingdom of the dangerous beast."

Ashtok set his chin on his stump. "And how much will that cost me?"

Dalbry gestured to Cullin, since the brave knight considered financial negotiations to be beneath him. "For his effort and to cover expenses, Sir Dalbry will require two sacks of gold coins," Cullin said. "I believe you call them *durbins* in this kingdom? I'm sure you'll find the fee to be quite reasonable."

Ashtok squirmed in his seat. "I can't very well have a dragon running around my kingdom, can I? I don't have enough extra knights that I can spare any to be devoured by a fire-breathing monster."

Dalbry lifted his chin. "None of your knights has the experience I possess."

Cullin piped up. "It's truly a bargain."

"Oh, very well. You shall be paid two sacks of durbins—but only *after* you have killed the beast and provided proof."

Dalbry bowed. "I vow to return here in five days with the dragon's head, or I shall never return at all." He turned around with a swish of his heavy dragonskin cape.

"We'll be back," Cullin assured the king before following the knight out of King Ashtok's throne room.

Behind them, the servants again rushed forward to polish the mud stains from the beautiful parquet floor.

CHAPTER TWO

PEASANTS LIVED MISERABLE lives, regardless of the kingdom.

Reeger knew it was not politically correct to refer to them as "slaves," but these indentured people toiled much longer than the standard forty-hour workweek that had been instituted by OODM, the Organization of Dwarven Miners. Peasants worked all year round, from dawn until dusk. They lived in decrepit huts made of sod or piled twigs daubed with mud. During winter, they huddled around smoky fires, red-eyed and coughing because they couldn't afford a contractor to install a chimney hole in the roof.

These particular peasants were so poor that when Reeger offered them a real coin, their eyes went as wide as saucers (not that any peasant owned a saucer, or a teacup, or any sort of china whatsoever). The coin was only a copper penny, but so shiny that when Reeger told the family that it was pure gold, they believed him. Having never seen either copper or gold, they were unclear on the relative values of precious metals.

"Just take the rustin' money and go! It's a new beginning, a fresh start." Reeger tried to move them along so he could be about his preparations. "Leave your shack, the goat pen, and the chicken coop to me."

When a mud-covered boy dressed more in patches than in clothes began to sniffle, Reeger said, "Don't cry, lad." He coughed and spat a lump of phlegm off to one side. "You'll find a better life."

"Don't wanna leave Lulu behind," said the boy, adding another sniffle.

The peasant father explained, "Lulu's our goat."

Reeger considered. "All right, take the goat. But leave the chicken. That's part of the purchase price." Since he was about to build large fires, he might as well roast the scrawny thing and get a good meal out of it.

The father crossed his arms over his chest. "If you're keeping the chicken, then I'll take one more of those gold coins."

"A gold coin for a *chicken*?" Reeger said. "Maybe if it was prepared, seasoned with herbs, and stuffed with truffles. I doubt that thing would even lay an egg."

"It's a rooster," the peasant wife pointed out.

"Of course it's a rooster. Crotchrust, that was the irony in my joke."

They haggled, and finally Reeger deigned to give them another copper coin, the smallest one. "Smaller coins denote larger denominations," he said. "That's the way currency works."

The peasant shook his head in confusion. "Never understood economics. I'm glad we're just indentured serfs to King Ashtok. It makes life simpler."

Reeger urged them away from the shack. "Now then, I haven't got all day. Off you go. Take your goat and don't show your face in this kingdom again."

With the boy leading the scrawny Lulu, the family hurried away from their squalid hut, the little corral, and their small garden plot, which was poorly watered but well manured, thanks to the goat.

When they were gone, Reeger set about catching the chicken, which gave him a more exhausting chase than he had anticipated. He repaid the effort by wringing the rooster's neck with great satisfaction, then cleaned, plucked, and spitted it for roasting. He'd have a good meal after all this was done, but he couldn't linger long. Someone would come to investigate the smoke and flames—which was, of course, the point.

Reeger opened his large sack and removed a pair of flat wooden "dragon feet," planks joined together and cut into the shape of a large, three-toed footprint. Everyone knew that dragons had three toes; anybody claiming otherwise had not listened to the proper tales.

Reeger strapped the wooden feet onto his worn shoes and proceeded to stomp around the area with great gusto. He spread his legs as wide as possible and took long strides, because dragons were huge creatures. He made prominent tracks in the garden, squashing a three-toed print into the soft and fragrant manure.

Once he made enough tracks to imply the monster's rampage, Reeger unstrapped the dragon feet, then removed cracked human femurs, a broken spine, several curved ribs, and even an eyeless old skull from the sack. He scattered the bones around the peasant grounds.

It wasn't a complete skeleton by any means, certainly not enough to account for the whole family and the goat Lulu, but a hungry dragon would have eaten all but a few remnants; the illusion should hold up well enough.

As the afternoon sun dropped toward the horizon, Reeger used his flint and steel to light the dry grass on fire, followed by the dilapidated hovel, and the dispirited plants in the garden plot. When the flames rose higher, Reeger roasted the chicken over the fire. The meat was tough and stringy with a distinctive aftertaste of goat manure—which was to be expected, since Reeger hadn't taken time to wash his hands since wiping down the wooden dragon footprints.

The fire spread across the grass before it died down, leaving singed patches; all the tossed human bones were charred and blackened. The rickety hut collapsed into embers. Reeger admired his handiwork: the peasants' hovel and the small plot of ground looked thoroughly wrecked by a dragon.

The ruins would still be smoldering by morning, leaving a smudge of smoke in the dawn sky, but he would be long gone. His sack was much lighter now that he had discarded the load of bones, but that could always be replenished from any convenient graveyard.

Before turning to go, Reeger pulled out a child's rag doll—well loved, battered, stained. It looked as if it had been used as a teething toy long past the time when a child's teeth had grown in. He positioned the tattered rag doll against the collapsed hovel, letting its head flop just so, and stepped back, nodding.

"How poignant." He picked a shred of chicken from between his teeth and licked his finger; it still tasted funny. He set off to meet up with Dalbry and Cullin at their camp.

Maurice is obviously skeptical. "If you weren't present in that scene, then how do you know what happened? Reeger was the only character there."

I'm glad that my son is less gullible than I thought. I finish my tankard and signal Reeger to bring another one. "I'm telling the story, son—I can choose the format and style. It's called an omniscient narrator."

Maurice snorts. "I know what omniscient means. Mother says you don't know everything."

"A king is allowed to be *omniscient* in his own kingdom. This story is inspired by actual events."

Reeger comes over with the tankard of ale and another small glass of cider for the prince. "Here's your second one, Sire. Did the queen cut you off again at two?"

"That's what she said," I answer with a frown.

"I'll have another one ready just in case," Reeger says and winks at the prince. "Never had any fancy schooling. Some nights I can't count higher than two."

"I can keep track," Maurice says. "I've got my own mathematics tutor."

Yes, he's my son and he'll be the next king someday, but Maurice can be too straightlaced for his own good. "You just let me worry about counting tankards."

Reeger leans over to the boy. "Listen to his story, lad. What Cullin tells you is true, every word of it. I'd never lie to you. I'm a trustworthy man."

Reeger hurries off before either the prince or I can dispute his statement.

CHAPTER THREE

NEITHER CULLIN NOR Dalbry was in any hurry to get on with the alleged dragon slaying. A good scam required time and careful attention to detail, and every step had to play out appropriately. The exciting parts were punctuated by long periods of relaxation—or boredom, depending on one's point of view.

The rumors had been carefully planted ahead of time—Reeger was particularly good at that. Once a few interesting tidbits were suggested, the stories took on lives of their own.

Cullin had been with Dalbry and Reeger for several years now, and he had played his usual role in front of King Ashtok, though little of it was true. The young man was lowborn and had never imagined that he might become a squire to a genuine itinerant knight, one with a coat of arms, armor, a sword, and all the ingredients that constituted knighthood.

Sir Dalbry was no fake; he had a real set of armor, had once ruled (and been scammed out of) a small fief, and he did have noble blood in his veins. On the occasions where Cullin had actually seen Dalbry's blood, however—such as when the old knight had nicked his face while shaving or caught his thumb on a thorn—it looked the same color as his own. . . .

When the two left King Ashtok's castle, the court had been in a flurry. The king summoned his advisors to discuss the horrific monster preying on the land and demanded to know why he had heard no tales of the dragon's depredations beforehand. The chamberlain responded by asking why King Ashtok had not been able to *predict* the dragon's arrival with his fortune-telling cards.

Cullin and the distinguished knight trudged away from the castle, following the main road into the surrounding forest. The only missing detail was that Sir Dalbry had no horse. Everyone knew that a good knight was supposed to ride a majestic mount, preferably a white stallion, but since Dalbry couldn't afford one, he and his squire both went about on foot.

After dark, they found the camp Reeger had set up in a nice hollow among the trees. The three had been here a week already, casing the town and subtly inquiring as to which peasants might easily be bought off and sent away.

Reeger's mule let out a loud braying when the knight and squire arrived. Cullin had never been able to tell whether the mule made the noise as a happy greeting or out of annoyance.

Reeger had strung a rope between two trees, rinsed some of his garments in a nearby stream, and hung them up to dry directly in the path of the smoke wafting from the campfire. He looked up at them with his cockeyed gaze. "Rust! You two took your sweet time."

"Nobility has its own pace," said Sir Dalbry. "But King Ashtok is hooked. I am officially hired to slay the dragon. I won't be able to collect our payment for a few days. We have to allow time for me to stalk and kill the monster."

"When we get paid, we could use some new pots." Reeger used a stick to nudge a battered pot over the campfire where several potatoes were boiling. "I killed a snake, skinned it, and added the meat to the broth. You two eat all you want. I'm not terribly hungry."

"You? Not hungry?" Cullin asked. "Are you sick?"

"No, but I just had a roast chicken before I came here."

Chicken sounded better than snake. Or their usual squirrel.

Dalbry fished out two chewy dried apricots from a pouch at his side. "I'll continue to eat the apricots from my magic sack, which never gets empty." He popped the leathery fruit into his mouth.

Reeger snorted and grabbed his crotch. "I've got a magic sack."

Dalbry rolled his eyes in distaste. "And that is why we can't let you be seen at court."

The other man picked at his teeth, found something there, and pulled it out. "That's why I'm good at the dirty work."

"I don't mind camp food for a few more days," Cullin said. "In the meantime, Sir Dalbry could share his apricots."

"If I do that, then my magic sack will get empty."

"I thought it was magic," Cullin said.

"Magic only extends so far. My magic sack never gets empty because I am wise enough to refill it when necessary." Dalbry chewed on his apricot, spat out the pit, and placed it in another sack on the opposite side of his waist. "I may have to put on a disguise tomorrow and go to market to buy some more."

Cullin found a green twig and poked at the simmering water, the lumps of potato, and the blobs of rubbery snake meat. Their nourishing stew wouldn't be done for some time yet.

Sir Dalbry wore his armor only when he had to play the part of dragon slayer; he changed clothes now into more comfortable camp attire. The companions had several outfits so they could appear as different strangers each time they went into town. In fact, the first time Cullin had met the two men, they were dressed as wandering friars.

He smiled at the thought. How that day had changed his life!

The two men had come to Cullin's town dressed in roughspun cloaks, barefoot, chanting a somber but well-coordinated song. They claimed to be holy friars with a heavy burden and an important mission, and everyone in town believed them. After all, who would lie about such a sacred subject?

Cullin had grown up in a town called—depending on who was asked—Miller's Folly or Honey's Folly; he had been only a boy when the village realized it needed a name at all. He was the son of the town's miller, a good man but a poor accountant, who never seemed to have any coins in his pockets. The reason for this, the miller eventually discovered, was that his pockets had holes in them, and each time he got paid, the coins would drop out along the ground; other townspeople had a habit of shadowing him wherever he went.

The miller's brother was a woodcutter who harvested dead trees around the mill. Fortunately for the woodcutting business, though not for the health of the forest, a beetle infestation had killed many of the trees, and the woodcutter could harvest plenty of wood without going far.

One sunny day, the miller was working on the top floor of his mill with the windows open to catch the breeze. His brother the woodcutter felled a large nearby oak, which turned out to contain a massive beehive. When the tree crashed down, the disturbed bees swarmed out in an angry buzzing thundercloud, seeking a target.

The woodcutter was wise enough to dive into the shelter of the fallen tree, so the bees swept away without seeing him. Instead, they flew across the stream and swooped in through the mill's upper windows. The innocent miller tried to escape. Flailing, he staggered out the open window, fell down into the waterwheel, and was never seen again.

Afterward, the woodcutter harvested several barrels of delicious honey from the hive he had discovered, and the bees took up residence inside the mill. Since they had proved themselves to be killer bees, no one dared disturb them, although occasionally the woodcutter would sneak inside the mill and harvest the honey, which soon proved to be quite a lucrative business.

Afterward, the villagers argued over whether to name their town Honey's Folly or Miller's Folly, and eventually settled on simply Folly.

Regardless, young Cullin became an orphan, with no means of supporting himself. His woodcutter uncle opted not to adopt the boy, telling him that it was good for his character—at age seven—to make his own way in the world.

From that point on, the boy existed as a scamp, finding berries in the woods and hoping that a kindly family of wolves might take him in and raise him as one of their pack. He had heard stories about that, but Cullin had no luck finding a receptive wolf pack.

He did get occasional work in town slopping out a pigpen, acting as a scarecrow for a farmer's fields, or hauling rocks from the quarry for the local castle, which was always under construction. And he was lucky to find the work. By the time he was thirteen, Cullin still had no other prospects.

Then two wandering friars came to town, Brother Dalbry and Brother Reeger. They asked for alms (even though the local currency was called a tuckus) or even a ladle of cool water from the town well. Brother Reeger emphasized that he preferred the alms over the water.

Brother Dalbry clutched a small silken parcel in his calloused hand. "Is there a church in this town? We have a holy relic that can only be given to the most pious parishioner or the most faithful priest. We have carried this burden for a long time, and it needs a true home."

The townspeople gathered around in awe, and Cullin worked his way close enough to hear.

"Of course we have a church—we are a town of devout people," said one man who fancied himself the mayor of Folly, although no one had elected him. "And we have excellent honey, too."

"We'd like some of that honey," said Reeger. "A jar or two, if you have it."

"It'll take more than honey to purchase our relic," said Brother Dalbry. He scanned the curious faces around him. "You'd better send for your priest."

He drank a ladle of water from the well as someone ran to fetch the priest. Despite the people's persistent questions, Dalbry and Reeger would say nothing more about the holy relic until the dark-robed priest bustled down from the ornate church.

Cullin had had his run-ins with the priest before. The man refused to respect the orphan boy until he cleaned himself up, got fine clothes and a decent job, so he would be in a good position to contribute to the collection plate.

When the priest asked about the mysterious relic, Brother Dalbry extended his silken packet, tugged at a bit of ribbon that held the fabric together, and opened the folds to reveal a dark sliver of wood about as long as a man's finger.

"We have come from the Holy Land," said Dalbry, "and endured many travails as we plodded from kingdom to kingdom, bringing this, our most prized possession. It is our holy quest to present this relic to one special church, one particularly worthy priest, in one pious town."

The priest frowned; clearly, he had expected something more extravagant to warrant all the fuss. "A piece of wood?"

"*Sacred* wood, if you please," said Reeger.

Brother Dalbry said in a voice pregnant with awe, "This piece of wood is a *splinter of the True Cross.* It possesses miraculous properties that are yet to be discovered."

The priest remained skeptical. "If the properties have yet to be discovered, then how do you know they're miraculous?"

"Because it's a miracle we survived this long," Brother Reeger interjected. "After all we've been through, we could not have survived without the grace projected by that splinter."

"We must have it!" said the town's self-proclaimed mayor. "The splinter will put Folly on the map."

The priest was unable to tear his eyes from the bit of weathered wood on the faded silk. "We would be happy to relieve you of your burden, Brothers. Rest assured that this sacred object will be prominently displayed in our church."

"Excellent," said Brother Dalbry with a smile. "But we must be assured of your church's commitment. Your townspeople must prove themselves worthy—nothing this precious comes without a sacrifice."

"What kind of sacrifice?" asked one of the local farmers.

Brother Dalbry lowered his voice and said with great import, "A *financial* one. It is impossible to place a value on a relic such as this, but if your people dig deep into their pockets and come up with as many gold coins as possible, we'll deem the sacrifice worthy."

"How will we know?" asked the priest.

"The splinter will know," said Brother Dalbry.

So the two friars remained by the town well, sipping water, while Brother Reeger kept asking for samples of the famous honey. Someone finally brought a small clay pot filled with honey, as well as half a loaf of leftover bread.

The townspeople were atwitter with the possibility that their very own Folly could become the home to a splinter of the True Cross. The people would consider it a great vindication, and a boost to their self-esteem, after having suffered a disappointment several years earlier:

Two men had come to town selling the actual skull of Saint Bartimund, a beloved local saint who was a hero to the people because he had cured sick sheep of a hoof blight. When the two strangers had offered to sell the skull of Saint Bartimund, the townspeople jumped at the chance. Such a relic could attract tourist trade and improve the local economy. The deal had been consummated, the two men were paid, and the town put the precious skull on display.

Just as the skull-sellers prepared to leave Folly, though, someone came riding in from the adjacent village with the proud claim that *they* owned the genuine skull of Saint Bartimund.

The townspeople of Folly grew ugly, believing they had been cheated. But the skull-sellers simply explained that there was no deception, no trick. They were aware of the relic in the adjacent village, but *this* was the skull of Saint Bartimund as a younger man, and therefore purer and more valuable.

Relieved and reassured, the people of Folly sent the men off.

And that had begun a "relics race" in the area, because each town wanted their own genuine skull of Saint Bartimund at varying ages. For miles around, every local church had a skull of the man at age sixteen, or seventeen, or eighteen. Before long, the relics covered most of the saint's lifespan, and some towns even split the hairs down to the months of Bartimund's life. . . .

Now, standing around the well, the supposed mayor of Folly said, "If we get a splinter of the True Cross, we'll have something even better than a skull of Saint Bartimund."

The excited townspeople scrounged up their savings, and by nightfall they presented Brother Dalbry and Brother Reeger with a sack of coins and gems. Even though the church had gold-plated and bejeweled candlesticks, baptismal fonts, ornate stained-glass windows, and gold chalices, the priest didn't see fit to contribute to the collection.

Brother Dalbry weighed the payment and consulted with his fellow friar. They agreed that the splinter deemed it a worthy sacrifice, so they left the sacred shard of wood, took their payment, and departed from town.

The priest held a celebratory mass and put the splinter on display at the main altar. The church was crowded as people took turns gazing with awe upon their new relic, which proved that Folly was special.

Scruffy Cullin, who had watched everything from the outskirts, stood at the door of the church, trying to gain entrance so he could glimpse the sacred object as well. Since he'd been paid a copper coin for slopping out a pigsty that day, he felt lucky.

But with one glance at his filthy appearance, the priest scowled. He looked as if someone had forced a pickle down his throat in his sleep. "What makes you think you deserve to have a look? Did you contribute anything? Did you help the town acquire these sacred objects?"

Cullin had not, so the priest shooed the dirty orphan boy away from the church. Disappointed and angry, Cullin ran into the surrounding forest, vowing to find a better life. The people of

Folly had never welcomed him, and he decided to try once again to find a kindly family of wolves who might take him in.

Instead, he heard voices, the crack of branches, the clink of a hatchet, and he came upon a man dressed in a plain tunic and trousers, hunched over a stump with his back to Cullin. There was a small smoky campfire over which a squirrel roasted.

The man used the hatchet to chip slivers of wood from an old downed branch. He discarded the slivers that he judged to be the wrong size, then dipped the appropriate pieces in the squirrel's blood before smearing them in campfire ash.

Sensing Cullin, the man looked up. It was Brother Reeger—but no longer wearing his friar's garb. Cullin saw the brown homespun cloak hanging from a branch on a tree. "You spying on me, lad?"

From the other side of the clearing, Brother Dalbry led a mule forward. "Who is this now?"

Cullin looked from one man to the other, trying to understand. "What are you doing?"

"Making more rustin' splinters of the True Cross," said Reeger. "Where do you think they come from? I sold the other one we had."

And that was how Cullin had fallen in with the two men, becoming part of their team, a friend, companion, and useful helper. Cullin had learned a great deal as they traveled together from kingdom to kingdom, year to year, selling saints' bones or splinters of the True Cross.

But those had just been small scams before they learned there was much more money to be made in the dragon business.

CHAPTER FOUR

THREE DAYS AFTER King Ashtok hired Sir Dalbry to remove the troublesome dragon, another knight arrived at court.

Sir Tremayne was a very impressive knight. Even though he did not have a dragonskin cape or a sword adorned with hardened dragon's blood, Tremayne had an air about him, as if his noble blood were closer to the surface. He wore thin, flexible plate armor that gleamed like a mirror in the sun. His perfectly fitted metal helmet showed the unmistakable shine of recent polishing, although no squire accompanied Sir Tremayne. When asked, the knight said, "I am currently unhindered by having a young life dependent on my own, therefore I am free to go wherever the obligations of honor take me."

Sir Tremayne's colors of indigo and white looked freshly laundered. Most knights avoided white for their daily fabrics, because they were so easily dirtied by sleeping on the ground, riding through rain and mud, and becoming blood-splattered during fights with ogres, werewolves, or less mythical opponents. Nevertheless, Tremayne wore his colors with a certain panache.

And he did have a white stallion, which he rode through the gates of King Ashtok's castle. He dismounted with a fluid grace, even in his plate armor; he tossed his white-and-blue cape over his shoulder, adjusted the sword at his hip, and handed his steed's reins to a wide-eyed stable boy who had never seen such a fine horse before.

"I've heard the rumors from afar, and I have come to rid your land of a horrific dragon," said Tremayne. "Take me to your king at once."

The stable boy looked confused, holding the reins. "Shouldn't I take care of your horse first, sir?"

"Good point." Tremayne looked around. "Who else can lead me to the king at once?"

"At once" took more than fifteen minutes, which exasperated Tremayne, but as he was a revered knight, he endured with patience.

The castle courtyard was a dusty place where peasants had set up a market. A blacksmith made a deafening clamor with an anvil and scrap metal; children played a game of tag that consisted of throwing handmade balls of mud and horse manure. Even so, not so much as a wayward speck of dust soiled Sir Tremayne's armor or garments as he waited.

Finally, he was summoned into King Ashtok's court. When Tremayne marched across the well-polished parquet floor, he left no mark—to the amazement and consternation of the servants who stood ready with polishing rags. His boots clacked on the hard floor, his sword brushed against his metal armor, but it made a sound like music.

Ashtok was impressed. Now, *this* was the sort of knight he expected to come save his kingdom. The one-handed king set aside his deck of fortune-telling cards and smiled at the visitor, while casting a sidelong glance at his chamberlain. "See, another knight arrived—exactly as I predicted!"

Sir Tremayne went to one knee in a deep and respectful bow. "Majesty, I come to your kingdom just in time. My name is Sir Tremayne, and I exist for honor and for glory. My life is dedicated to promulgating the mystique of the knighthood."

"I am most impressed, Sir Tremayne," said King Ashtok. "I've never heard anyone use the word *promulgating* in a sentence before."

Sir Tremayne regained his feet without even a clatter of his armor. "I vow to slay the dragon that has been plaguing your subjects." He bowed his head, as if a weight of grief pressed down upon him. "I saw the devastation myself, a peasant hovel burned to the ground, blackened bones strewn all around. And enormous three-toed footprints."

He reached into a pouch at his side and removed a filthy rag doll. He shook the limp doll so that its stuffed arms and legs dangled. "Only this remains of that poor family." Tears stung his eyes. "Such a beast must be killed before it murders more innocents!"

The chamberlain interrupted, "And what do you charge for your services, Sir Tremayne?"

The knight drew a deep breath, offended. "I am a knight. It is my duty to slay dragons. I offer my services because your kingdom requires it. Honor requires it." He growled deep in his throat, "I cover my expenses. I am a nonprofit enterprise."

King Ashtok perked up. "You mean you'll do it for free?"

"Exactly. No hidden fees, no fine print . . . although, a bed and a meal would be most appreciated."

The king grinned. "That sounds like an excellent deal."

Just then, the throne room doors were flung open, and Sir Dalbry marched in with his dragonskin cape over his shoulders.

He looked dusty and smudged, with singed hair, but he had a triumphant glint in his eye. He strode ahead of Squire Cullin, who had to struggle to keep up, because of the bulky burlap sack slung over his shoulder.

"Too late." Dalbry gave the other knight a dismissive glance. He and Cullin left muddy footprints on the parquet floor, but the throne room servants were too astonished by this new arrival to do their work. "Mission accomplished. The foul dragon is no more."

Cullin stepped up to the throne, opened the heavy sack, and dumped a hideous reptilian head onto the beautiful inlaid floor.

"Careful, lad," Dalbry said. "Dragon's blood can damage fine wood."

The squire tucked protective folds of cloth under the severed head. With a long snout and sharp fangs, it was impressive and ugly, although not quite as immense as one might have expected a dragon's head to be.

One of Reeger's shady associates imported stuffed crocodile heads from the arid lands across the Desert Sea. To make the creature look more fearsome, Reeger had adorned the crocodile's head with artificial horns made from sanded-down antler nubs.

King Ashtok, though, saw what he wanted to see, as did the Chamberlain and the curious courtiers, including the young virginal ladies who still worked on their embroidery. When Cullin revealed the dragon's head, a cheer echoed throughout the throne room.

King Ashtok rose to his feet, spilling his fortune-telling cards again. "You did it, Sir Dalbry!"

"As I promised, Majesty. The vicious creature gave me a terrific fight. It breathed flame, thrashed its wings, and struck at me with its powerful claws. But my sword and my skill were too much for it! Once I had pierced its throat with the tip of my blade, fire vomited out—killing the beast and starting a small blaze in the forest. I brought its severed head directly to you, according to the terms of our contract."

"Yes, you did fulfill your end of the bargain," Ashtok said, as the financial reality set in. "Our minstrels must hear the full story so they can sing appropriate songs."

"Do you have Nightingale Bob playing at your court, by any chance?" Dalbry asked. "I hear he's quite talented."

"He was through here last month, but we don't expect him back soon," said the Chamberlain. "He's on an extensive tour."

Ashtok proclaimed, "We'll have a grand celebration throughout the kingdom! Sir Tremayne, you are welcome to stay."

Disappointed to be upstaged, the shining knight muttered his excuses. He bowed to the king. "Apologies, Majesty, but I must be on my way, for there are other dragons to slay."

Cullin was eager at the prospect of a feast, as well as getting to look at pretty ladies of the court. Sir Dalbry saw the glint in the young man's eyes and turned to King Ashtok. "My squire and I would be honored to take part in the celebration, Majesty."

Cullin was thrilled by the party that evening. He drank too much wine—one goblet—and his head was spinning. He listened to the music and watched the dancing, although he had never been taught. (And he had a tendency to trip in the presence of a lady.) Many of the women fawned over Sir Dalbry, but the older knight seemed immune to their affections.

Giggling and blushing, some of the serving girls flirted with Cullin. He adored their attentions, but didn't quite know how to respond. He was barely sixteen, and his experience with romance was limited to the coarse jokes Reeger made. (And Reeger himself didn't seem to have much experience with sex, despite his bluster.)

Even with the pageantry around him, Cullin thought of his friend in the forest. Reeger claimed that such finery was beyond him, and he was not interested in that kind of life, but Cullin could picture him outside, looking up at the well-lit ballroom windows and imagining the feast.

He surreptitiously pocketed stolen bits of roast and pastries from the table. They would be smashed by the time he could give them to Reeger, but his friend would appreciate the treat, nevertheless. It was bound to be better than potatoes boiled with snake meat.

Next day at the break of dawn—at Sir Dalbry's insistence, though Cullin would have liked to sleep in—the two gathered their things. The knight graciously accepted his reward, two (small) sacks of gold durbins, which he let Cullin carry. They departed to resounding cheers and headed down the road, on foot.

Off to the next kingdom . . .

CHAPTER FIVE

BEING A PRINCESS wasn't all that the fairy tales made it out to be.

Princess Affonyl had no one to complain to, certainly no one who would understand what she had to endure. Her ladies-in-waiting were tittering girls whose heads were unburdened with complex thoughts. They all found great excitement in stitchery techniques, dress designs, and gossip. Affonyl was much more interested in alchemy, astronomy, and specimen collection than she was in fashion trends.

But her father, King Norrimun the Corpulent, insisted that she meet expectations. "A princess is a princess," he said. "Don't go thinking of yourself as a person." How could she respond to that? Her father told her to pick out the finest autumn gown—it was only late spring, but the new model year started early—and to be content with her lot in life.

After much study, Affonyl concluded that varying clothing styles from kingdom to kingdom was a devious conspiracy. The fashion industry wanted to foster constant demand for changing hemlines, sleeve styles, lacings, bodices, gloves, corsets, or lack of corsets. Recently, a scandal involving the land's primary corset manufacturer had shut down his factory, and the man was put into stocks in the public square for restraint of trade (when his true business should have been restraint of waistlines).

The princess cared little for frilly dresses, and she had no desire to make herself more beautiful for Duke Kerrl, whom she would soon be forced to marry. When she told her father she would rather study at a university, he responded that being a dutiful princess, and then a dutiful duchess, was her homework assignment.

Affonyl's ladies-in-waiting swooned when they thought of Kerrl, his thick black mustache, his dashing features, his black hair swept back in a ponytail, his rich eyebrows that looked like woolly caterpillars on his brow. Affonyl didn't care about him, or about marriage. There were frogs to dissect and alchemy experiments to conduct.

Alas, Duke Kerrl was a man of great wealth and power, and he was deeply in love—with her father's kingdom, which had fallen on hard times. Although the treasury was nearly depleted, Norrimun's land butted up to an adjacent kingdom, against which Duke Kerrl wished to wage war—which constituted the primary source of his attraction to Princess Affonyl.

King Norrimun considered it a fine business opportunity, a chance to get his kingdom out of financial discomfort. Affonyl didn't think much of it at all, and no one else—except maybe her ancient nursemaid, Mother Singra—understood why. The deal looked good on paper.

Affonyl sat in her tower room fumbling with her hoop and stretched linen fabric, dipping a needle and thread to create unrecognizable patterns. The ladies-in-waiting were dismayed by the princess's embroidery, but fortunately she had studied art criticism and learned the erudite vocabulary. She could speak with her nose held high in the air. After pretending to contemplate the tangle of thread, Affonyl would say, "This is my abstract work, a composition meant to symbolize the chaotic nature of unexpected events that can occur in a conventional life. Note the intensity of contrast between simple flow and the disruptive tangles in the lines of possibility. Yes . . ." She nodded, poking the needle and thread through again, coming back up with a cross-stitch that trapped several threads. "I believe I've captured the paradigm perfectly." Affonyl even quoted the maxim of many art and literary critics, that if a work was comprehensible to anyone but critics, then it hardly qualified as art.

The ladies-in-waiting discussed it amongst themselves, and agreed that Princess Affonyl's vibrant artwork hit the mark precisely and was quite exceptional.

Affonyl was not interested in embroidery. She would rather have spent her afternoon reading the many books and scrolls sealed in Wizard Edgar's old library. Even though the wizard was long gone, she had access to his tomes, as well as natural history treatises, astronomical charts, chemistry tables, alchemy tables, and hand-transcribed horoscopes from old newspapers. She wanted to read it all, learn it all.

King Norrimun didn't understand the strange girl's curiosity. He was sure it must be some passing fad, and she would become a true princess, sooner or later. While Mother Singra covered for her, Affonyl played with spare vials from Wizard Edgar's chemistry sets, conducting experiments that often left her with stained fingers and stank up the castle's corridors with the smell of brimstone, rotting flesh, rancid butter . . . or even, once, petunias.

At night from the top of a high turret, she loved to gaze skyward and pick out the constellations, find the fuzzy veil of the Milky Way, or trace the planets moving along their courses. Alas, when she brought her ladies-in-waiting outside to show them the universe and listen to their complaints about the tedium of stargazing, she was reminded of the emptiness between the stars.

She had shared such a close bond with Wizard Edgar, but he had left the kingdom years earlier, and although her old nursemaid was sweet and understanding, Mother Singra's curiosity ended at the castle walls.

Bored with embroidery, Affonyl sat in her tower chamber looking out the window across her father's kingdom: the rolling hills dotted with cottony puffs of sheep, the patchwork of grain fields, the crowded darkness of forests, the narrow river that wound down to the port of Rivermouth and the sea. She let herself daydream about the wide world.

A princess is a princess. Don't go thinking of yourself as a person.

As soon as she sat still, one of her cats—a gray tabby—jumped onto her lap and situated himself, forcing Affonyl to move her embroidery aside. She stroked him, scratching under his chin. The white cat jumped up next, fighting for a position, and was followed by a tuxedo cat. The chorus of purring drowned out the ladies' chatter about buttons and beaus.

"How cute!" cooed one of the young women. "Your cats are so adorable, Princess. Won't you tell us their names?"

"They don't have names. They just come to me—from all around the kingdom, I think. I'm like catnip."

"They certainly like you," said one of the other ladies.

"Of course they like her," snapped another companion. "She's the princess—she's likable by law."

"I like rainbows," said another. "Especially when the colors are in the right order."

"Rainbows and butterflies," agreed another, which led to a lengthy discussion of the merits of rainbows and butterflies. Affonyl sighed. She had tried, she really had, but their conversations did not engage her.

Four more cats swarmed around her ankles, awaiting their turns to be petted.

"Do you like puppies, Princess?" asked one of her companions.

Affonyl was rescued when Mother Singra knocked on the door. "Time for lunch with the king, dearling."

The frail old woman claimed to have served six generations of Affonyl's family—six generations? Affonyl questioned the endearing woman's counting ability, because that meant Mother Singra was either extraordinarily ancient (a possibility, considering her appearance) or the royal family's generations were alarmingly short. Affonyl decided to study genealogy for a while once she finished the natural science tomes she was currently reading.

She left her ladies-in-waiting to continue their discussion of the fine points of embroidery, rainbows, and butterflies, and closed the door behind her before the drowsy cats could decide to follow her wherever she went.

"What's for lunch today, Mother Singra?"

The old woman sucked in her cheeks, which made them look even more hollow. "The chef's invented something new—two slices of bread with a piece of lettuce, a slice of tomato from the New Lands, and strips of fried bacon, all in one big pile. Accompanied by potatoes sliced thinly and fried crisp in oil."

"More fried food," Affonyl muttered.

"And bacon," Mother Singra said. "But at least we might trick the king into eating a piece of lettuce."

"That's a start."

"Norrimun was always a finicky eater even as a boy, never liked his vegetables. Just like his father before him. And his grandfather."

"I'm glad to be the exception."

"Oh, dearling, you are an exception in many ways."

Although Affonyl took care to exercise and eat a healthy diet, her father was called King Norrimun the Corpulent for obvious reasons, and he showed no signs of wanting to get in shape. She worried about his health. Their kingdom was woefully short on leeches, barber surgeons, and cardiac specialists.

Mother Singra led her to the dining hall where her father sat in a double-wide chair at the head of the table, ready to devour a tottering stack that consisted of two slices of bread, then tomatoes, then lettuce, then strips of bacon. King Norrimun struggled to balance his food as he took a large bite.

Affonyl saw what was wrong. "It might work better, Father, if you placed the bread on the top and the bottom, sandwiching all the material in between."

"You may be right, my sweet," said the plump king, "but the last thing I want to see before it goes into my mouth is the bacon, which makes the whole mess much more palatable."

"As you please, Father." She sat down at her own place, and Mother Singra brought her an identical lunch.

King Norrimun wiped his mouth. "We must finalize the formal wedding preparations between you and Duke Kerrl. I can't let this opportunity slip through my fingers."

Affonyl had been stalling for months. "Aren't there complicated legal matters that need to be discussed first? Paperwork, fees, contracts? It could keep our lawyers busy for years." In fact, she had hired additional attorneys to guarantee exactly that.

"It's a simple merger. They have standard forms for situations like this. My kingdom needs this marriage—you understand that—but I want to make you happy in every possible way."

"Except for making me marry a man I don't want to."

"Yes, except for that, but it's a minor detail. A princess is a princess. You'll still have your ladies-in-waiting, you'll be able to do all the needlepoint you wish, and you won't need to worry your pretty little head about politics, economics, education. I insist on making your life simple, without all those headaches. See how fortunate you are?"

Affonyl picked at her lunch. "Father, how long have you known me?"

"Why, all your life! You're my princess, my darling little girl. You're my star in the heavens."

"There are countless stars in the heavens. I could take you out to look at them some night."

"Not much point in that," Norrimun said. "They're just confusing."

"They don't have to be. There are patterns, even maps of the stars. Think of star groups like the kingdoms of the land," Affonyl said. She had tried to educate him, help him, but he simply wasn't interested. She knew what the duke was up to, but her father couldn't see it. "You should study maps to know where your kingdom's boundaries lie, where Duke Kerrl's dukedom is, and where all of the adjacent duchies, princessdoms, baronies, and principalities are."

King Norrimun took another bite of his disorganized sandwich. "I've been looking at maps a great deal of late, my sweet. Duke Kerrl has been kind enough to bring in his own mapmakers to help me. It seems there are some errors in our assumed boundaries. Would you believe that many of the iron mines and the richest agricultural acreage that I thought belonged to me actually fall within Duke Kerrl's borders? It's embarrassing."

Affonyl frowned. "We should hire our own surveyors."

"We can't afford that, my sweet. I'm glad that the duke did it for us." He asked Affonyl if she intended to eat her bacon (he was not interested in the lettuce). "But it's no matter—once you and the duke are wed, my kingdom and his dukedom will be joined into one large happy land, and your children will be heirs to it all."

Affonyl had looked over her father's finances, and she knew the kingdom was weak and poor. Duke Kerrl's takeover was a more polite method than an all-out invasion with his military forces—which he could certainly do. But it was less expensive and more efficient for him to marry Affonyl, especially in light of the fact that the father of the bride was expected to pay for the celebration.

Duke Kerrl had even suggested eloping (once the numerous treaties and legal documents were signed, of course), because that would save money for the treasury he intended to absorb. Fortunately, King Norrimun the Corpulent refused. Affonyl was his only child, and he wanted the finest fairy-tale wedding for her. No elopement would do.

Affonyl also rejected the idea of running away for a quick marriage, because that would hasten the very fate she hoped to escape, and she still had plans to make. If an elopement was in her future, it would certainly not be with the unpleasant Duke Kerrl!

Though her father insisted on making her wear lacy gowns, Affonyl was prone to being a tomboy. She liked to sit on tree branches or to climb the castle towers by scrambling up the tangled vines. She had learned all of Wizard Edgar's chemical and wizardly tricks, and she grasped *reading*, which her father neither enjoyed nor encouraged. "Why read poetry," he would ask, "when we can just bring in a minstrel to do all that tiresome work for you?"

"Why indeed?" She would slink off to her rooms and slip through a secret passage to the wizard's library, where she spent her evenings studying natural science. Affonyl had become quite good at sneaking about, so she could have some measure of freedom in King Norrimun's castle. She explored whenever she could get away with it.

Though not a particularly romantic person, Affonyl had found the man she wanted to marry. Down in the port of Rivermouth (though she rarely went to the seedier districts known as Sewermouth and Guttermouth), she had met a dashing young merchant prince named Indico, who had a fabulous sailing ship with gold leaf on the rails and figurehead. The sails were of colored silk, and his men wore the finest clothes. Indico was a handsome young man with a maroon leather doublet, a gold belt buckle, very tight and very flattering leather breeches, and boots that went all the way up to his knees.

Indico had thought he could melt Affonyl's heart with a smile and a flower, but she was actually more interested in hearing about the places he had visited, the cultures, the landscapes, the species of birds and sea mammals. She even took notes.

After learning that she was a princess, Indico took a much greater interest in her questions, and was eager to hear about King

Norrimun's lands and castle. For the past six months, Affonyl had rushed down to meet his ship each time it came into Rivermouth.

Indico spent many hours describing the wide seas and exotic lands he had visited. He talked about sea monsters, showed Affonyl his charts of the coastline, all the kingdoms in the vicinity, as well as his own island principality just beyond the horizon. He brought her special presents: hand-painted charts of distant tropical islands, exotic shells, iridescent beetle specimens, even a wicked-looking tooth from a sea serpent. He told her how the monster had bitten down on the prow of his ship and left the tooth embedded in the wood after his crew fought back the creature with boat hooks and oars.

He told her the stars were different above his private island principality, that he had constellations all his own. She was fascinated by the possibility, although she felt that changeable star patterns must make long-distance navigation difficult. Indico promised that if she were ever to visit his island beyond the horizon, he would build her a private observatory so she could study the stars all day long if she liked.

"All night long," she corrected.

"Possibly," he said in a voice that oozed suaveness, "but I may be keeping you otherwise occupied during the night."

Realizing that he was trying to seduce her—outrageously—Affonyl giggled, but when she thought she sounded like one of her ladies-in-waiting, she stopped. All in all, she decided this merchant prince would be a much preferable husband than the boorish Duke Kerrl.

Indico's ship was due back within a week, and she couldn't wait. She needed to set up her plan and work out the details for her flight. She'd have only one chance at this, if she meant to escape marriage to the duke. There had to be much better things in store for her. . . .

"You don't look hungry, my sweet," King Norrimun said. "Think of all the starving peasants and eat it for *them*." Affonyl dutifully took a piece of honeyed fruit, which was much too sweet for her. The king was very fond of the special honey from a distant village called Folly.

She decided to try one last time, pulling a father's heartstrings. "As a hypothetical question, Father, let's say I have a friend who's a princess about to be married to a duke she doesn't love. She feels she has more significant things to do with her life than being wedded to a brutish man who wants to take over her father's kingdom so that he can finance his wars."

"Oh, dear, that sounds terrible. Who is your poor, dear friend?" King Norrimun said. "I didn't know you had other princesses for friends."

"I said it was *hypothetical*, Father."

"Ho-hum, yes you did. Unfortunately, princesses have certain obligations—as you know full well. For instance, you're marrying Duke Kerrl because it's best for the kingdom. Fortunately, he's a charming, powerful, and wealthy man . . ." He ran his finger along his chubby lip. "Wait a minute—I think that hypothetical princess is you!"

Affonyl had the good grace to blush. "You caught me, Father. I really don't want to marry Duke Kerrl."

"*Want?* Hmmph, it's your duty. A princess is a princess. Your only other choice is to be sequestered in a nunnery, and no one wants that."

Affonyl considered. "Don't nunneries have large libraries?"

"Being sent to a nunnery is supposed to be a punishment, and

I'll not punish my darling daughter. You are going to marry Duke Kerrl, and that will save our kingdom."

"It'll lose our kingdom, by making it part of Kerrl's dukedom."

"I prefer to consider it a win-win situation. I win, and the duke wins."

"And I lose," Affonyl said.

"Don't think of yourself as a person, my sweet," he reminded her. Frowning, he scratched beneath his multiple chins. "Princesses have been forced to marry against their will since time immemorial, but you could have it much worse. After all, other kingdoms are plagued by *dragons*."

I've been so carried away with my story that I just now realize that others are listening in. They all love a good tale, but few of them have ever heard of King Norrimun, or Duke Kerrl, or that entire subset of my adventures.

Appreciating the audience, I raise my voice as I continue. Maurice, though, is eyeing me suspiciously as the story sinks in. "Now, wait a minute. How do you know that part? You weren't there with Princess Affonyl or King Norrimun. Are you speaking as the omniscient narrator again?"

I drain my second tankard. If we had met the young prince on our travels, Dalbry, Reeger, and I would have considered him a tough nut to crack. "Who's to say that Affonyl didn't tell me the story afterward? A good audience participates in the tale through willing suspension of disbelief."

The boy brightens as if someone had lit a candle over his head. "I see where the plot threads are coming together! Is Princess Affonyl my mother?"

This startles me. "You mean, you don't even know your mother's name?"

"Why, she's . . . she's Mother, and the queen, and Her Majesty."

I sigh. My own son needs more education on important matters, and I intend to give it to him. I sit back on the bench, ignoring the din of the tavern crowds. "You'll find out soon enough. Just let me tell the story."

CHAPTER SIX

THANKS TO THE reward from King Ashtok, Dalbry, Reeger, and Cullin could live high on the hog for a while. None of them owned a hog, although Cullin did manage to leave the castle with some wrapped salt pork.

On foot, the three followed a forest path that led to a wider road. Having seen Sir Tremayne's proud stallion, Dalbry hefted the bag of durbins and did some calculations. "It might be time to invest in a good steed—preferably a white one, but the color doesn't matter. A knight needs a horse. The role demands it."

Reeger rolled his unevenly set eyes. "Crotchrust! How would we afford to care for a horse?"

"Sir Tremayne has one."

"Who knows about Sir Tremayne's rustin' bank accounts? He was offering to slay a dragon for free; maybe he's independently wealthy—a trust-fund kid." He shook his shaggy head. "Fools like that bring down the market value of dragon slaying."

"We have our mule," Cullin pointed out. The beast grumbled and wheezed, perhaps as a sign of recognition that they were talking about him, or perhaps to share his misery at being overloaded with pots and pans, camp gear, Dalbry's armor, and all the "sure to be useful" items that Reeger picked up along the way.

"If I had a horse, Cullin could take care of it," Dalbry said. "That's fitting work for a squire."

The handsome young man sighed. "Back in my village, I always dreamed of being a stableboy with a warm place to sleep and slightly used straw, but that was above my station as a feral orphan boy."

"Let's think about this," Reeger said. "True, a fine white stallion would make brave Sir Dalbry more dashing, but horses come with a lot of hidden maintenance costs. You have to feed them, shoe them. And then there's the saddle—good saddles don't come cheap." He looked over at the knight. "An impressive warrior like yourself could never be seen with a bargain-basement saddle. And then there's the stabling fees whenever we hit a town."

"At least I wouldn't have to walk," said Dalbry. "I'm old enough that my knees and feet ache most days. And it's awkward to claim I'm an important knight when I come into every town on foot."

Reeger flashed his brown smile. "Simple enough explanation, Dalbry—your mount got devoured by a dragon during your last combat. You fought and wounded the ferocious monster, but you yourself were injured, your armor damaged. You fell to your knees and held up your sword, desperately trying to stay alive. The dragon lunged toward you, and all seemed lost—but then your brave steed . . ." He paused, tapping his lips as he thought of a name. "*Lightning* charged in to distract the beast—rearing up, striking the scaly monster with his front hooves! But the dragon roasted your valiant horse with a gout of fire. In that moment of distraction, though, you drove your sword into the monster's throat. Alas, the valiant steed was mortally injured. There, on the blasted ground, next to the dead dragon, you cradled the head of your horse until he died. Poor Lightning . . ." He hung his head, then snapped his gaze up again with a bright smile. "And that, Dalbry, is why you don't have a horse."

Cullin grinned. "Reeger, you're good at that."

They all agreed that a good story was more cost-effective than buying and maintaining a real horse.

The trio headed to the next kingdom, which was ruled by a king legendary for his rotundness: King Norrimun the Corpulent. Traveling through a sparse forest where there were more stumps than trees, Dalbry reached into his magic sack that never got empty and pulled out a dried apricot to munch on. Feeling a certain largesse after his successful dragon slaying in Ashtok's kingdom, he offered Cullin a handful of the apricots. They tasted delicious, but gave the young man such bad gas afterward that Reeger made him walk in the rear, even behind the mule.

As they entered the fringes of a woodcutter's territory, they came upon a wiry man sitting on a weathered stump, strumming on a lute. For musical variety, he also owned a ukulele and a mandolin, which sat at his feet.

"You're a one-man band," Cullin said.

"I am a versatile minstrel," said the versatile minstrel. "My name is Nightingale Bob, known throughout the land for my repertoire, my singing voice, and my witty lyrics." Nightingale Bob was a short, round-faced man with blond hair, blue eyes, and nimble fingers—obviously not nobleborn, but handsome enough and with a pleasing voice. He sized up the three men and saw something in Dalbry's eyes. "I do take commission work."

"We've heard of you," said Cullin.

The minstrel continued to strum, picking out a tune.

"There was never a knight so brave,
when he rode down the lane,
as the dashing knight Tremayne."

Dalbry couldn't hide his surprise. "Why are you writing a song about Sir Tremayne? Has he done anything noteworthy?"

"He believes so." He strummed again, adjusted a string.

Cullin said, "The rhyme of *brave* and *Tremayne* seems a little forced."

"They both have the long 'a' sound," said Nightingale Bob.

"Nothing else, though," Cullin said. "It doesn't sound right to me."

Reeger grumbled, "Rust, if minstrels start singing songs about Sir Tremayne across the kingdoms, it'll hurt our business."

Dalbry pressed further. "Exactly what did Tremayne say his accomplishments were, minstrel?"

"He wasn't specific, but he didn't pay much—only two copper coins. Still, he gave me carte blanche, the sort of artistic freedom a minstrel likes. He says a minstrel is honor-bound to promulgate the legends of brave knights." Nightingale Bob snorted. "He actually did use the word *promulgate*. Try finding a rhyme for that!"

"Minstrels should be able to make a living," said Reeger. "You've got a mouth to feed, even if it's your own. With all the walking from town to town, you must need new soles for your boots every few months."

Sitting on the stump, Nightingale Bob lifted his feet so he could look at the worn soles. "I wish I could afford my own horse so I didn't have to walk everywhere."

"Beware of the hidden costs," Dalbry cautioned. "We were just discussing that ourselves."

Cullin said brightly, "Sir Dalbry here is a knight. I'm his squire."

Nightingale Bob reassessed the older man. "Shouldn't a knight have a shield, sword, and armor?"

"Casual Friday," said Reeger. "These are just our traveling clothes."

"Sir Dalbry slew the terrible dragon preying on Ashtok's kingdom and delivered the monster's head to the king's court," Cullin said. "I placed it right on his parquet floor."

Nightingale Bob chuckled. "Oh, I'll bet he didn't like that."

"We were careful not to stain the wood."

The minstrel nodded. "I thought Sir Tremayne was going to kill that dragon."

"We got there first," Reeger said.

Dalbry was distracted by other thoughts, however. "Now that you mention it, we could use the services of a good minstrel. Would you like another commission—a more lucrative one?" He opened the sack of gold durbins he had received as a reward, took out a large coin, and held it up so the minstrel could see its yellow gleam.

"Now, I do like that color better than copper," said Nightingale Bob.

"Write a song about me and play it often—the tale of brave Sir Dalbry."

Nightingale Bob hesitated, as a negotiating stance. "It'll be a challenge. Nothing much rhymes with Dalbry."

"Hallway," Cullin suggested. "Fallberry . . . you know, like a winterberry."

"Paltry?" Reeger said.

"We should avoid *paltry*," said the knight. "Doesn't set the proper tone."

When the others couldn't come up with any viable alternatives, Reeger picked something out of his teeth. "Bloodrust, for a gold piece he can make up his own rhymes. Just be sure Sir Dalbry sounds impressive."

"I'll need material about his exploits, but you can expect I'll take a little poetic license," said the minstrel. They told him about the dragon slaying for King Ashtok, complete with the heart-rending tale of the demise of the knight's valiant horse Lightning.

To make sure Nightingale Bob had enough fodder for several verses, they told him about the ferocious basilisk of the gravel pit, which was so hideous that anyone who dared to gaze upon it turned to stone. Sir Dalbry lifted his chin, "When I slew the monstrous monster, I felt the splash of its hot blood and heard the groan of its dying breath, but I could not look upon my kill. Alas, my squire at the time, Norby, risked a peek—and promptly turned into a statue. Though I was grieving, I brought the poor boy's stone head as proof to the king."

In truth, it had been no more than a marble bust they had found in some old ruins. Nevertheless, the perfect stone head convinced their benefactor, and so they rode away with the reward.

Then, for good measure, since they still had Nightingale Bob's attention, they made up a story on the spot, this time about the "slavering ogre of Ragnok." The minstrel took notes.

"The ogre story should be the third verse," Dalbry suggested. "But add as many verses as you like, so long as you sing my song far and wide. I want people to hear of my exploits so they know whom to call for assistance with their dragon problems."

The minstrel accepted the gold coin, bit it to make sure it was real, then slipped it into his pocket. He seemed quite satisfied.

"Just for the sake of full disclosure, as an artist I own the complete copyright to the song and lyrics."

Reeger shook his head. "We commissioned the song—it's a work for hire. We paid you for it. We retain the rights."

Nightingale Bob dug in his heels, and they dickered for an hour before resolving to grant the minstrel the rights to the music itself and a nonexclusive but unlimited-term license to the lyrics, while "Sir Dalbry" (as an entity representing Dalbry, Reeger, and Cullin) retained all other rights to the story, adaptations, remakes, musicals, novelizations, and other media, whether now or yet to be invented, throughout the known universe or portions of the universe yet to be discovered, whether mythical, legendary, or otherwise.

It was a good deal.

The minstrel traded his lute for his ukulele and experimented with a tune. Picking out a melody, he began to sing.

"The dragons died,
and the king said Hi!
to brave Sir Dalbry . . .
in the hallway."

He frowned and played with other lyrical combinations.

"Just make sure it's a catchy tune." Reeger tugged on the mule's halter rope. They moved along the forest road, and Cullin kept trying to imagine words that rhymed with Dalbry.

CHAPTER SEVEN

THE THREE COMPANIONS set up camp in an isolated section of forest. They cooked the salt pork in a pot with some dried beans and ate a satisfying repast, although much inferior to the post-dragon-slaying feast King Ashtok had thrown. Reeger found flavorful herbs to add to the pot along with some wild mushrooms that he and Cullin decided were probably nonpoisonous.

While their meal cooked over the campfire, Dalbry withdrew his fine sword, inspected the obsidian chips in its hilt, lifted it, tested the balance. In slow motion, he swept the weapon from one side to the other. He bent down to stretch his calf muscles, twisted at his waist to make himself limber. When he finished his warm-up, he swished the sword in painstaking patterns, contorting his body to make dramatic moves. He paid close attention to his form.

"I hope you fight with more speed than that in a real battle, Dalbry," Reeger said. "An opponent could die of old age or boredom while waiting for that blade to strike."

The knight held his perfect pose. "My father taught me that form is just as important as substance." He crouched, lifted one foot, balanced there. "This move is called Raven on Corpse." He lurched forward, pushing the sword in front of him. "And that's Oxcart Through Mud."

Reeger sat down on a stump and used a stick to stir the cookpot. "And this one's called Frog Sitting on Lily Pad."

Cullin retrieved his practice sword, a workmanlike unadorned blade with a dull edge. Since it mostly remained in its scabbard, the training sword served its purpose. He lifted his own weapon and stepped in front of Dalbry. "Should we practice? If I'm going to be a knight someday, I need to know what I'm doing. Even if I'm not a real squire, I still have to play one in our performance."

Dalbry lifted his sword, ready to defend himself. "Your move first."

Hoping to surprise the knight, Cullin charged forward, flailing his practice sword from side to side. Dalbry easily parried, and the ringing sound of metal-on-metal disturbed a group of birds that had settled into the trees overhead. They squawked in annoyance, but Cullin considered it a fair payback for all the times birds had woken him up far too early in the morning.

He swung again, and his practice sword clashed against Dalbry's blade. The impact vibrated all up his forearm. The older knight just frowned at him. "Swordplay depends on more than just enthusiasm, lad. If you're trying to startle me or distract me with that clumsy flurry, then you succeeded."

Cullin stepped back, holding up his sword and trying to imitate Dalbry's stance. "I was trying to lower your expectations so that you'd underestimate my skill. Then I hoped I might get lucky."

Dalbry considered. "A valid strategy, though not one that my father ever taught me. He made me learn many accepted standards of chivalrous behavior." He gave a wan smile. "Some of it sank in."

They practiced for a few more minutes, but Dalbry didn't have his heart in it, preoccupied by other thoughts. The older knight wiped sweat from his brow, nodded to Cullin. "You keep practicing with yourself. I'll watch from here."

Cullin swished the training sword in the air. "That won't do any good against real enemies."

"Think of it as preparation for the day when you have to fight an invisible foe."

Sir Dalbry sat by the fire munching on dried apricots, slipping each pit into the other sack. His expression was distant and wistful, as if the apricots triggered memories for him.

"In the next town, maybe we should buy some dried peaches or prunes," Cullin suggested after he had worn himself out fighting imaginary invisible foes. "Just for variety."

Dalbry shook his head. "No, it has to be apricots."

"It's about time you told him the rustin' story," Reeger said. "The lad's been with us long enough. He deserves to know."

Cullin was surprised. "There's a story behind the apricots?" He slid the practice sword back into its scabbard.

"Special apricots. The best ever grown on this Earth, from the most beautiful orchard you've ever seen, in a fief that is no more." The older knight heaved a deep sigh.

Reeger said, "Go on, tell the whole thing. If nothing else, it'll help you get into the role."

"It's not a role—it's my history."

"And if you want to get your revenge, then you have to play that role."

Dalbry looked at the fresh apricot pit in his fingers. "I prefer to think of it as balancing the scales instead of revenge, but that's just a matter of semantics."

Reeger stirred the beans. "Crotchrust, don't be so damned honorable about everything! You were screwed, Dalbry. They're all corrupt—that's why I never feel guilty about scamming them. They're gullible. They're fat, lazy."

"Not to mention vindictive," Dalbry added. "I suppose you're right."

"Now you've really got me interested," Cullin said. "I know you once had your own fief, but you lost it. If Reeger can make up a story at the drop of a hat about a dragon eating your horse, why are you hesitating now?"

"Because this is a true story, lad—therefore it's harder to tell. It's a tale of machinations and treachery, of how an innocent and good-hearted young man was cheated out of everything he owned."

"Ooh," Cullin said. "I'm all ears."

Dalbry was raised as a lord and trained as a knight. From his early years, his father hammered into him a solid sense of honor—not that it did him any good in later life.

Dalbry's father was himself a great knight who had fought in six wars and earned just the right amount of praise and respect. When his leg was injured in a great battle and he had to hobble with a walking stick, Dalbry's father was granted a permanent fief, a manageable domain with thick forests and arable land. He built a cozy castle—words that don't usually go together. He married a pretty woman who made him happy, and they managed to make the castle into a home.

Dalbry's father planted an apricot orchard and tended it. Because the retired knight had a good heart and because the land was blessed, the apricot trees produced a wealth of fruit. All year long Lord Dalbry, his wife, his young son, their servants, and everyone else in his fief ate apricots and more apricots. They stuffed themselves on the fresh fruit before it spoiled, then they ate dried fruit and apricot jam, roast pig with apricots, apricot tarts, apricot bread spread with apricot chutney. Life was good. And the apricots made Lord Dalbry comfortably wealthy.

The old man died when Dalbry was twelve. After all of the great battles he had survived, the monsters he had killed, and the villains he had slain with his sword, Lord Dalbry had succumbed to an infection in his finger after scratching himself on a rusty nail.

Thus, young Dalbry found himself in charge of the fief, aided by a freelance regent who offered his services and presented a long scroll of references. In order to "streamline the leadership," he suggested that Dalbry's mother be sent to a nunnery, where she wouldn't interfere with the regent's advice; she was content enough to do so, for by now the very sight of apricots made her weep.

Even at the age of twelve, Dalbry was proficient with a sword as well as his letters. His wise father had ingrained in him that a knight should help other people, show mercy whenever possible, and be generous. Though the fief was relatively small, as fiefs went, young Dalbry had not explored it all.

One day, a bedraggled man came to the cozy castle, claiming that his small village on the far side of Dalbry's fief had been devastated by a flood, the hovels washed away, the fields ruined, the livestock drowned. The village was in terrible shape and needed to rebuild, and the poor suffering people required help to survive the coming winter.

Dalbry's heart was torn by the anguish on the man's face. The story struck him to the core.

The freelance regent bent close to advise him. "My Lord, what these people need is money from the treasury. Gold will help them establish their homes, rebuild their paddocks, buy new livestock, and replant their fields. Think of the children!"

Since he had been raised to think like a knight, Dalbry was generous to a fault. He requisitioned enough gold from the treasury to rebuild the village and sent the bedraggled man away with it. The man thanked him profusely, bowing and weeping. Dalbry thought he saw a glance pass between the freelance regent and the flood victim, but he thought nothing of it. At the time.

As soon as the new Lord Dalbry's generosity became known, other supplicants arrived: people whose villages suffered from a deadly fever, houses blown down by storms, crops wiped out by a mysterious blight. Since Dalbry had helped one flooded village, how could he say no to his other subjects? It was not for him to choose whose plight was worthiest. And so he gave each supplicant an equivalent amount of gold.

Then the freelance regent reported that the adjacent principalities were showing signs of war, and he strongly advised that Dalbry defend his borders. Since the young lord did not know how to do that, the regent brought in a group of his outside friends, mercenaries who were eager to "help."

The brotherhood of mercenary knights demanded in the name of Dalbry's father and the honor of their order that he grant them hospitality. They moved into the cozy castle, taking over the rooms, kicking out the servants, emptying the larders. Young Dalbry didn't know what to do. The brotherhood of mercenary knights boasted about their fellowship with old Lord Dalbry, telling stories of great battles that did not sound familiar at all to the young man, although his father had told him many war tales.

The regent talked about funding the defense of the fief, and he rode off with a donkey and a cart filled with gold. As the young lord rode around his fiefdom to inspect the results of his charity work, poor Dalbry learned that there had never even been a flood, nor a fire, nor a plague, nor any of the disasters for which he had funded relief.

By the time he grew suspicious enough to question what they were doing in his castle, it was far too late. When he returned to the cozy castle, Dalbry found out that he was bankrupt and that the mercenary knights had taken over the castle, the grounds, everything. Laughing, they ran him out of his own castle and seized his property.

But because he was the son of a knight, they dubbed young Dalbry an honorary knight as their special gift before he left. They let him keep his father's sword and armor as well as his name.

As he was driven from his own home, he watched the mercenary knights chop down the apricot orchards and use the wood to build wagons and siege machines, which they trundled off to war. . . .

As he finished the story, Dalbry popped another dried apricot into his mouth. The magic sack looked nearly empty now. He carefully stored the pit in the other sack.

"I don't even like apricots anymore," he admitted, "but they remind me of my cozy home, my heritage, and everything I lost. I keep these pits in hopes that someday I can plant another orchard of my own."

"Bloodrust and battlerot, I always get angry when I hear that story," Reeger said.

Dalbry seemed resigned. "Nevertheless, the experience taught me a valuable lesson and set me on my path in life. Not the path I would have chosen, but . . ."

Reeger busied himself around the camp. "We've got our own work to do and business to attend. We'll get your lands and your orchards back one of these days, Dalbry." He grinned, showing off his bad teeth. "And we'll have fun while we're at it."

CHAPTER EIGHT

When Reeger found an abandoned graveyard on their way to King Norrimun's castle, he could barely contain his glee. Neither Cullin nor Sir Dalbry could drag him away from the treasure trove. "Bloodrust, never waste resources! A good skull and a rib cage are worth their weight in . . . well, in bone. And every cemetery's got plenty to spare."

Sir Dalbry indulged him. "Do what you need to do, Reeger. It is a distasteful but important part of our business."

Reeger bent over the rough grave markers, the worn stones, and the uneven mounds that indicated double-decker sites, communal family-style graves from times of heavy plague. Occasionally, witches and hanged men were also buried in a jumble to keep them from stinking up the forest, unless ambitious medical researchers cut them down first.

Reeger bounded from one grave to the next, counting. "What a haul! This makes my day."

"We all have to dream big, Reeger," Dalbry said.

Reeger pulled out two hand spades from the mule's saddlebags and handed one to Cullin. "Come on, lad. You're well practiced by now."

"A well-practiced grave robber." The young man still felt squeamish, although he had long since crossed the line of things he thought he would never be willing to do. "Once I put that on my business card, just imagine the prospects I'll have."

"It's not grave robbing—it's harvesting materials no longer being used by their original owners. A sort of recycling." Reeger was cheery about the work. "Acquiring items necessary for our trade, thus guaranteeing us gainful employment. Rust! Even the stingiest lord should applaud that."

"Let's not put the question to the test." Dalbry looked cautiously around. "Do your excavations so we can be on our way."

The old knight would not soil his fingers with grave robbing; he made that plain from the outset. Instead, he stood by the mule and took inventory of the saddlebags, ate more dried apricots, and prepared his armor. Though he wouldn't wear his full knight regalia until he appeared in public, Dalbry liked to keep his possessions in good order.

Cullin found a likely mound, stuck the hand spade into the ground, and began digging, sure he would strike yellowed bones soon enough. Early on, when he first started helping Reeger, the young man had eagerly chosen a fresh mound where the dirt was brown, soft, and loose. He thought the task would be easier than digging into one of the older, packed graves. Offering no advice, Reeger had hidden his knowing smile and let Cullin dig wherever he wished. When the young man did strike a body that had been in the ground only a week, the putrid worm-infested mess was such an unpleasant shock that Cullin slipped and ended up covered with worms and rotting flesh.

"Why didn't you warn me?" he had demanded.

"Best way to learn a lesson, lad. Now you'll never fall for that again."

Cullin had not appreciated his uncouth companion's instructional methods, but he did learn. . . .

"Put your back into it. The best bones are usually deep." Reeger began to fling dirt in all directions. "If you work hard, you'll build up those scrawny arms, get yourself some muscles."

Cullin felt his bicep, which was tough if not overly large. "I've already got muscles. So far, you haven't given me the pampered life I was hoping for."

"You'll want bigger muscles, lad. Girls like muscles."

Cullin blushed. "What makes you think I've been looking at girls?"

"Because I was your age once." He kept digging.

The girls in King Ashtok's court certainly hadn't snubbed him, and Cullin knew he was halfway handsome once he cleaned himself and put on his best squire clothes. But by digging down into a muddy grave, there wasn't much chance of him getting cleaned up.

When he was just a boy, back when his father was still alive at the mill and his uncle chopped down trees that were not infested with killer bees, Cullin had been content, with few aspirations. His future had looked clear and stable, and he was sure he'd grow up to be the town's next miller. By age seven, he had learned how to haul sacks of grain, how to watch the millstones, and how to pinch just the right amount of flour from a customer's load so the loss would never be noticed.

Now all that had changed, though, and Cullin had different dreams—none of which included digging up old graves to acquire bones for a long-running scam.

"Found a femur!" Reeger said. "That's a good start."

Cullin kept digging, loosening the dirt with his shovel and then moving clods with his fingers. He realized he had uncovered a skull when he accidentally stuck his hand into the bony mouth and knocked loose an old tooth. "Skull here! That trumps your femur."

"I've got three rustin' vertebrae and a pelvis—ha!"

They both continued digging while keeping score.

"Now that we've got the reward money from King Ashtok," Cullin mused, "what should we do with it—so we don't spend it all commissioning songs from minstrels?"

"One song," Dalbry said. "Hardly an extravagant expense. We're still wealthy."

At the moment, busy digging up a broken skull, Cullin didn't feel wealthy. He often mused about taking his share of profits from the dragon business and going to the port city of Rivermouth, where he would book passage to the New Lands—not volunteer as a cabin boy, but pay for a real stateroom and his very own chamber pot to puke in if he got seasick. Cullin longed to seek his fortune in the New Lands, where the whole continent was free and available, with plenty of homesteads for the taking.

Someday, he wanted to have his own farm, set up his own cottage, plant his own fields, find himself a wife, and lead a happy and comfortable life. But such a sea passage was expensive, and dragon slaying—especially when the proceeds were shared with two others—wasn't as lucrative as most people thought it was.

Sir Dalbry was in charge of the budget. First and foremost, he set aside a portion for their own needs; afterward, because it could never be washed out of him despite his many disappointments, the old knight gave some of their coins to genuinely poor and desperate peasants or orphans. After his years of experience with cons and scams, Dalbry was no longer so easily fooled.

Reeger was more interested in hitting each town's taverns. He would talk to the innkeepers, the barmaids, and the patrons—and not just as part of setting up their next scheme. He was interested in the business aspects of tavern administration. "Someday I might settle down. No harm in that. I want an inn of my own, and I'll need to know how to manage it."

Neither Cullin nor Dalbry believed it would come to pass, but the young man didn't mock his friend for having unrealistic dreams, because he had plenty of his own.

While excavating his second grave, Cullin yelped with delight. "A full rib cage—intact!"

"Skull, too?" Reeger asked.

"Skull, too."

The other man came over to pat him on the back, getting graveyard dirt on his tunic. "You are my true protégé, lad. Crotchrust! Someday you'll be just like me. Every young man needs high hopes."

Cullin wanted to aim higher than that, but since it was a happy moment, he didn't complain.

Reeger retrieved the large sack from the mule's saddlebags and held it open. "Put the femurs on the bottom and then the rib cage. Skulls go on top."

Cullin was no longer squeamish at all. "How did you get to be so good at this, Reeger?"

"Plenty of practice. Been doing it a long time." Although his hands were covered with grave dirt and a few smeared earthworms, he plucked something from between his teeth. "Where do you think all those bones of Saint Bartimund came from? The ones we sold to your old town of Folly."

"I suppose they had to come from somewhere," Cullin admitted.

"The world is full of opportunities." He tossed up another skull and a fibula that might prove useful. "Never pass up a good skeleton."

By the mule, Sir Dalbry watched the activity. "Sometimes one must do what has to be done."

"A job is a job." Reeger spat. "I've been a ditchdigger, a manure hauler, even a manure hauler in a *swamp*, which is far worse—take my word for it."

Cullin rearranged the bones in the large sack. "I'd think being a ditchdigger in a swamp would be worse."

"Done that, too, lad. Bloodrust and battlerot, it's no fun, believe me. One of the worst jobs, though, was my stint as a latrine refurbisher."

Cullin wiped his hands on his trousers. "Sounds exciting. What is it?"

Reeger put his hands on his hips. "Oh, some lord has a nice latrine in a perfect place—maybe with a good view from the wooden seat, or a confluence of fresh breezes that makes the entire latrine-going experience a pleasant one. But lords, being lords, are so full of shit that they fill up those latrines faster than you might imagine. Rather than having a new one dug, which would upset the feng shui of the outhouse placement, they hire a professional—someone like me—to empty and refurbish the latrine, good as new."

Cullin understood. "And that's how you got a job as a manure hauler."

"Rust! Not just any manure either. I only sold guaranteed *noble* manure. I even advertised that it smelled like roses and was filled with little gold flakes, if a customer took the time to sift through it."

"Was there gold in it?" Cullin asked. "Did you sift through it yourself?"

"I wouldn't fall for that, but I did convince quite a few

customers to try. Ah, you should have seen the looks of disappointment on their faces."

Dalbry said, "Reeger, you sound nostalgic. Are you trying to say those were the good old days?"

"Not at all." He cinched the bone sack tight, adjusted the saddle on the mule, which brayed in either appreciation or complaint. "I'm just saying this job is no worse than other career opportunities I've had."

"The castle and town are just ahead. It's about time we make our separate ways," Dalbry said. "I shall learn the politics at court, and how best to sell our services to King Norrimun the Corpulent. Cullin will acquire provisions—nothing too expensive."

"And what are you going to do, Reeger?" Cullin asked.

"Got some reconnoitering to do, ply the peasants for information, spread some rumors. First, though, I've got to find a suitable dragon's lair."

In order to drum up business at the Scabby Wench, Reeger and Wendria advertise live music on Saturday nights. Wendria wants to attract a different sort of clientele for the tavern, while Reeger's just interested in selling more ale and questionable meat pies. (The pies are fine, but the meat is questionable. Still, we ate plenty of unusual game when our group traveled the land; we settled for whatever we could catch or dig up in between alleged dragon slayings.)

Tonight, this is going well. I'm just getting to the part of my story about Princess Affonyl, King Norrimun the Corpulent, Duke Kerrl, and that whole business with dragons and treachery. I don't mind the few eavesdroppers listening to my tale, but they are all restless for the minstrel to arrive.

Hob Nobbin is set to play tonight.

On weekday afternoons, Reeger endures minstrel auditions, lining up acts. Since the Scabby Wench pays half a pittance for each performance, he can only book minstrels who aren't ready for prime time on the main stages inside a king's court—even my own court.

As the hour grows later, the people in the tavern are emptying their tankards slowly, drawing the ale out so it lasts until the performance starts. And the minstrel is late, which does not please Reeger at all. He has little patience for prima donna acts, minstrels with some talent but questionable punctuality. Wendria is in the back making more pies and scraping leftovers from wooden plates (to make more pies).

Because of Hob Nobbin, many of tonight's customers are younger women, buxom bakers' girls, seamstresses, candlemakers' daughters. Though I've never heard of him before, I realize the minstrel must be one of those teen idol acts—not my favorite, but then most minstrel songs are a load of crap, sometimes sweetened with flecks of gold . . . like the noble manure Reeger once sold.

Hob Nobbin finally throws open the tavern door and casually strolls in. He's a wisp of a boy with stringy tangled hair, pale skin, and altogether too much angst, but the young girls seem to find that attractive.

Thank heavens Prince Maurice hasn't turned out like that. I can tolerate a bookish dreamer, someone with imagination but innocent in the ways of the world, but I despise those depressing existentialist "life is a vale of tears and then you die" bores.

A collective, though high-pitched and feminine, gasp goes through the crowd as Hob Nobbin regards the venue. He has a battered lute over his shoulder, rumpled clothes, and poor hygiene that probably started out as an affectation, or maybe out of necessity, but now has become part of his distinctive "look."

"It's about rustin' time!" Reeger pushes through the crowd to meet the minstrel and herds him toward the stage without further ado.

Prince Maurice looks at the young singer, and his eyes sparkle. "Now we'll have some real entertainment."

I frown. "I haven't finished my story yet."

"I meant, some *more* entertainment, Father." Maurice is blushing.

The minstrel sits on a stool, crosses his gangly legs, and props his lute on a knee. He strums, picking out a melody that's not familiar to me. The candlemaker's daughter and the baker's girl both sigh. "I love that one!"

Hob Nobbin doesn't deign to raise his eyes; he pays them no attention whatsoever with a studied indifference, which only seems to encourage his audience.

I lean closer to Maurice. "I can keep talking while he's warming up."

But the minstrel doesn't seem to care about practicing his voice or tuning his lute. He requests a tankard of ale, but Reeger will give him only water until he finishes his first set. Hob Nobbin begins to sing a ridiculous ballad about a blond-haired knight and a quest across seven lands and seven seas to find the perfect raspberry for his lady to garnish her breakfast cereal. Somehow, the raspberry remained fresh and sweet over the years of the knight's travails.

Even more unbelievable, the crowd loves the song and applauds, whistles, and cheers. Maurice pays rapt attention.

I just roll my eyes. "You know life isn't like that."

"Don't ruin the entertainment, Father," my son says. "Don't you have any imagination? Any sense of wonder?"

I blink at him. Hasn't he been listening?

During the lull, I call toward the stage, "I've got a request. Do you know 'The Tale of Brave Sir Dalbry'?"

"Never heard of him." The minstrel looks at me as if I am no more than a green bottle fly on a pile of dung. "And I don't do requests."

He plays another song. I make a mental note to inform the queen that we will not be hiring this particular minstrel at court. Ever.

CHAPTER NINE

AFTER CULLIN FINISHED procuring their supplies, carefully adhering to the number of gold durbins in his budget, he went to find the town's primary tavern for his rendezvous with Sir Dalbry.

The older knight had donned his armor and orange sash, although he left his alligator-skin cape behind because he didn't want to draw too much attention to himself, not yet. Cullin again played the part of Dalbry's loyal squire. Reeger was already in the tavern, one hour and two tankards ahead of them, but they pretended not to know one another. Reeger hunched at a table, chatting with patrons, getting information about local legends and geography.

Dalbry and Cullin each ordered the pewter-plate special, a dry loaf of bread soaked with lumpy gravy. Everyone could see that Dalbry was a knight, but he didn't introduce himself by name. "I came to your kingdom because of the troubles," he said to no one in particular.

"We have troubles?" asked a large blacksmith who sipped from a tiny glass of white wine.

Dalbry turned to the blacksmith, amazed. Cullin took his cue and piped up, "The dragon, of course! A big nasty one wreaking havoc all over the countryside."

"Haven't heard anything about that," grumbled the blacksmith and took another delicate sip, extending his pinky into the air as he did so.

"No surprise—all the witnesses were eaten and burned, or burned and eaten . . . it's hard to determine the exact order," Sir Dalbry said. "But I assure you, it's true. I've seen the evidence."

From his table, Reeger coughed loudly. "I've heard of the attacks. Shepherd's cottages burned to the ground, flocks devoured in a single night. I came by one such place—you wouldn't believed the stench of roast mutton and burned wool in the air." His face twisted in disgust.

As the uneasy people mumbled into their tankards, Cullin sopped up the lumpy gravy with his bread and assessed the room. At one table a group of rangy men—by the look of them, they were professional cutthroats, not amateurs—played a game with dagger points, spread fingers, and optimistic coordination. When one cutthroat's finger was sliced open, to howls of laughter from his comrades, they paused the game long enough to use the leaking blood to draw a smeared map on the wooden tabletop. They discussed their next scheme before scraping away the evidence with the edge of the knife.

At another table, a man ran a game of chance with fast hands, three small half-skulls, and a hard-boiled egg. He placed the egg under one skull then spun it around, mixing it up with the other two skulls, jabbering all the time to distract his marks. He switched and slid the skulls back and forth, around one another, toward himself, then away. Then his audience placed bets, guessing which skull hid the egg. The observers lost every time, even though Cullin could plainly see the egg through the gaping molar socket in one skull.

Outside, a ragamuffin rube from the countryside led a cow so scrawny that rows of ribs protruded and its udder hung like an empty glove. The young rube had spiky hair, a straw hat, a freckled face, and a broad astonished grin. Obviously, he'd never been to the big city before.

As soon as he arrived at the tavern and tied the family cow to a post outside, the people inside the tavern perked up, sensing an easy mark. The man with the skulls and the hard-boiled egg was so distracted by such a golden opportunity that he slipped up, and one of his marks guessed the correct skull. The winner claimed the hard-boiled egg as a prize, which he ate, thereby ending the game.

Before anyone else could make a move on the rube and his cow, another fast-talker got there. He hurried over to the grinning country boy, pulled a pouch from his waist, and began extolling the virtues of his rare collectors' edition magic beans.

The rube's eyes went wide. "Magic beans?" He held out a hand to look at them. "They look like normal beans."

"That's part of their magic—the power of disguise," said the fast-talker. "See, it's proof of what I'm saying."

The fascinated rube listened to the story about the magic beans, while Cullin eavesdropped, looking for pointers, since this man seemed to be a master. Before long, the fast-talker shook the rube's hand and walked back out of the tavern. The fast-talker took the cow's halter rope and led the beast away toward the town's butcher shop and tannery.

The rube regarded the three beans in his hand with reverence and awe. He looked so thrilled with his good fortune that Cullin shook his head at the young man's gullibility. Sir Dalbry appeared disheartened, but resigned. "Our scheme will do well in this place, Cullin. These people will believe anything."

Reeger left his table, saying he had to go to the outhouse to drain some of his ale. He walked past Cullin and Dalbry, feigning drunkenness (or maybe not feigning it). He stumbled into their table, leaned close, and said, "I've learned what I need. There's a haunted cave in the hills nearby. The locals call it Old Snort. Foul smoke and vapors, scary sounds."

"Sounds like a real dragon's lair," Cullin said.

"Definitely something I can work with," Reeger said. "I'll tell you more back in camp after I've had a look."

He staggered out the tavern door, and Sir Dalbry continued to hold forth about the rampages of dragons. "My former kingdom was plagued by the creatures. The fields, orchards, and forests were laid waste, burned to the ground, my people killed! That's why I'm a wandering knight—I vowed to walk the Earth and never rest until I've slain the last of the foul reptiles."

The wide-eyed rube listened, his mouth half open. "Would magic beans help?"

Frowning, Dalbry took pity on the young man. "Why, yes, I think they might—I'll buy them from you." He reached into the pouch, counting how many gold durbins remained of Ashtok's reward. While Cullin groaned, Dalbry paid the rube more coins than his scrawny family cow would ever have been worth. "Take this money back home; use it to keep your family fed and warm throughout the winter."

The rube clutched the gold coins and said, "I'm just glad I

could help you slay dragons. Those magic beans are very powerful, or so I've been told."

With a somber nod, Sir Dalbry pocketed the beans. "Yes, they are. I'll count on them to protect me from a monstrous attack."

The rube left the tavern, light on his feet.

Upset, Cullin leaned toward him and kept his voice down. "Why did you do that? That was our reward money! It could have helped me buy passage to the New Lands."

"That poor young man was cheated. Sometimes a good deed is more important than a few extra coins." Dalbry was content with his choice. "We'll earn more money."

A minstrel entered the tavern, and Cullin recognized Nightingale Bob with his lute, ukulele, and mandolin. He said, "I'm here to perform my first set, matinee show."

The people in the tavern shifted their benches and stools, and the barmaid poured more tankards of ale. The minstrel gave Sir Dalbry a knowing smile, took his seat, and started singing the still-rough lyrics of "The Tale of Brave Sir Dalbry."

The rhymes didn't work, but the song captivated the audience nevertheless. They had never heard of Sir Dalbry, but soon they would repeat the story throughout the town. Cullin saw the glow of pride in Dalbry's eyes. The old knight folded his hands on the table. "Yes, I think we'll do well here."

Though Cullin had consumed only a small glass of ale, he felt the need to pee and excused himself, heading out the door for the outhouse marked "Customers Only." A few minutes later, he emerged with an empty bladder and sore lungs from holding his breath against the stench of the pit. Reeger could have sold his services to refurbish the latrine.

Before re-entering the tavern, though, he was surprised to see the rube with his straw hat meet up with the fast-talker who led the scrawny cow. Both were smiling. After the rube held up the coins Dalbry had given him, they high-fived each other and strolled out of the town together, taking the cow with them.

When he went back inside, Cullin decided not to mention the incident to Sir Dalbry.

CHAPTER TEN

WHEN THEY ENTERED the court of King Norrimun the Corpulent, Cullin adjusted Sir Dalbry's dragonskin cape and his apricot-colored sash. The knight had spent the previous evening getting into his role, reshaping his personality as the honor-bound knight he would have been, if his life had turned out differently.

By now, rumors of a monstrous dragon had spread. In the tavern, Nightingale Bob had played "The Tale of Brave Sir Dalbry" twice more for an encore, and magician-entrepreneurs were designing and selling dragon-proof charms. The blacksmith (who had finally finished his dainty glass of white wine) went to his shop to make armor and swords to equip what would surely be a rush of eager dragon slayers coming to save the kingdom.

Sir Dalbry and his squire entered the court, where bearded King Norrimun reclined on his special double-wide throne. Cullin looked at the princess who sat beside the throne and was smitten in an instant.

Her name was Affonyl—a willowy young woman who looked like a fairy princess in a lacy blue gown. Her blond hair hung in a long braid down her back, like straw that had already been spun into gold. Four cats prowled around her feet, two more on her lap, and she took care to stroke each one, although she wore an absent expression as she did so.

Courtiers, ladies, lordlings, wannabe knights, an ancient matronly woman, and other staff members hovered in King Norrimun's hall. They listened as Dalbry and Cullin presented their case about the horrible dragon. The knight drew his sword and said, "I have come, therefore, to offer my services as a dragon slayer, Majesty. You'll find my fee to be quite reasonable, in light of the terror and destruction the monster has already caused."

King Norrimun stroked his curly beard. "While that's very kind of you, Sir Dalbry, my kingdom is currently experiencing financial difficulties. I've had to impose austerity measures, limiting feasts to once a week—which is quite a hardship, believe me." He patted his stomach.

"But what about the dragon, Majesty?" Cullin said. "You must think of your people."

"I have everything under control. We are in the process of an important merger that will greatly benefit the economy, but right now we can't afford to hire the services of a dragon slayer."

"Our prices are quite reasonable," Dalbry said. "Satisfaction guaranteed."

Norrimun continued, "Just yesterday the itinerant knight Sir Tremayne offered to kill our pesky dragon as part of his knightly duty, and to . . ."—the king paused, snapping his fingers as he searched for the word—"and to *promulgate* the mystique of knighthood throughout the land."

"I know Sir Tremayne," Dalbry said in a clipped voice. "So you've dispatched him to slay the creature? How much did he charge?"

"We couldn't reach an agreement, but it was not necessary. I have my own champion on staff—Sir Phineal. And dealing with any dragon problems that might arise in the kingdom is part of his job description. Since we're already paying his salary, it's easier on the treasury not to engage other services."

At the edge of the room a skittish knight cleared his throat and stepped forward with all the confidence of a poet facing a horde of ogres in single-handed combat. "It—it is my duty, Sire. I have always w-wanted to slay a dragon, never got the ch-chance."

"Dragon slaying is a skilled profession. It shouldn't be left to chance," Cullin interrupted, though he knew Sir Dalbry was supposed to do the talking. "If Sir Phineal is your champion, then let him try, by all means, but my Sir Dalbry is the greatest dragon slayer of all. I'm sure you've heard the songs about him?"

King Norrimun touched his lip. "No, I can't say that I have."

Cullin couldn't tear his eyes from Princess Affonyl, although she hadn't actually noticed him, which only made her all the more desirable. He suddenly felt bold. "If cost is an issue, then instead of a fee, perhaps whoever slays the dragon could win the hand of Princess Affonyl in marriage?"

"Slay a dragon and win my daughter's hand?" Norrimun spluttered. "How *medieval*!"

Now the young woman looked at Cullin for the first time, and his heart leaped. A calculating look came to her eyes. "It might be worth considering, Father. Wouldn't you rather have your daughter marry a famed dragon slayer than any old duke?"

"Not any old duke, my sweet, but a wealthy and powerful one." Norrimun shook his head and looked at Cullin. "Princess Affonyl is already betrothed, young man. We're looking into that new-fangled printing press so we can send out wedding announcements, since it's so costly to hire the monks' transcription services."

Sir Phineal cleared his throat, looked longingly at Dalbry, then turned to the king. "Isn't tonight a f-feast night, Sire?"

Norrimun sighed. "Every night *used to be* a feast night . . . but yes, it is the feast of Saint Bartimund. Sir Tremayne will still be here. Perhaps you and your squire would join us at dinner, Sir Dalbry?"

"We would be honored, Your Majesty."

Mother Singra, the ancient nursemaid, turned and shuffled at the speed of a glacier out of the throne room. "I will see that two more places are set."

By now, with most of their durbins spent, neither of them would turn down a large meal. Cullin planned to squirrel away enough food to keep Reeger happy. More importantly, he was glad for the chance to keep making eyes at Princess Affonyl, in hopes that she would ignore him again to show how much she cared.

As Cullin and Dalbry washed themselves in the courtyard using water from a bucket, the older knight gave him a curious look. "What was all that about? You've never shown interest in marrying a princess before."

"You and Reeger taught me to be ambitious." Cullin splashed water on his face. "I, um, was hoping I could be the one to slay the dragon this time and earn my chops, present the head to King Norrimun."

Dalbry's gray eyebrows shot up as he understood. "You think the princess is pretty!"

"And she likes me, too—I can tell by the cute way she ignored me. Think about it. If I marry the princess, then we have

Norrimun's kingdom. I'll live in the castle, and I can hire you to be my number one knight."

"And what about Reeger?"

"Oh, he'll be number two."

"Reeger's not a knight and could never pass for one."

Cullin shook his head. "Not my number two knight, just *number two*. We could set him up with his own tavern like he always talks about."

"An interesting scheme, though I wish you'd consulted me about it first."

"It just came to me. I had to improvise."

Dalbry clapped his hand on Cullin's shoulder. "Well, nothing to be ashamed of—it showed initiative, but in this particular case it won't do us any good. King Norrimun seems to be fond of the coins in his treasury or all too aware of how little money he has." He made a slow turn so Cullin could inspect him. "How do I look? Good enough for the evening's feast?"

"Dashing as always, Sir Dalbry. And what about me?" He ran his hands through his hair, brushed the dust off his tunic.

"You look like a scamp, and you need a haircut."

"I'm aiming for the roguish look," Cullin said. "Girls like the bad boys."

"Good luck with that, lad, but the princess looks to be all finery and lace, cats and embroidery. I doubt she'd know what to do out on her own."

The banquet hall was full of noise, people, and food. Sir Tremayne had joined the crowd, dazzling in his flexible polished armor, his white-and-indigo cape, and features too handsome to be rendered properly by the crude artistic techniques of the period.

Tremayne seemed displeased with the interloper Dalbry, but the two knights no longer had to consider each other competition, since Sir Phineal was assigned the task of slaying the nonexistent dragon. Cullin thought that with enough continued depredations, set up by Reeger, the corpulent king would have no choice but to reconsider hiring a professional dragon slayer and his apprentice.

For the feast, a roast pig sprawled on the table with a potato in its mouth (because apples were out of season). A roast goose accompanied the pig on its own platter, and the two eyeless heads looked forlorn, as if wondering how they had ended up there. Squash and bread and tarts completed the feast—at least this course.

Princess Affonyl looked cool and bored at the banquet table. At her left sat a dark-haired, mustachioed lord with long hair tied in a ponytail and a heavy gold chain at his throat, his shirt unlaced to show off his wiry dark chest hair.

Sir Phineal had been served hunks of meat, but ate little. King Norrimun noticed. "You've barely touched your food—eat up! You need your strength. Dragon slaying is a hard business."

"I—I feel ill, Sire. Perhaps I need a few days of b-bed rest."

"Nonsense, there's a dragon afoot. No time to lose."

"All the more reason why *I* should be dispatched to slay the beast," Sir Tremayne interrupted. "For the honor of your kingdom."

"Phineal is my chosen champion," Norrimun said. "I need to get my money's worth."

Cullin sat at a smaller separate table for the squires and pages, and he felt a twinge of jealous resentment as Duke Kerrl reached over to clasp Affonyl's hand in a crushing grip. She was holding a fork in her other hand and looked as if she could barely restrain herself from sticking it into Kerrl's wrist.

"King Norrimun, we should be realistic," said the duke. "My attorneys have already negotiated the terms for our wedding and our merger, but a dragon devalues your property. I wouldn't want anything to harm my investment—or the beautiful princess, of course. Now is the time to make a Plan B, put these other two knights on retainer. After Sir Phineal is devoured by the dragon, we'll need a fallback position."

"*If* Sir Phineal is devoured by the dragon," Norrimun said.

The skittish knight looked as if he had found too many curds in his whey. "There's altogether t-too much talk of slaying and d-devouring. I'm losing my appetite."

"*Being* slain and *being* devoured," Affonyl interrupted. "In this instance you must use the passive voice."

Phineal did not find the language lesson terribly heartening.

"My champion will get the first chance to slay the dragon and win my gratitude," the king said. "If he should fail, then I'll take applications for a new champion. There seems to be a sizeable candidate pool."

Sir Tremayne reached inside his doublet and withdrew a small white scroll neatly tied with a ribbon. "Here is a copy of my résumé, Your Majesty."

At the table, the skittish knight looked down at his plate of untouched food. A manservant took it away and gave him a fresh serving, for which he also had no appetite.

"First, we have the evening's entertainment," Norrimun said. "Let's have a round of applause for Nightingale Bob."

Everyone at the feasting tables cheered. The famous minstrel entered and began plucking out a tune on his mandolin. He sang "The Tale of Brave Sir Dalbry"—with new bonus verses—to the amazement of the audience and the extreme annoyance of Sir Tremayne.

CHAPTER ELEVEN

THE SAINT BARTIMUND'S feast was so long and so extravagant that Cullin quickly understood two things: (1) why King Norrimun was so corpulent, and (2) why the kingdom had so little money. At least they could listen to Nightingale Bob while they ate and ate and ate.

A pile of roasted beets came around, so red and dripping that they looked like fresh raw organs from a slaughterhouse. Seeing Cullin's stunned expression at being offered yet another plate of food, one of the young pages leaned close. "Oh, this is nothing—and the feast is only half over. You should see what King Norrimun does for the annual feast of Saint Melbicore. It's coming up next month."

"Since the king doesn't want to hire my master's services, we won't be around that long," Cullin said. "The dragon should be taken care of by then, regardless." He didn't see much chance of becoming a brave young hero in his own right either, which would help him claim the hand of Princess Affonyl in marriage.

Observing Affonyl's frigid demeanor next to her fiancé, Cullin was sure the beautiful princess would rather have him as a husband than the duke (although judging by Affonyl's unhappy expression, she might even have preferred Reeger to Kerrl).

While Nightingale Bob sang about a mermaid and an unromantic fisherman who preferred fish filets to half of a beautiful woman, Dalbry excused himself from the table and headed to one of the back hallways. He signaled Cullin with his eyebrows, and the young man got up as well.

Cullin said to the page next to him, "I have to attend to my master, but you can have my beets if you like. Eat all you want."

As he slipped out of the banquet hall, he saw Sir Phineal also get up from the table. Attendees familiar with King Norrimun's feasts probably understood the need for a mid-banquet intermission.

Cullin left the heady smells of multiple courses, the buzz of conversation, and the tragic yet pragmatic lyrics about the unromantic fisherman. He wandered down the corridor looking for Sir Dalbry in the hallway. (The two words really did not rhyme at all, he realized.)

Torches guttered in wall sconces, shedding a smoky orange light. Half the torches remained unlit; with the kingdom's budgetary concerns, King Norrimun had instituted energy-conservation measures.

He found Dalbry coming out of a side corridor, looking confused. "I found the ladies' garderobe, but not the lords'. I went into that one by accident—do you know the women's privy has sofas, makeup benches, and mirrors?"

Cullin was amazed at the extravagance. "All we ever get is a splintered seat with a hole underneath it."

"That's all a man needs," Dalbry said. "As a knight, I've suffered worse hardships."

Cullin pointed down another dim corridor. "Let's try this way. You'd think they'd have signs."

They bumped into a wide-eyed and fidgety Sir Phineal, who hurried toward Dalbry. "My dear knight, I b-beseech you! I require your assistance."

Dalbry squared his shoulders. "A knight is honor-bound to offer assistance wherever it is necessary. You must be familiar with the demands of chivalry, Sir Phineal."

"Yes, I've read the Knight's Manual . . . but at the m-moment I require utmost discretion. As a d-dragon slayer, I'm not quite as experienced as you. I haven't had the opportunity, you see."

Dalbry nodded. "Judging from your demeanor, I can tell your monster-slaying experience is limited. I take it you've killed fewer than, say, ten dragons?"

Cullin barely restrained a snicker.

"Substantially f-fewer than that," Phineal said.

Dalbry remained cool. "But surely you've slain at least one dragon?"

"Um, I'm afraid not. This has been a p-peaceable kingdom with a marked lack of dragons—until recently, alas."

The older knight nodded. "Alas."

"And it is r-rather late in my c-career to change my focus. D-dragon slaying is a specialized skill."

"Indeed, it should only be attempted by a professional. Considering the size of the beast plaguing your kingdom, which can be accurately estimated by measuring the claw separation distance on the footprints, I would suggest you not attempt it yourself."

The skittish knight looked both nervous and relieved. "I c-couldn't agree more! But King Norrimun has put me in an awkward p-position." He glanced back down the corridor as if he expected spies to be peeping through tiny holes in the stone walls.

"And that is why I require your discretion." He narrowed his eyes at Cullin. "Is your s-squire trustworthy?"

"He would no more tell a lie than I would."

Cullin tried to look as honest as possible, and Sir Phineal took heart. "You see, my life story has not t-turned out the way I imagined it."

"Many of us could say the same," Dalbry said. "But is this a long story? They'll be expecting us back at the banquet. I believe the turnip course is next."

"I can tell an abbreviated version. The g-gist of it is that I never wanted to be a knight. Most boys dream of it, but I was railroaded into the career. My parents had several sons who all became doctors and lawyers, but Mom and Dad always wanted a knight in the family. So I got my suit of armor and became a knight, thanks to a technicality."

"A technicality?" Cullin hadn't known the option existed.

"In jousting matches, I was adept at dodging, though I never m-managed to strike an opponent. The 'Phineal Squirm' became an acknowledged move on the jousting lists. I could b-bend my body away from any oncoming spear with such proficiency that p-people began to say I had no backbone whatsoever. Only now do I realize that it m-might not have been a compliment. . . .

"King Norrimun made me his champion after I beat him in a game of dice. I thought it was a triumph, but now I realize that the title is a great b-burden. This kingdom is quiet, and we haven't gone to war in almost a century. I've never b-been in battle myself, never slain an ogre, never even seen a dragon. I was beginning to wonder if they existed."

"Oh, they exist," Cullin interjected. "That's been scientifically proven."

"I d-don't doubt it," Phineal said. "But I wouldn't have the slightest idea how to slay one, what tricks to use, or even how to find the m-monster."

"We could sell you magic beans for protection," Cullin said. Dalbry gave him a quick glance, and the young man fell silent.

Phineal pulled out a purse of coins. "I would be greatly indebted to you if I could hire your services as a d-dragon slayer. On the side. In secret."

Cullin was delighted with the offer. Even if King Norrimun did not pay them, they could accept Phineal's bribe and conduct their dragon business that way.

Dalbry, though, reacted with indignation. "You want me to be a dragon slayer by proxy? Are you suggesting that I not take credit for killing the monster?"

Phineal shuffled his feet; prominent beads of sweat appeared on his forehead. "Just this once? I b-beg you to take pity on me. With your fame and your career, do you need to add another d-dragon to the list? I heard Nightingale B-bob's song about your exploits."

"And those were only a fraction of Sir Dalbry's adventures," Cullin added.

"Exactly my p-point," Phineal said. "What's one more victory on top of all that? This would be my first slain dragon. I wouldn't b-brag about it overmuch, I promise, but it would mean the world to me."

"I suppose it could be done." Dalbry looked at the size of the pouch. "As a special favor to a fellow knight."

"I'd do the same for you, if the boot were on the other f-foot—if, for instance, you found yourself trapped in a deadly competition of statistics or m-mathematics."

"I've heard those can be treacherous," Cullin said.

"If I take this contract engagement, the fee will be off book, correct?" Dalbry asked.

Phineal looked about to collapse with relief. His knees were quaking. "Yes! And when you've k-killed the monster—assuming you survive—we can arrange a rendezvous for me to deliver the severed head to King Norrimun with n-no one the wiser."

Dalbry extended his hand for the pouch, and Sir Phineal placed the gold coins in it. Cullin realized their scam was going to turn out well after all.

A loud throat clearing echoed in the hallway behind them, and Cullin turned to see the very upright Sir Tremayne regarding the transaction with disgust. "Sir Phineal, did you actually just hire Sir Dalbry to perform your sacred task?"

The skittish knight fidgeted, cleared his throat. "I w-was, um, delegating responsibility."

"And I was helping him to retain his honor," said Dalbry.

Tremayne waggled his finger from side to side. "Appalling! When Nightingale Bob hears of it, he'll add a new verse to his song that will change the tone of the tune."

While Dalbry and Phineal were both dismayed, Cullin thought fast. "And why were you spying on your fellow knights, Sir Tremayne, slinking through the hallways like a footpad or a thief?"

Tremayne sniffed at the squire. "I was looking for the men's garderobe. I never expected to come upon a heinous bribe in progress." He knew he had the upper hand. "Dragon slaying is serious business and not to be undertaken by cowards. King Norrimun made a mistake in picking his champion." A stormy expression crossed Tremayne's face. "But I expected more from you, Sir Dalbry—you're a real knight."

Phineal snatched the purse of coins out of Dalbry's hand and thrust it toward Tremayne. "I can offer significant c-compensation if you keep this embarrassing m-matter private."

Now Tremayne was even more deeply offended. "Those coins are tainted by the stench of bribery."

Even more embarrassed, Phineal pocketed the pouch. "You can't b-blame me for trying."

Tremayne turned to Dalbry. "The dragon must be slain, and Sir Phineal is obviously not up to the task. Politics and messy embarrassments aside, Sir Dalbry, the deed falls to the two of us. We shall go together, as freelancers. And by accompanying you, I might learn a few pointers—while also keeping an eye on your activities."

"That is not necessary, Sir Tremayne," the older knight said. "King Norrimun doesn't want our help."

"I can convince him otherwise," Phineal broke in, too quickly.

Dalbry looked at the skittish knight. "I am willing to do my chivalrous duty, but I work alone." Cullin knew that the last thing in the world Dalbry wanted was the annoyingly honest and honorable knight at his side.

"The Knight's Manual allows brothers-in-arms," Tremayne said, "so long as each knight faces the dragon individually. I can cite chapter and verse, if need be. I am very familiar with the Manual."

Dalbry frowned. "I have no doubt of that." He seemed to be searching for other excuses, but not for any cowardly reasons. Cullin understood that Tremayne had to be taken out of the picture. Somehow. "I have no horse, however. My valiant steed Lightning was killed by the last dragon I slew."

"I c-can arrange a new horse," Phineal said. "The king will allow it—for dragon-slaying purposes only."

Cutting off further debate, Tremayne said, “We will set off at dawn.” Scorn dripped from his voice. “*If* we survive this interminable feast! There must be hours left.”

He wandered away in search of the garderobe, and Cullin politely directed him toward the women’s privy down the adjacent corridor.

IT WAS A perfect cave. Reeger concluded that as soon as he made his way through the sinister rock formations and at last found Old Snort.

He could smell brimstone and steam long before he actually saw the cave. Even from a distance the reek from the cave was so strong his eyes stung. He sneezed, coughed, and spat out a wad of phlegm, but clearing his nasal passages did not help. "Rust, it's like the foul breath of a real dragon!"

Yes, he could work with that.

The locals shunned this cave. The rotten-egg smell, the wafting steam, the burbling sounds—Old Snort was indeed a scary place. His sources were already so fearful that they had given him conflicting directions.

For the time being, he left the mule and the supplies in their camp while he trudged through the trackless hills looking for Old Snort. Now he would have a long trek back. Such was his life, doing all the work while Dalbry reveled in feasts, listened to minstrels, and endured fine ladies fawning over him. On the other hand, in order to play his role properly, Dalbry had to bathe more often than Reeger thought was healthy. He had to brush his hair, add a dab or two of perfume, and speak courtly language. Reeger snorted to himself. Given the choice, he preferred refurbishing latrines.

Around the cave, the steam was so thick it hung like a yellowish fog in the low-lying areas, and the ground was a lifeless brown color. A few thorny weeds had struggled to survive but failed. It looked like a bleak wasteland.

It looked like a dragon's lair.

Proceeding with caution, he entered the cave, where he was engulfed by fetid and stifling shadows. Moisture trickled down walls that were covered with greenish slime. "Oh, even better!" He smeared slimy fingers on his trousers before venturing forward. Towering rocks had fallen together to create the talus cave, but cracks in the ceiling let in enough light that he could make his way through the dim twisting passages.

When he heard rumbling and hissing ahead, a shiver went down his spine. Yes, gullible people would believe a monster lived here. Fortunately, Reeger knew enough insider tricks to cure him of gullibility.

He crept forward, worried about what he might find and glad that no one else accompanied him, because then he would have to pretend to be dismissive. On the other hand, he could have made Cullin go first, just in case something with large snapping jaws lay ahead.

Reeger wasn't afraid of dragons—they were just creatures of myth. *Bears*, though, were certainly real.

When the tunnel opened to a large grotto, the steam was so thick that Reeger could barely see. The sulfurous stench was heavier here, and sweat dripped from his dark hair.

After the steam cleared, he encountered a large pool—a hot spring! He had heard of luxurious steam baths where lords and ladies would soak away the joint aches caused by a rich lifestyle. Nobles often suffered from acute gout. Since Reeger usually ate boiled potatoes seasoned with snake or salt pork, he didn't have to worry about gout.

Reeger stood at the edge of the hot spring and dipped his fingers into the water before yanking them back with a yelp. Who would want to bathe in water as hot as a cauldron? How could lords and ladies stand it with their delicate skin? Maybe nobles had a toughness he didn't understand.

As he hunched there, a gurgling came from deep in the pool. The water churned and roiled, and two huge bubbles of rotten-egg stench spewed into the chamber. Reeger recoiled from the smell. Then an idea occurred to him.

"Dragon farts. We can sell that."

More bubbles churned up, and the steam thickened in the grotto. When a rumbling hiss grew louder from deep underground, Reeger decided it was an appropriate time to make his way back outside. He retreated quickly, winding his way back out of the passage as the rumble grew to a roar. He scrambled faster. His worn boots slipped on the slimy rock floor. Why did algae have to grow in such inconvenient places?

The hissing and grumbling became an explosive sound behind him, and superstitious fear yammered in his head. It couldn't possibly be a real dragon—but *something* was emerging from under the grotto.

He bolted outside just as the churning reached a crescendo, and an explosion of steam and vapor vomited from the jagged mouth of Old Snort. Scalding water pattered all around him like a rainstorm from hell.

The column of steam died down within seconds, and Reeger blinked, catching his breath. He still didn't understand what had just happened . . . and suddenly he knew what it was.

He had heard of geysers before, a matter of simple hydrogeologics: an explosion of boiling water caused by underground volcanic activity, surface water percolating down and striking hot rocks, then being ejected through a vent in a high-pressure column.

Yes, there was always a rational scientific explanation. A good con man never let himself be too caught up in his con.

If Reeger could predict how often Old Snort erupted, that would be an even more useful bit of information for Dalbry and Cullin. This was getting better by the moment!

The mule brayed loudly in either complaint or delight as Reeger returned to camp. He patted the beast on the head, ate some squirrel jerky, and gathered the sack of props. He had to trudge all the way back to Old Snort, since the mule would be much too skittish in the vicinity of the geyser.

Reeger headed for the ominous cave at sunset. Already the convincing abode of a monster, Old Snort needed little work from him to crystallize the picture, but Reeger took his work seriously. Small details mattered.

Outside the geyser cave, he selected from among the femurs, rib cages, and skulls they had harvested from the graveyard. He cracked a few of the bones for effect and scattered them in a pattern to imply the dragon's satisfaction.

He explored the area thoroughly, climbed up and around the rocks, poked through the cave, and found another crack, a second entrance where he could slip in through the side. It was always good to have an emergency exit.

Satisfied, he built a campfire near the smelly cave and settled down.

Three times during the night the geyser erupted with a spectacular show. Reeger was impressed, although he didn't appreciate the interruptions to his well-earned sleep.

CHAPTER THIRTEEN

MEANWHILE, BACK AT the castle . . .

The men's garderobe was a spacious two-seater, but by the time they found it, Sir Tremayne had arrived moments earlier. He swung the door shut, carrying one of the kingdom's monk-transcribed newspapers, which implied he would be in there awhile. Cullin and Dalbry decided they didn't have to go after all.

As the two headed back toward the banquet hall, Sir Dalbry seemed embarrassed by the encounter. "Tremayne wants to accompany me on the hunt." He frowned. "The last thing I need is a squeaky-clean knight with a disproportionate sense of honor breathing down my neck. How are we going to do our dragon business?"

"Tremayne chafes my smallclothes," Cullin agreed.

Dalbry lowered his voice, sounding troubled. "He isn't a bad sort. A true knight in shining armor, filled with an unshakable sense of honor. In fact, he reminds me of what I should have been." He plucked at his sleeve. "Not this pretend knight performing pretend quests for gullible people."

Cullin suddenly got an idea. "Why don't we find a way to rescue Princess Affonyl from marrying that man she obviously despises? Would that make you feel honorable?"

"Nothing we can do about it, lad. Getting married against your will—it comes with being a princess. That's one advantage to our lifestyle, footloose and fancy-free, never pinned down. Neither of us has to worry about being married to a spouse we despise."

"But what if Princess Affonyl and I were happy together?"

"You've been listening to too many of Nightingale Bob's sappy songs."

Cullin shrugged. "There's nothing wrong with being innocent and romantic."

"Right now my main concern is how to deal with Sir Tremayne. If he follows me on the dragon hunt, it'll cramp my style."

A slow grin slid across Cullin's face. "How much longer do you suppose the feast will last?"

Dalbry stroked his beard. "Only another few hours or so. I've been warned they still have several more root vegetables, second salads, plus at least two dessert courses. And coffee."

"Plenty of time, then. You leave Sir Tremayne to me."

Fortunately, the castle's apothecary kept extended evening hours, so the shop was still open. Due to King Norrimun's frequent feasts and his corpulence, the apothecary stocked digestive aids of all varieties and potencies.

When Cullin entered, a tiny bell jangled on top of the wooden door. The apothecary behind the counter was a wizened old man with very little hair on top of his head, but eyebrows so large they made up for the lack elsewhere. All around the shop, shelves were loaded with clay jars, blown-glass beakers, tied leather pouches.

The gift section offered scented candles, birthday scrolls, and potpourri for sale.

The apothecary squinted at him with a compassionate and earnest expression, as if he truly felt the pain of all the maladies his customers suffered. "I'm so sorry for your misery," he said, as if Cullin had already told a tale of woe. "You look like such a strapping young man . . . yet, not all infirmities are obvious to the naked eye. How can I help? Is it the pox? The, er, *private* pox? When I was your age, I visited many a saucy wench, heh-heh. One must practice safe copulation."

He clucked his tongue and kept talking before Cullin could even wedge in a word. "Now, is it the kind with just a rash, or the one with erupting pustules? Oh, that's nasty. You have to lance the pustules with a needle, then cauterize them with a hot brand. Try finding someone to help you with *that!*"

Cullin managed to interrupt, "It's not for me—it's for a friend."

Again, the apothecary looked painfully sincere. "Naturally, it's always for a friend. But I have cures here—magic cures, specially formulated unguents prepared under the light of a full moon, sprinkled with holy water, and touched by a virgin's kiss. Guaranteed to cure all sorts of sexual pox."

"It's not a sexual pox," Cullin interjected. "And it really is for a friend. Actually, for my master—Sir Dalbry."

The apothecary looked alarmed. "Sir Dalbry suffers from a pox? Yes, I can see why he might want to keep that a secret."

"It's *not* a pox," Cullin said again. "But his condition is . . . embarrassing, and requires discretion."

"But of course." The apothecary patted his chest, searching the pockets of his smock for a notepad. "So long as you tell me all the details."

"Sir Dalbry is renowned for his prowess on the battlefield and his skill as a dragon slayer, but he also suffers from . . ." Cullin made every effort to look uncomfortable and embarrassed. "Severe and chronic constipation, and it is exacerbated when he rides all day in the saddle. Fortunately, his horse was eaten by a dragon, so he's been walking for the last week or two."

The apothecary nodded. "Exercise will often get the bowels moving."

"I can tell when my master is regular by his improved mood," Cullin said. "But tonight he has been sitting through King Norrimun's long feast. He was already plugged up, and now I fear the worst."

"Oh, dear." The apothecary's tone of voice expressed even deeper sympathy.

"I was hoping you might have something that'll help? An extremely potent laxative? No need for it to be gentle, so long as it's effective."

"Ah, you need waterweed. One good dose will clean him right out."

Cullin smiled. "That sounds like just the thing. Can it be added to food or drink?"

The apothecary rummaged among his clay pots and beakers. "Yes, the best delivery system is in coffee or some other hot beverage."

He glanced at a sundial mounted on a countertop, but since it was nighttime, the sundial didn't operate properly; the wizened apothecary brought a candle close, looked at the shadow, and said, "Yes, I can see by this hour King Norrimun should be ready for the dessert course."

"Perfect timing. Give me a good strong dose of waterweed extract—in fact, make it two doses. Sir Dalbry is very plugged up. Most distressing."

"Poor man. I hope he feels well enough to slay a dragon. Between you and me, I think Sir Phineal might require a little help."

"Oh, he will," Cullin said in a bright voice. "He would never let a little thing like constipation keep him from his duty."

The waterweed extract came in a small vial. The apothecary cautioned him about the potency of the drug. "Use only half of this, or he'll be quite miserable."

After thanking the wizened old man, Cullin made his way back to the banquet hall, where the castle chefs were gathered in the serving corridors like an army about to launch a military assault on the dessert course. The ancient Mother Singra paced about, lining them up in ranks, sorting the treats into alphabetical order.

Seeing the cakes, tarts, pastries, and cookies, the bowls of clotted cream, scones and jam, pickled fruits, oozing honeycombs (with a special stamp indicating that it was genuine honey from the town of Folly), Cullin couldn't understand how Princess Affonyl remained so slender. Perhaps it was worry over having to marry Duke Kerrl, or maybe she had a metabolism as beautiful as her features.

He reentered the hall amidst the flurry of serving dishes and the smell of sweets. Typically, diners would have celebrated such marvelous desserts, but after hours of a constant food assault, they groaned at the prospect of consuming even more.

Dalbry sat next to Sir Tremayne, both knights looking cool and formal to each other. On the other side of the table, Sir Phineal looked miserable and ashamed. Apparently, they had already announced they would go out on an independent dragon hunt in the morning, and King Norrimun had grudgingly allowed that—*if* they actually killed the monster—he would allow a small honorarium, then got distracted with anticipation of the impending voluminous desserts.

As the servants rushed forward with trays of apple pie, egg custards, lemon cake, and poppyseed cookies, others followed with pots of strong coffee brewed from beans brought into Rivermouth, imported from the fabled continent of Atlantis. Recently, a merchant ship filled with magically decaffeinated beans had gone down in a storm, and King Norrimun apologized that he could not provide decaf for his more sensitive subjects.

Cullin approached Dalbry as if he wanted to speak with his master, but he timed his movements so that as he came close to the two knights, servants were just pouring the coffee. Dalbry read something in his squire's eyes, and Cullin surreptitiously flashed the glass vial.

Dalbry cleared his throat to distract Tremayne. "If you and I go out dragon slaying tomorrow, I'll ask King Norrimun to grant me a loaner horse."

When Tremayne glanced at the other knight, Cullin dumped the entire vial of waterweed extract into his coffee.

The shining knight said, "You must have a horse, Sir Dalbry, so that you can keep up with me. Together we will show them how dragon slaying is done." He picked up the coffee and took a gulp. "That is a bitter brew." He looked down the table. "Could someone please pass the sweetener?"

FOURTEEN

NIGHTINGALE BOB WAS still singing when the second dessert course came around. The minstrel had an astonishing repertoire that covered a range of comedies, tragedies, heroic deeds, and epic debacles. Out of consideration for his patron, he sang "The Tale of Brave Sir Dalbry" two more times. By now, the drowsy, overstuffed banquet attendees paid little attention to the music.

Sir Tremayne noticed, however. "Why do you have to sing that song again?"

"It's my current hit." The minstrel struck up the same tune on his ukulele. "This time I'm doing an unplugged version. Gives it a whole different sound."

"When are you going to finish 'The Ballad of Sir Tremayne'?"

The minstrel fidgeted. "I've got an artistic block. Genius can't be rushed."

Tremayne frowned into his coffee, while Sir Dalbry tried not to show his pride; Cullin still found the rhymes problematic.

As Nightingale Bob played song after jaunty song about legendary knights who met horrible ends, Sir Phineal turned paler than sour milk, tinged with a faint shade of green. In the songs, one hero was gutted by wolves, but he crawled eviscerated for miles through a forest, dragging his entrails behind him, so he could return a lost handkerchief to a beautiful lady. Another knight fought hand-to-hand with a ferocious bear and had his eyes gouged out by the beast's claws. But even blinded he was able to smell his foe and kill it by ramming his fist down the bear's throat; the beast choked to death just after it bit off the knight's arm; the elbow was too much for it to swallow.

"Ah, glorious," said King Norrimun, applauding.

Another knight had climbed a tall tree during a thunderstorm to rescue the queen's kitten, and in his metal armor he was struck by lightning and killed. But—happy ending—the fluffy kitten fell into Her Majesty's arms and was safe.

In song after song, knight after knight slew monster after monster. But in order for the tales to be properly poignant, each hero had to suffer a tragic mortal wound in the process. Sir Phineal swallowed hard. "I see a p-pattern here."

The great feast of Saint Bartimund wound down after a mere seven hours. Overstuffed and exhausted, Cullin said to Dalbry, "I'll prepare your sword and armor for tomorrow's hunt, oil your dragonskin cape, set out your boots and socks, make sure everything is ready for our departure at sunrise."

On Cullin's way out of the banquet hall, Sir Tremayne raised a hand and spoke privately to him. "Hold, boy."

He hesitated. "What is it, sir?"

Tremayne shot a sidelong glance at Dalbry, but the older knight was paying attention to King Norrimun and Duke Kerrl.

Servants had cleared away the plates and dessert bowls so the two men could spread out maps of their respective dukedom and kingdom.

"I've been watching you, young man—and I'm impressed. You do good work." He lowered his voice further. "I could use a skilled page."

Cullin sniffed. "I'm a *squire*, sir. I'm too old and too well trained to be a mere page." He had never been a page either, nor a real squire, but he had the role down quite well.

"Apologies; I should have known. What are you doing with a washed-up, has-been knight like Dalbry?"

"He is my master, sir. He took me in when I most needed it, gave me the opportunities a young boy dreams of." Cullin wondered where this was going.

"Good help is hard to find. I'd like to have your name and contact information."

"At the moment I am happy with my employment."

Tremayne narrowed his eyes. "It never hurts to have a fallback position. There's no telling what might happen when we hunt the dragon. You might need a new master sooner than you think."

Cullin wanted to escape this conversation. "I'll leave my information with the castle's human resources department."

Sir Tremayne's expression suddenly twisted, and he put a hand on his stomach. The honorable knight's Adam's apple bobbed up and down as he swallowed. He squirmed, held his stomach again, and a sheen of sweat broke out on his forehead. His stomach gurgled so loudly it sounded as if a small dragon had slipped into the castle and was growling underneath the long table.

"Maybe it was something you ate," Cullin said.

Meanwhile, Duke Kerrl unrolled a large map in front of the king, pulled a dagger from his waist, and used its sharp tip to trace the boundaries of his dukedom. Outside of the immediate area drawn on the chart, the cartographer had doodled ferocious beasts and marked "Unknown lands—Here be monsters" . . . even though detailed maps of the surrounding kingdoms were widely available in any monastery library.

Princess Affonyl sat next to her rotund father, studying the maps herself. She looked up at the duke with an icy glare. "Those boundaries aren't correct. This line of hills is drawn much too far into your dukedom, sir. The tin mines are over here, not there." She pointed with her delicate finger. "And the lumber road goes through this valley, which is definitely *not* in your territory."

Duke Kerrl let out a brittle chuckle. "How charming you are, my dear. You shouldn't bother with such details. I have it on the greatest rumored authority that my maps are correct and that your father's need updating."

"It's not a matter of rumors," Affonyl said. "It's a matter of plain geography, cartography, and trigonometry."

Kerrl rolled his eyes. "Where does your daughter learn such big words, Sire?"

Exasperated, Norrimun patted Affonyl on the hand, but she snatched it away. "What did I tell you, my sweet? Be a princess. No young man wants to date a woman who shows off her intelligence."

"Intelligence is obvious to anyone who bothers to look," Affonyl said. "I dispute Duke Kerrl's claims to this territory. His maps are incorrect. We have other maps in our castle archives, and I can prove what I say."

A dark expression crossed the duke's face. "And who is to say that your ancient maps are accurate?"

Affonyl's expression tightened. "Our court surveyors say it. We can send out teams to remap the kingdom if you like."

King Norrimun forced a chuckle, stroked his curly beard. "Ho-hum! There's no cause for debate, since it won't matter once you two are married. With the duke as my proud son-in-law and you, dear Affonyl, as his radiant and faithful wife, our lands will be joined, and any disputed borders merely a matter of historical interest."

Duke Kerrl relaxed and rolled up his map. "We'll make sure all the proper documents are finished, signed, and sealed, so I can begin to absorb your kingdom into my lands."

"I thought we were joining as equal partners?" Affonyl said.

Kerrl chuckled again. "My lovely princess, I can see you have far too much time on your hands. Once we're married, you won't have the time or energy to worry about books and alchemy and astronomy and cartography. You'll be too busy having my babies—brave sons to grow up into powerful knights! And of course you'll be mending my fine clothes. I've heard you're proficient in embroidery with a new technique of abstract designs?"

Affonyl stood from her chair, like a rising thunderhead. Her expression darkened, her eyes flashed. Cullin thought she looked absolutely beautiful when she was feisty—so long as her wrath was not directed toward him. "Father, I feel ill. I'm going to my chambers."

The old nursemaid Mother Singra hurried up to attend her, and the two of them stalked out of the banquet hall, followed by a herd of adoring cats. The princess went to her tower room and locked herself inside.

CHAPTER FIFTEEN

LONG AFTER MIDNIGHT, most people in the castle were asleep. The hallway torches had been extinguished, except for a few small candles to serve as night lights.

Three manservants had steered King Norrimun off to his bedchamber. After overindulging, the banquet attendees lay restless in their beds; many had staggered to the castle apothecary's shop, which observed extended post-feast hours and offered a "St. Bartimund's Day Special" of antacids, heartburn remedies, and hangover spells.

Cullin and Sir Dalbry had a guest room not far from Sir Tremayne's. Outside in the courtyard, the rooster had been set to wake them at dawn.

But the young man couldn't sleep, and Dalbry lay silent on his bed. "Remember, stay flexible," the older knight said. "I'm sure Reeger has done his part by now."

"And I've done mine." Cullin lay back, grinning in the dark. "By morning, the only thing Sir Tremayne will be riding is a chamber pot."

Suddenly, the castle was rocked by a scream and a horrific explosion from Princess Affonyl's tower chamber.

Cullin scrambled for his breeches, stumbling in the dark. "What was that?" He yanked them on after tangling his foot in the left leg.

Dalbry was already off his pallet, searching for his sword. "It sounded like a dragon attack to me."

He and Cullin bounded down the hallway, bumping into walls and into each other, unable to see because the torches had been extinguished. Others emerged from their rooms, chattering in terror. The two ran up the winding staircase, pushing ahead of gawkers.

When they reached Affonyl's chamber, Sir Phineal stood shuddering out in the corridor, too frightened to approach. Smoke curled from beneath the barred wooden door and through a splintered gouge in the planks.

Cullin pounded on the door. "Princess! Princess, are you all right?"

They heard no sound except for the crackling of flames and the yowling of distressed cats. Again a woman screamed, but it did not sound like Affonyl. Dalbry used the pommel of his sword to hammer the latch, then stood back and gave the door a sharp kick with his boot. Cullin added a kick of his own, anxious to save the princess.

When Sir Tremayne made it to the top of the stairs, he looked winded and shaky. He had taken the time to don his shining armor, and had done it in only a few minutes. Driven by duty, he stepped up, shoulder-to-shoulder with Sir Dalbry and Cullin, and added his own kick against the door, which finally resulted in a crack. They all threw their shoulders into the blow while Sir Phineal supervised, and finally the door crashed open.

Affonyl's chamber was filled with smoke and the stench of sulfur. Cullin stared in amazement: the window had been torn away, leaving a great hole in the stone wall. Her furniture had been toppled over. Smoldering bits of draperies lay singed on the floor among hoops with sketched embroidery patterns.

Cullin felt a sharp chill as he spotted long gouges in the stone wall, parallel tracks in sets of three as if made by . . . dragon claws! "Princess Affonyl!" he shouted again.

They heard a whimper, and Cullin found the old nursemaid cowering against a large wardrobe. Mother Singra hunched down, covering her gray hair with her hands, and the several cats sniffing her seemed very concerned. Cullin crouched at her side. "What is it? Can you tell us what happened?"

The old woman looked up, as if to be sure others were listening, and wailed, "A dragon! A dragon smashed through the balcony and seized the poor, dear princess. It flew off with her in its monstrous claws. Look!" She gestured toward the deep gouges in the stone wall.

Once the room was shown to be unoccupied by either princess or dragon, Sir Phineal dared to enter. "What a t-tragedy! She's been d-devoured."

Cullin's heart ached, but Dalbry pointed out, "I see no blood. Maybe the dragon just carried her off to its lair."

Mother Singra wailed, "She's dead!"

"Why would a d-dragon attack here?" asked Phineal. "And why go after f-fair Affonyl?"

Swaying and unsteady, Sir Tremayne stood next to Dalbry. Though queasy, he snorted at the cowardly knight. "Everyone knows that dragons have a fondness for beautiful princesses. The monster probably added her to its treasure hoard."

Cullin pointed out, "Affonyl did have beautiful hair of gold."

Mother Singra sniffled and moaned.

Dalbry moved cautiously through the room, nudging aside embroidery hoops, studying the debris on the floor. Cullin bent down to pick up something that caught his eye—a triangular-shaped scale, obviously from a reptile. He looked at it in disbelief. "This must have come from the dragon."

As he held the large scale in his hand, his entire world was spinning. He thought of the scams that he, Dalbry, and Reeger had perpetrated, selling splinters of the True Cross, or the bones of Saint Bartimund at different ages, all of which had culminated in the dragon business. It had been good fun and occasional profit, but he didn't *believe* any of the stories.

He was not prepared for a real dragon.

Curious bystanders crowded the corridor outside the princess's room, but they parted when King Norrimun pushed his way in. The corpulent king wheezed, exhausted from the climb.

Duke Kerrl accompanied him, looking surprised but pleased. He had urged the gasping Norrimun to great speed up the steep stairs, and now he stroked his thick black mustache, assessing the situation. Cullin disliked him even more, realizing that if King Norrimun were to collapse from a coronary, and Princess Affonyl were kidnapped or devoured by a dragon, the duke would no doubt consider it a productive day.

The king gazed around the ruined chamber, his mouth agape as he saw the blasted hole in the wall, smelled the smoke, spotted the long claw marks. Several disturbed cats milled about the room. "The dragon has my sweet princess! Now who's going to marry the Duke?"

Sir Tremayne staggered forward with a groan, bravely clutching his abdomen. The defiant words on his lips faded, and he could barely manage a thin voice, "I am ready to go fight the dragon—in just a little bit! Excuse me, Majesty." He raced off, pushing his way through the crowds, and rushed down the spiral stairs to the nearest garderobe.

Without even a glance at Cullin, Dalbry squared his shoulders, seizing the opportunity. "I came to your kingdom offering my services as dragon slayer, Majesty, and I still vow to kill the monster for you. Sir Tremayne is obviously indisposed, and no one can better care for a knight than another knight. I suggest that Sir Phineal remain behind in the castle to ensure his swift and full recovery, while I take on this quest."

Through chattering teeth, Sir Phineal said, "Yes! W-we need to be sensible about this. P-poor Sir Tremayne looks so ill."

King Norrimun looked confused, still out of breath. "Yes, go rescue my little princess. I would prefer her back intact."

Mother Singra sniffled and moaned some more.

Dalbry said, "My squire will accompany me, and we'll leave at dawn's first light. Provided you can give us horses?"

"Yes, yes. That seems a reasonable request."

Cullin had never thought they would ride out to fight a real dragon. He felt dizzy.

Looking intent rather than sympathetic, Duke Kerrl hauled the shaking old woman to her feet. "Come with me, Mother Singra. I'll comfort you, and we can talk about what you saw. *Exactly* what you saw." He led the crone away, and she seemed unsteady on her feet.

Norrimun shouted out calls to arms and hurried off, leading the crowds down the spiral staircase, while Cullin and Dalbry remained behind at the scene of the attack. "We need to study our nemesis," the older knight said, and no one argued with him.

As soon as they were alone, Cullin turned to him, "Why did you volunteer, now that we know a real monster is on the loose?

This isn't what we do! You don't know how to kill a real dragon, and neither do I."

Dalbry sniffed. "Young Cullin, sometimes the course of honor is the most appropriate. After seeing what has happened here, I am convinced of what we must do."

Cullin swallowed hard. "But . . . but—"

Then Dalbry smiled. "But I'm not worried, lad. Look carefully, and you'll see for yourself." He gestured to indicate the hole ripped in the wall, the smoldering curtains. "Those claw marks are obviously fake, chiseled into the stone. And note the characteristics of the explosion: the windowsill and the stone wall were blown *outward*. There's almost no debris inside the chamber—it's all strewn on the ground below. If a real dragon had attacked from the outside, the stones would have been smashed *inward*."

Cullin scratched his head, his curiosity piqued. He hurried to the windowsill and saw that the older knight was indeed correct. "But what does all that mean?"

"I think Affonyl set this up to look like a dragon attack. She must have blown the hole in the wall herself."

Cullin ran his fingers along the shattered edge of the stone, and his eyes widened when he found an iron eyelet hammered into one of the cracks. "This is how Affonyl dropped herself down to the ground!"

Dalbry took a closer look at the "dragon scale" Cullin had retrieved. "And this, carved and shaped from a tortoiseshell, no doubt." He raised his eyebrows and smiled. "It seems the princess is perpetrating a scam of her own."

Cullin let out a gasp. Then, understanding how much Affonyl had wanted to get away from her father and Duke Kerrl, he chuckled. "I think I like this girl a lot."

In the Scabby Wench, Hob Nobbin finishes playing a short set but he pays little attention to the crowd. The young girls from the town still swoon and fawn over the aloof minstrel, pressing closer to the stage. One opens her bodice and flashes her breasts, but Reeger hurries over and makes her cover up. "Rust, none of that! We run a family establishment here."

Maurice divides his attention between the minstrel and my story, but at least he finally seems interested. Every father wants his son to like and respect him, and I have realized that I need to make more of an effort. I rule the kingdom, sure—I meet regularly with peasants, sign decrees, keep my army ready to defend our borders, but the prince's interests and mine have diverged. He spends more time with his mother than with me, and I never invite him out into the courtyard so we can toss a ball back and forth or whack at each other with wooden swords—you know, the sort of father/son bonding experience that nonroyal families enjoy.

By exposing Maurice to the rough camaraderie of common folk, the concerns of everyday people, and my friends from times past, I'm hoping to warm things up between the two of us. Alas, Maurice has been brainwashed by too many unrealistic stories.

He isn't impressed with the attitude of Hob Nobbin, however. After a couple of his better-known songs, the dreary minstrel starts to sing atonal experimental tunes, none of which please the audience. His girl groupies scream and swoon only out of habit, though without any sincerity.

At their table, the mercenaries grumble and call out, "Play 'The Goose and the Noose'!"

The other mercenaries laugh and add their shouts, "Yeah, 'The Goose and the Noose'!"

Hob Nobbin stops and looks at them as if they are no more than dungheaps in clothes. "If you want that kind of musical crap, go to some other establishment."

Yes, the minstrel certainly knows how to be a crowd pleaser.

The tough mercenaries are taken aback by his attitude. "But everyone loves 'The Goose and the Noose,'" growls one of the shaggy men.

"'The Goose and the Noose'!" someone else cries.

Soon, a groundswell of people add their voices, not because they have much fondness for that particular song, but because they're fed up with the minstrel's attitude and want to hear anything other than what he's been playing.

Hob Nobbin remains oblivious to the rising tide of anger. "I am practicing my art. I won't sell out and perform commercial drivel. You might as well ask me to play 'The Fart in the Park'!"

One of the mercenaries yells, "Yeah, 'The Fart in the Park!'" Others take up the shout.

The minstrel sets down his lute and lifts his pointed nose in the air. "I can't perform under these conditions."

Two mercenaries rise from their stools. "We'll make you perform under these conditions, or maybe you'd rather play your lute strings with broken fingers?" Three more mercenaries join them and encroach on the stage.

Maurice's eyes are wide and white. "Father, aren't you going to do something? You're the king."

"Not here I'm not." I give a dismissive wave. "These things have a way of working themselves out. Besides, that minstrel's being a jerk."

The baker's girl throws herself in front of the threatening men. "Don't you hurt him." The nearest mercenary knocks the girl out of his way, and she goes sprawling on the floor.

The town blacksmith—who is nearly as muscular as the mercenaries—lurches to his feet with a scowl and a growl. The blacksmith is no fan of the minstrel's songs, but won't let the thugs push a young lady around. He doesn't threaten, doesn't wait, simply cocks back his arm and throws a punch like a sledgehammer into the mercenary's face, breaking his nose and spraying blood and teeth.

The other mercenaries bound forward, roaring, while the townspeople draw together to defend the blacksmith.

The minstrel pulls his lute close to his chest, tiptoes off the stage, and starts toward the safety of the bar.

Just then Wendria appears from the kitchen, an apron across her wide hips, a cast-iron skillet in one hand, and flour all over her square face. Reeger looks at her. "Crotchrust, my lovely, looks like this is getting out of hand."

"I'll deal with it. As usual." Wendria snatches an oaken clout from beneath the bar and moves like an avalanche into the fray.

Reeger glances at me, and we share a smile. We've both seen Wendria in action before. She swings the cast-iron pan with one hand and clubs sideways with the oaken staff in the other. Within moments she has scattered the mercenaries and townspeople, leaving a room full of groans, bruises, and cowed expressions.

"I won't abide rowdy customers," she says. "You all know the rules. The Scabby Wench is a classy place."

The people mutter their apologies.

Maurice has been watching with an amazed expression. Reeger chuckles and picks at his teeth.

As Hob Nobbin tries to slink away, Wendria sets the oaken club aside, grabs him by the collar, lifts him off the ground, and swings him back to the stage. His lute strings jangle as the instrument thumps onto his lap.

"You! We hired you to play music, and that annoying noise you've been making is not music by my definition." She shakes a finger at him. "First, you'll play 'The Goose and the Noose,' then 'The Fart in the Park.' Afterward, you will take requests for the rest of the evening. Have I made myself clear?"

Hob Nobbin trembles, his carefully cultivated arrogance dribbling away, as if from an emptying bladder. "Yes, ma'am."

She looks around the tavern. "Now don't make me come out here again. I've got pies to make." She stills the entire crowd with her stare, then stalks back into the kitchens.

"That's my lovely wife." Reeger grins. "Now, who's ready for another tankard of ale?"

I look at Maurice. "And I'll get on with my story."

CHAPTER SIXTEEN

AS WAS USUALLY the case after monster attacks, no one in the castle got much sleep. The members of court could talk about nothing other than preparations for Sir Dalbry's upcoming dragon hunt and possible (though optimistic) rescue operation. Old Mother Singra delivered tea to anyone who wanted a cup, though her trembling hands spilled much of it. She looked haunted and dismayed, and her private chat with Duke Kerrl had not calmed her a bit.

With Affonyl gone, Cullin was too agitated to sleep. Even before the screams and the explosion, he had lain awake, plagued by undeveloped romantic fantasies. The beautiful blond princess had so flirtatiously ignored him. And now that she was perpetrating her own scam to rival anything that he, Dalbry, and Reeger could make up, Cullin found her more intriguing than ever.

Unfortunately, before dawn Duke Kerrl came up with an idea that caused another round of complications and consternation.

Kerrl frowned, stroking his long black mustache. "Sire, now that we know the magnitude of the threat, we also have to think of history. Brave Sir Dalbry is experienced, to be sure, but this is a more personal matter for you and me. She is my betrothed and your daughter. We must both join the dragon-slaying party."

Norrimun balked. "I'm sure that's not necessary."

"Oh, but it is, Sire." Duke Kerrl proved he could be quite persistent. "Just think about Nightingale Bob's lyrics." His dark eyes were intense. Cullin wondered what had changed the duke's mind.

Cullin and Dalbry were alarmed by the added complication. "Dragon slaying is a profession best conducted alone—or with no one but my apprentice, Squire Cullin. Your company is not required."

Norrimun was unprepared for a dragon hunt, even an imaginary one, and the duke seemed less devastated than annoyed that his plans had been thrown off-kilter. He took the loss of the princess with an undukely lack of grace, as if dragons were an inconvenience that should not be tolerated.

"The king and I must insist," Kerrl said, and bullied Norrimun into agreeing. Dalbry could no longer argue. He and Cullin sighed in unison and tried to readjust to the new circumstances.

The rest of the court remained on high alert. The fires in the castle kitchens were stoked and pastry chefs roused early so they could create a memorable pre-dragon-slaying repast.

Now that the king had been pressured into going along, Norrimun's armorers and clothiers met in an emergency session to perform immediate alterations so the corpulent ruler could join the quest. He required armor that provided a modicum of protection for his bodily enormity, while also allowing him to look stylish, as befitted a king. (The clothiers engaged in a grammatical debate as to whether the proper declension of the verb was "befitted" or, in King Norrimun's case, whether the word should be "befat.")

Amidst the bustle, a shaky-looking Tremayne had stumbled out of his chambers. Though his skin was gray and sweaty and his knees wobbly, he declared, "I am ready to slay the monster and avenge the princess!" Then he turned green again and rushed back to his room for more quality time with a chamber pot. Sir Phineal bravely hurried to attend him.

Cullin followed Sir Dalbry, as a good squire should. "We have to play out the princess's game, while also finishing our own," Dalbry said in a low voice. "Fortunately, Sir Phineal and Sir Tremayne aren't going to cause problems, but the duke and the king certainly are."

"We're not actually going to rescue her, are we? I mean, if Princess Affonyl staged being devoured by a dragon just so she could run away, it would be a grave disservice to drag her back to court and force her to marry that evil man."

"We have no evidence that he's evil," Dalbry said. "Other than the fact that she doesn't wish to marry him."

"He does have a black mustache," Cullin pointed out.

"Granted. But we have been engaged to slay a dragon—that is all. Any bonus quests are beyond the scope of our employment, especially if we're only getting a modest honorarium."

Cullin knew it would be difficult enough for them to find a way to sidestep the persistent and unwanted company, meet up with Reeger, and perform their required dragon-slaying duties without prying eyes.

Troubled, Dalbry paced the castle's great hall while the rest of the court kept busy. "Before we set out, our first order of business is to remedy the situation that I am currently unhorsed."

"You've been unhorsed as long as I've known you."

"True, but at present it's more of a hindrance than usual. The duke and the king will be riding, so it would be unseemly if I, the only dragon slayer among us, had to go on foot."

"And I'm a squire," Cullin pointed out. "It's important that your apprentice dragon slayer should also ride."

"Just make sure your horse is less impressive than mine. Perhaps a pony."

Cullin decided to be satisfied with a pony.

Since they already had King Norrimun's blessing, the two went to sign out a pair of rental steeds. The stablemaster came out, bleary-eyed and harried; he had had a busy night. He didn't appreciate dragon attacks and unexpected quests, which threw off his entire schedule.

Dalbry presented himself. "I require a horse for myself and a pony for my squire, preferably recent-year models."

The stablemaster grimaced. "What happened to your own horses?"

"My valiant horse was devoured by a dragon," Dalbry explained.

"Poor Lightning . . ." Cullin said.

Dalbry put an edge in his voice, since the stablemaster didn't seem inclined to move. "I am in the business of slaying dragons and hunting down the beast that stole Princess Affonyl."

"Poor Princess Affonyl . . ." Cullin said.

Dalbry put his gauntleted hands on his chain-mailed hips. "We can get a written order from King Norrimun, if you like."

The stablemaster pursed his lips. "I'll let you look at my selection, but don't expect much. My inventory is low right now."

The selection of loaner horses was indeed limited. Most of the stalls were empty, although horses had been there recently, judging from the level of manure and scraps of hay. Cullin wondered if the surplus horses had been eaten during the previous night's feast.

Dalbry frowned at the stablemaster. "This is all you have?"

"We had more last night, but twenty lords rode out this morning."

Cullin feared that they all had gone out on a pell-mell dragon hunt, which would mess up the scam even further.

"They fled when they heard a dragon had attacked the castle," the stablemaster explained. "Grabbed their possessions and saddles and raced away before dawn."

Dalbry raised his bearded chin. "I am a knight, and I deserve a white stallion. It's a mandatory accessory for dragon slaying."

"I have one for you, but it's not a stallion, just a gelding."

"That'll do. As long as it's white."

"It is white—underneath all the gray spatters and black spots." The horse looked as if it had rolled around in the cold ashes of a campfire. "Best I can do."

Dalbry sighed. "My other brave steed was named Lightning. He held a dear place in my heart before he sacrificed himself so that I might live."

"Poor Lightning . . ." Cullin said.

"So I'll name this one Lightning as well, for continuity and for nostalgia."

The stablemaster shook his head. "We already have a Lightning on the stable rolls. Can't have two horses with the same name. That would be confusing."

"Very well. The alternative would be to name him Thunder."

Cullin agreed that was an impressive name.

"Sorry, sir. We already have a Thunder as well."

They went through a succession of meteorological alternatives until finally settling on the best available name. Sir Dalbry's horse was henceforth called Drizzle.

For himself, Cullin had to make do with a pony that already looked exhausted. The creature's condition was understandable: its previous owner had seven children, each one more rambunctious than the last, all of whom loved their pet pony and insisted on riding him all day long, every day, until the pony's patience and life essence had been drained away.

When the two mounts were saddled (all tack bore a label that stated, "Property of King Norrimun the Corpulent"), Cullin and Dalbry rode to the castle gate, tied up their horses, and went back inside to see what was taking King Norrimun and Duke Kerrl so long.

The king had rushed through breakfast, consuming only three pastries, four eggs, a bowl of porridge, and a tray of scones slathered with jam. Still at the table, Norrimun looked haggard and dismayed. Duke Kerrl was at his side with a stack of official-looking documents as well as two prissy men who seemed less suited for armed combat than for bean counting (magic beans or otherwise). They were the duke's lawyers.

The duke stroked his mustache. "The loss of your daughter is a tragedy, to be sure—we can agree on that—but no need to be overly saddened by these events, Sire. I was looking forward to the bonds of holy and lucrative matrimony, but all is not lost. There's no need for our agreement to be null and void just because Affonyl is no longer part of it. I want you to think of me as your son. We can still sign the paperwork, with appropriate revisions and addenda."

Norrimun's shoulders slumped. "I wanted Affonyl to give me grandbabies, cook at your hearth, darn your socks, patch your armor. You would have given her something to occupy herself other than those silly books and scrolls and charts." He let out a sad sigh. "Without you, she would have become an old maid, I'm sure of it. She should have been married to you."

"And our lands should have been joined," said the duke. "We can salvage that part at least, in her memory. She was a princess through and through, and she would have wanted it that way. My attorneys have redrafted the documents, and I assure you they are fully licensed in the use of whereases and wherefores. We must be prepared before you and I ride out to face the monster. Once you sign this and affix your seal, I will be your true son and heir, all nice and legal. Your kingdom and my dukedom will be permanently bound together, for the good of everyone."

King Norrimun sniffed. "A dukedom and a kingdom . . . but what shall we call it?"

Kerrl brushed his black mustache. "Why, a *dukingdom*, of course."

"Yes, I think dear Affonyl would have liked that." Norrimun grabbed a goose quill, dipped its tip into an inkpot, and scrawled his name on the documents. Duke Kerrl's lawyers promptly fetched a lit candle, poured a blob of wax onto the paper, and affixed the appropriate seal. King Norrimun's notary came forward and placed a stamp on the document.

Kerrl's entire demeanor changed immediately. "Now that the important but unsavory matters have been dealt with, we can get on with the rest of the day's activity. Off to slay a dragon!" He looked up and saw Dalbry and Cullin. "Ah, and here are our companions."

Cullin could see the masked disgust on Sir Dalbry's face. "Reminds me of what happened to my fief," the old knight muttered. "But there's nothing we can do about it. The papers are signed."

"I can't see that King Norrimun is much better than Duke Kerrl," Cullin muttered.

But the high politics of dukedoms and kingdoms, machinations and cartographical bargainings, were beyond him. He just hoped that after this job was finished they would find Princess Affonyl.

CHAPTER SEVENTEEN

FOR THE FIRST time in her life, Princess Affonyl was free to do whatever she liked. A princess might be a princess, as her father always said, but now she was also a *person*. It seemed to be the best of both worlds.

She wanted to pursue her dreams, a career path of her own choosing—natural investigations, exploration, experiments—all the fun stuff. She was a young woman with imagination, and she had her wits about her. Affonyl knew she was destined for more than marrying some brute who considered her part of an inventory sheet.

Now, the opportunities seemed limitless. The world was her oyster, except she didn't care for oysters. Better yet, the world was her *raspberry*. She liked raspberries.

The plan she had developed with old Mother Singra had exceeded her wildest expectations. Sir Dalbry and Sir Tremayne couldn't have come at a better time with their stories about dragons.

The whole evening had played out perfectly. At the banquet, Duke Kerrl had given her ample reason to storm off and lock herself in her chamber, as she had known he would. The man was a chauvinistic churl, unfit for any woman with more brains than air between her ears. (Alas, she knew that many of her ladies-in-waiting would have been delighted to have the duke for a husband.)

After barring her door, she had made dragon claw marks on her wall with a chisel, hammering deep parallel lines into the stone blocks, while Mother Singra finished fashioning three impressive-looking "dragon scales" from river-turtle shells that Wizard Edgar had kept in his storage unit. It was certainly enough to provide the illusion.

As Affonyl prepared the explosion for the simulated dragon attack, Mother Singra had herded all the cats to the shelter of a sturdy wardrobe. After the princess lit the fuse, she crawled under her heavy bed and waited for the cask of alchemical powder to detonate. The explosion was remarkable, more energetic than her previous experiments had suggested. The deafening roar caused great damage to her chamber, blowing a hole right through the balcony, and creating much confusion among her cats.

After the interminable songs and tales about dragon attacks, her father and the duke would have few doubts.

Suffocating smoke filled the room, and Affonyl waved the stinging fumes from her eyes. When Mother Singra emerged from the wardrobe, the cats sought comfort and reassurance, and the princess quickly petted each one, but she didn't have much time. She would miss them, too, but cats tended to be good at caring for themselves.

"Someone will soon be pounding on the door, dearling," the old woman had said. "You have to hurry. I know what to say to them, but you must be away from the castle." The old woman seemed to revel in helping the princess with her scheme. She grinned, and Affonyl realized how unusual it was for a woman her age to have such a large percentage of her teeth intact. "Time for you to start your new life. Ah, I wish I'd had the nerve to do that, many decades ago."

Affonyl felt a pang in her heart; despite all the advantages of her new circumstances, she was going to miss the old woman who had cared for her (and for so many previous generations).

She grabbed her sack of necessary items, everything she and Mother Singra had thrown together while planning her escape. Affonyl had already changed into comfortable breeches and a loose-fitting peasant jerkin that gave her arms room to move. What a relief to be unencumbered by a corset!

Hurrying beside her, Mother Singra helped her pound a small iron eyelet between blocks in the blasted windowsill, and Affonyl threaded a rope through the hole, tested the strength of the cord, and gave the old woman a last longing look. "Goodbye, Mother Singra, I'll miss you." She kissed her cheek and saw a bright tear trickling down the obstacle course of her friend's facial wrinkles.

"You were a bright spot in the castle, dearling. But off you go, now. I understand that a young girl needs her adventures."

"Thank you for everything."

The old woman shooed her off. "I'll cover for you—but you'd best get going."

Affonyl had swung herself over the crumbling edge, walked down the castle wall to the ground, and retrieved the rope. Her pack of necessary items was already cumbersome, but a girl never knew when she might need a rope; she slung it over her shoulder and hurried away as the fires died down and the shouts rose louder.

She felt sorry to be leaving her father, but what choice had he left her? "Don't start thinking of yourself as a person." Indeed!

Affonyl felt perfectly ready to take care of herself. She used a rag to wipe away the last smudges of makeup the ladies had dabbed on her face before the feast. To complete her disguise and to throw off the last chains of her princess life, Affonyl used a dagger to cut off her long braid, leaving her hair a shaggy mop.

She glanced behind her at the castle tower in the moonlight and the gaping hole that had once been her window. Yes, that dragon had done plenty of damage.

The small silhouette of Mother Singra waved, then ducked back inside to set the scene.

Affonyl headed down the main road, making her way to the port city of Rivermouth. She could barely contain her excitement. Prince Indico's ship was due to dock within a few days. He would take her off to the life she really wanted.

Incognito, Princess Affonyl arrived in Rivermouth the next day. Mother Singra had packed snacks for her, along with coins and a few changes of clothing. While she trudged through the night, Affonyl concocted an entire new life story: from now on, she would claim to be a specialist in exotic herbs, potions, and spells, although she had to be careful not to be confused with a witch, for which she was not licensed.

Since Affonyl had grown up listening to constant gossip about anything and everyone at court, she was surprised that no one in Rivermouth seemed to care about who she was or what she did, so long as she had the coin to pay for whatever she purchased. It was refreshing.

Walking through the streets of Rivermouth, she enjoyed all the "normal" sights. Down at the docks, she listened to the fishmongers yelling out special sales, seaweed seamstresses hawking waterproof though odoriferous garments, and tourist boats offering full harbor tours of Rivermouth and the subdistricts of Guttermouth and Sewermouth.

Affonyl listened to the townspeople talk about how a dragon had broken into the tower, devoured the princess whole, and torn half the castle into rubble. The story grew more exaggerated each time she heard it, which was silly, since anyone could go up the main road and have a look for himself or herself to see that the castle was still mostly intact.

In her father's kingdom, stories were often more important than facts.

She wished the intrepid dragon slayers good luck, meanwhile. Maybe they would find a monster after all. Maybe Duke Kerrl would be accidentally devoured. It didn't matter to her—soon, she would be sailing away with her dashing merchant prince to begin a new and much happier life, doing exactly what she wanted. . . .

She ate food that was inferior to the worst leftovers at her father's court and enjoyed it. She stayed at an inn with pallets of straw and prickly sheets, but she slept soundly the next night, without a care. She had much to learn about being a *person* instead of a princess and decided it was worth the sacrifice. Once she met up with Prince Indico, they would sail together to his private island principality where he would build her an observatory and a well-equipped laboratory so she could conduct her alchemical experiments. He would make just the right sort of husband.

Indico had promised her the moon and any constellations she could name if she eloped with him. At first, it had seemed only a distant dream; now, it was going to become a reality. Indico would be completely surprised when she arrived to take him up on the offer.

His ship pulled into port the next morning, with its colorful silken sails and gold trim, a well-dressed crew, and a cargo of exotic supplies. Merchants hurried to the docks to be the first to bid on the merchant prince's wares.

Affonyl decided to wait until the rush was over, although she was anxious to see her handsome explorer who would sail with her beyond the horizon, dodging sea serpents and mysterious storms to reach his magical island. There was going to be so much to see. She realized she needed to buy a notebook.

She spotted Indico on the gangplank of his ship. He wore a clean black shirt unlaced halfway down to show off his bronzed and muscular chest. A blue bandana wrapped his head, and his thin mustache was neatly trimmed and waxed; it looked so much more civilized than Duke Kerrl's villainous mustache.

The merchant prince directed workers to offload barrels of imported wine, bolts of fabric, and salted lye-cured fish that Indico insisted was a rare delicacy in his kingdom; he sold it at a premium to Rivermouth merchants, though they had difficulty selling it to anyone who tasted it.

Unable to hide her grin, Affonyl walked toward the gangplank. When Indico glanced up, his gaze skated right over her. With her hair shorn, wearing a drab jerkin and peasant's trousers, no wonder he didn't recognize Princess Affonyl. He was going to be in for a shock!

She bounded up the gangplank and called out, "Indico—it's me!" She threw herself into his arms, but a startled Indico pushed her away and held her at arm's length.

His crew paused while hauling the heavy rope and cargo. They snickered. "Another one?"

Affonyl ignored them. "Prince Indico, it's me. *Affonyl.*"

"Prince?" said one of the sailors and let out a guffaw.

Indico seemed to be trying to recall her name. "Affonyl?"

"*Princess* Affonyl. The daughter of King Norrimun."

He blinked. "Ah, of course! But what happened to you? Your hair, your clothes, your makeup." He sniffed. "Your perfume."

"I don't need to worry about any of that now. You and I can be together without courtly obligations or politics." In a rush she spilled out the story of how she had faked her death by blaming it on a dragon attack. "I gave it all up, my clothes, my kingdom, my treasure, my jewels." She hefted her sack of necessary items. "I've got all I need right here. My books, chemical samples, a few changes of clothes, some walking-about-the-harbor money, but that's all. We can elope, just like you wanted. We'll sail away to your merchant island and set up my alchemy lab, observatory, maybe even a library."

Indico's crew were quite amused. The merchant prince kept her at a cool distance. "But if you're no longer a princess . . . Why, dear silly girl, I can have any penniless peasant wench I like."

"And he often does," muttered one sailor.

Affonyl's dreams and plans crumbled.

Indico shook his head. "If you were heir to Norrimun's kingdom, it would be a different story, but . . . Here, I'll give you my card. If circumstances change again, you can look me up when I'm back in town."

On deck, the captain's cabin door swung open, and a beautiful raven-haired woman sashayed out, swinging her hips to swirl the scarlet skirt she wore. Her corset was cinched so tightly that her bodice practically erupted with breastly bounty. She looked as if she had graduated with full honors from the nearest Saucy Wench Academy. Her eyes flashed upon seeing the ragamuffin Affonyl. "Indico, honey, is she bothering you? Would you like me to scratch her eyes out?"

Fuming, Affonyl yanked herself out of Indico's grasp. "That won't be necessary. I'm obviously on the wrong ship." She spoke out of the corner of her mouth to the raven-haired beauty. "There may come a time when you want my help to scratch this bastard's eyes out." She stalked back down the gangplank and away from the ship.

It was a change of plans, but Affonyl remained undaunted. She would just have to come up with a different set of dreams.

She had no regrets. If her merchant prince—who likely wasn't even a prince—didn't want her, then Affonyl certainly didn't need him. She could take care of herself. She would forget princes and dukes and nunneries. From now on this princess would be a person—her *own* person.

CHAPTER EIGHTEEN

DUKE KERRL AND King Norrimun agreed that Sir Dalbry should lead the hunt for the dragon, since he was the only one with experience. Cullin couldn't understand why Kerrl was so eager to accompany them, or why he had pressured the obviously ineffective and corpulent king to go along. It was going to cause problems.

Sir Dalbry sat tall on Drizzle, imagining himself on a proud white stallion rather than one with unsightly speckles. Cullin rode his even-less-inspiringly named pony, Pony. They followed the road into the sinister forest, and Dalbry dismounted to look in the underbrush. Putting on a show, he lifted his nose to sniff the air and peered into the trees. "I believe the dragon went that way."

The duke frowned. "I don't see anything. How can you tell?"

"Dragons leave a subtle but unmistakable mark of their passage. I can show you, if you'd like to join me?"

King Norrimun was exhausted and uncomfortable from just sitting in a saddle. "I'll take your word for it, Sir Dalbry." Back at the castle, it had taken several men and a small crane designed for loading sacks of grain to lift the corpulent king onto his horse.

When they camped at night, Cullin wondered how they would ever get him off his horse, let alone back on again. He swung down from his pony. Since he was unpracticed in dismounting, he landed on the ground with less grace than he had intended. Cullin knelt beside the knight as he stirred the shrubbery.

Dalbry spoke in a loud voice for the benefit of the others, "As you can see, Squire Cullin, the leaves of this bush have curled inward in a natural reaction to the fumes a dragon exhales. You've seen a dragon's fiery breath, but few people realize that dragons have just as deadly an exhaust from the other end. Come, let's venture into the forest so we can better determine the monster's direction."

They slipped into the underbrush, and Dalbry whispered to him, "While I keep leading them westward, back and forth, I'll send you off to hunt game for dinner. King Norrimun will insist on it."

Cullin understood. He knew Dalbry would stretch out the wild-goose chase for at least a day or two. "Good plan. Meanwhile, I'll track down Reeger and tell him what's going on. He needs to know this isn't a typical scam. I'll find out where we should guide the king and the duke. He's bound to have prepared a dragon lair by now."

Cullin arranged a meeting point, then went off hunting on foot, while the others led Pony on a guide rope. The young man had his dagger and practice sword, but for hunting he was better off throwing rocks. He expected he could gather up a brace of quail or a fluff of squirrels without too much effort. First, though, he had to find Reeger's camp, which took more than two hours of wandering through the forest.

Cullin tried to sneak in and surprise his friend, but the mule brayed as soon as he came close. Reeger was roasting a badger on a spit over a campfire. Cullin's mouth watered, since roasting badger with onions and sage had a distinctive smell. "Crotchrust, Cullin! You took your sweet time. Where's Dalbry? I found the most beautiful dragon's lair, best one we've ever used. There's something special about that cave. It'll be like the cherry on top of a plum pudding."

Cullin had never had a cherry on top of a plum pudding before.

"There's been a complication, thanks to Princess Affonyl." He couldn't keep the admiration out of his voice as he described how the beautiful princess had pulled off her scam.

"Sounds like an impressive young lady," Reeger said, "except she mucked up our plans."

Cullin hunkered down near the fire. "I prefer to see it as an opportunity, since her setup in the tower room makes our story all the more convincing. After we show your dragon's lair to the king and the duke, Dalbry just needs a little privacy so he can 'slay' the monster. We'll deliver one of our stuffed crocodile heads, and Nightingale Bob will have to add another verse to his song about brave Sir Dalbry."

Once he had all the information he needed, the young man was anxious to get back to Sir Dalbry and the others, since he still had to hunt their dinner. He was not anxious, though, to be there when they attempted to haul the corpulent king from his mount. Norrimun would be sore and stiff with his feet back on the ground again, and his horse would certainly be relieved.

Reeger didn't want him to go so quickly, though. "Rust, lad! Stay awhile. I've got a nice roasted badger, and I can't eat it all myself."

He realized that Reeger was just lonely. During a scam like this, Cullin and Dalbry got to spend time at court talking with lords and ladies, while Reeger was stuck by himself out in the forest, working. "Well, it does smell good. And I suppose the longer I stay away, the more they'll worry that a dragon got me."

So they split the badger, licked their fingers, and sat relaxed and satisfied for a while. Reeger adjusted his seat. "Before you go find Dalbry, you and I have some work to do."

"As long as it isn't excavating skeletons from graveyards."

Reeger made a rude sound. "Already distributed those. You can help me replenish our supply in the next kingdom, but right now, I've got something fresher."

Cullin didn't like the sound of that

Reeger stretched and cracked his back. "I found a dead body, and I know just what to do with it."

Reeger had discovered a hanged man at a forest crossroads and was very excited by the condition of it, while Cullin thought the corpse's condition left much to be desired. Even in the deepening dusk, he could see that crows had pecked out the man's eyes and shredded his face; other vermin had snacked on his fingers and his neck. The corpse's clothes were in tatters, and his feet were bare. A legal certificate tacked onto the hanging tree identified the executed man as a proven thief and rapist.

Reeger gestured upward with the torch he carried. "Go on, lad—climb up there and cut him down."

Cullin grimaced. "He's awfully ripe. Why should I have to do the disgusting work?"

Reeger tilted his head. "You want to keep score, disgusting for disgusting? Is that really a game you want to play?" Cullin decided not. "Besides, you're more nimble than I am."

So, the young man clambered up, grabbing branches and footholds until he could crawl out onto the limb where the noose was tied. He sawed the rope with his pocket dagger. Reeger stood under the corpse and held out his arms to catch the hanged man, but the rotting body broke into several pieces in his arms, dripping putrescence as it fell.

Reeger spluttered, dumped the body parts on the ground, and wiped his face. "You still sure you got the disgusting part of the job, lad?"

"You win, as usual." Cullin climbed back down the tree.

"For what I have in mind, a body's more effective if it's got some meat on the bones," Reeger said. "I found just the right spot for the scene, and I'm ready to make my dragon tracks."

They hauled the hanged man's remnants to the chosen location; Cullin bore the heavier parts, but Reeger carried the juicier ones, so Cullin didn't complain.

They set up a fake camp and concocted their story, deciding that this poor man must have been a wandering tinker who enjoyed the natural beauty of Norrimun's kingdom. "Alas, his vacation was cut short when a dragon attacked his camp and ate most of him," said Reeger. He set fire to the deadwood around the camp and put kindling close to the body so it would be properly blackened and roasted.

With an indulgent smile, he let Cullin don the wooden footprints this time, and the young man stomped around the smoldering scene, smashing twigs, leaving clear three-toed imprints in the black ash. When they were done, Reeger inspected the "massacre site," satisfied. Cullin agreed it was convincing.

"Now, lead the duke and king here to show them the evidence of another dragon attack. After you've got them worked up, your next stop will be the dragon's lair, a cave the locals call Old Snort. You're going to love it."

CHAPTER NINETEEN

WHEN CULLIN STUMBLED into the clearing at dawn, he felt as exhausted and bedraggled as he intended to look.

Sir Dalbry rose to his feet, delighted and relieved. "Squire Cullin, you're safe! We were so worried when you never returned from hunting our dinner."

Norrimun scowled. "We had to eat pack food. All of our supplies are gone."

Cullin was surprised. "We packed enough for a week."

"Gone!" the king cried.

Dalbry made a show of embracing the young man, which gave him an opportunity to whisper, "Did you find Reeger?"

"Yes, and I helped him prepare something special, like a cherry on a plum pudding."

Dalbry frowned. "Who puts cherries on plum pudding?"

"Did you bring breakfast?" asked King Norrimun. The fat ruler was glad to see that Cullin carried a skinned woodchuck and a game hen, then disappointed to realize that he had neither his kitchen staff nor kitchen equipment on their quest.

"We decided you must have been eaten by the dragon," Duke Kerrl said. "These woods are dangerous."

Cullin hadn't rested at all, and he'd gotten no sleep the night before either. Now, his unkempt appearance only heightened the effect of his story. "I was lost, and then stalked—I'm sure it was the dragon. Then, just when I thought I was safe, I found another victim."

"Dead?" King Norrimun asked.

"Yes, a dead victim! I can take you there. It might give us clues about how to find the dragon."

"We set out at once," the king announced. "Immediately after breakfast."

As the lowest-ranking person in camp, it was Cullin's job to prepare the woodchuck and game hen. The king was disappointed in the quality of the food, although Cullin did his best.

After breakfast, he wanted nothing more than a nap, but Sir Dalbry called for his horse Drizzle, and the squire had to saddle it for him. Meanwhile, King Norrimun's horse cringed at the ordeal it would have to endure for yet another day.

Oddly, Duke Kerrl seemed more enthusiastic than before. "I look forward to a productive day of dragon hunting." He smiled at Norrimun and added, "*Dad*."

The king seemed startled by the reminder about who would be heir to the dukingdom. Since Duke Kerrl had what he wanted, Cullin doubted the man had any interest in finding the princess alive. Affonyl certainly didn't want to be found.

The group did not set out until late morning, much to Sir Dalbry's frustration, but Cullin, overburdened by performing duties for three men plus tending Pony, took all the time he needed. "You can't rush a good dragon hunt."

He led them toward the site of the dragon attack he had "stumbled upon" the previous night, but the forest looked much different in the daylight, and he had to backtrack. Cullin finally found the location by the stench of burned wood and roasted flesh. Dalbry moved along with his gaze to the ground, studying the evidence and deconstructing the crime. He inspected the blackened bones and charred skull of the hanged man's body, while the frightened king hung back.

Duke Kerrl sniffed around curiously. "It's not Affonyl, is it? Doesn't look much like her."

"No, Majesty," Cullin said. "This was a wandering tinker who enjoyed the natural beauty of your kingdom. Alas, his vacation was cut short when a dragon attacked his camp and ate him."

Dalbry responded with a grave nod. "This dragon has proved its appetite for human flesh. It destroyed part of your castle, took the lovely princess, and murdered this poor tinker."

Kerrl held up the blackened skull, then dropped it to the ground. "I am very impressed. Others would have shivered beneath their blankets, like Sir Phineal, but you, Dad, are brave enough to face the danger in person. Even though the risk is greater to you than to anyone else here, you still do your duty. What a king!"

Cullin asked, "Excuse me, aren't we all in danger? Why is the risk to King Norrimun greater than to the rest of us?"

The duke gave a flippant wave of his hand. "Think about it. Who would make the heartiest meal for a hungry dragon?"

Neither Cullin nor Sir Dalbry could argue with the logic.

King Norrimun was distraught that he hadn't thought of it himself. "Maybe I should just go back to the castle now and leave the hard work to you. I can be back in time for lunch. It will be all the same to Princess Affonyl, if you do manage to find her. A princess is a princess, and she knows her duties."

Dalbry quickly said, "Agreed, Majesty. Squire Cullin and I can finish the job. We will report to you if you and the duke wish to return to the safety of the castle."

"Nonsense," Kerrl interjected. "A king is a king, too, and your obligation is to go on honorable quests, like this one, despite the tremendous hardships."

The corpulent king was not pleased by this, but he did seem to know his responsibilities.

"We may be done with this soon enough, Majesty." Sir Dalbry pointed out the three-toed dragon footprints, garnering clues from bent twigs in addition to the whispered instructions Cullin gave him on how to find the cave of Old Snort.

Sir Dalbry took the lead, guiding them in the general direction of the cave. Cullin tried to think of a way to separate Dalbry from his unwanted companions, so they could complete their plan, and return with a dubious trophy. Once they claimed to have slain the dragon, they would collect their small honorarium. The duke remained close to King Norrimun throughout the day—too close. Cullin struggled to figure out what he was up to. Kerrl had already forced Norrimun to sign over the kingdom to the duke. Maybe he planned to arrange for an expedited inheritance?

And terrified King Norrimun now needed protection more than he needed dragon slayers. He refused to be far from Sir Dalbry, and Duke Kerrl refused to go far from the king. It was an awkward situation all around.

Throughout the day, Cullin glimpsed the shadowy figure of Reeger following them, keeping tabs. When they camped that night, Cullin was glad for a chance to sleep at last . . . but just as the young man drifted off, a horrific roar shattered the stillness—a guttural, reptilian bellow that sounded suspiciously Reeger-like.

Then a tree crashed down in the darkness near the camp: a rotted old trunk that Reeger had no doubt pushed over.

King Norrimun was so alarmed that he demanded the party pack up camp and leave to find a safer spot—which they did.

They moved three more times throughout the night, and Reeger kept making loud dragon roars and knocking down nearby trees. It was a very effective and convincing scare tactic, but Cullin didn't appreciate it one bit.

When they finally bedded down for what Cullin hoped would be the last time that evening—Reeger had made his point!—the king was so skittish that he commanded Squire Cullin to remain awake and stand watch until dawn.

CHAPTER TWENTY

AFTER THAT STRESSFUL, sleepless night, Sir Dalbry led the intrepid and not-so-intrepid dragon hunters to the sinister cave without further ado. Seeing the older knight's bloodshot eyes, Cullin assumed Dalbry was also growing impatient with the runaround. He doubted King Norrimun could tolerate the stress, hardship, severe exercise, and lack of usual diet for much longer, either.

Dalbry continued to track, pretending to spot subtle details of the dragon's passage. Whenever the knight got sidetracked, Cullin corrected him, which made his own abilities seem more proficient. He hoped that minstrels might even include his name in a few songs. Maybe Princess Affonyl would hear about him, wherever she was, and wonder what had happened to the handsome young man she had ignored during the Saint Bartimund's feast. . . .

As they approached the cave of Old Snort, the landscape became bleak and charred. The soil was poisoned; vegetation had died; trees stood in tall brown dismay as if all the life had been sucked out of them by the roots.

"It smells like the devil's breath." King Norrimun's lower lip trembled. "Affonyl must be even closer to that stench, and she has a sensitive nose."

Duke Kerrl made a helpful comment. "More likely she's in the belly of that dragon, where she can't smell a thing."

The horses were reluctant to go farther. Pony, not to be outdone, tried to bolt away, and Cullin had to wrestle the reins.

"We'd better leave the horses here and approach on foot," said Sir Dalbry.

"On foot?" Norrimun sounded as if the prospect of huffing and puffing along the steep ravines was more frightening than facing the dragon itself.

"It's the only way, Majesty—and we must be cautious so the monster doesn't sense us."

Cullin swung down and tied Pony to a tree, before helping Sir Dalbry secure his ash-speckled gelding. Duke Kerrl didn't bother to wait for the squire's assistance. It took the three of them together to wrestle King Norrimun out of his saddle.

Sir Dalbry placed a gauntleted hand to his ear, listening intently. He whispered back, "Follow me, but tread lightly. We must not alert the monster to our presence." They set off, and King Norrimun stumbled through the underbrush. Although he tried to keep the crashing sounds to a minimum, he did not at all succeed.

The brimstone stink grew more intense, and they found a small poisoned spring, a trickle of water oozing out of a crack in the soil, smeared with slimy algae. Steam bubbled up.

"See the evidence of the dragon's presence," Dalbry whispered. "Its excrement taints the water supply."

Their timing couldn't have been better. Even before they reached the cave, a loud roar and hissing gurgle erupted like a contained thunderstorm. Clouds of dissipating steam rolled across the landscape, and the men scrambled for shelter among the dead trees. Norrimun yelped, "The dragon!"

Thanks to Reeger, Cullin knew about the hot spring and geyser, but since none of them carried an accurate timepiece, they had no way of predicting when the next explosion would occur.

For the first time, Kerrl sounded anxious. "We're exposed here. If the monster flies out, it'll see us."

"That sound is probably just indigestion from the poor man it devoured two nights ago," Dalbry suggested. "Or maybe even a sheep it consumed last night."

"It was hunting *us* last night," Norrimun reminded them. "We heard the crashing trees close to the camp."

"All night long," Cullin added.

Dalbry said, "Nevertheless, we're probably safe at the moment. Giant reptilian monsters tend to sleep during the daytime."

"I wish Sir Phineal were here," the king said.

"I don't," said Duke Kerrl.

After the geyser sounds died away, the four men crept forward until they reached the dragon's lair. The cave of Old Snort was as magnificent a location as Reeger had promised: blasted soil, dead trees, spare human bones strewn about—Cullin even recognized a few of them—and a low cave that exhaled hot miasmic odors.

"Typical dragon's lair," said Sir Dalbry, "straight out of a natural historian's fieldbook."

Norrimun swallowed hard. "So, are we . . . are we going in to kill it? Right away? I'm not sure I have the energy. I didn't have any breakfast."

"We should scout the area first," Cullin said. "Sir Dalbry and I need to make our plan of attack."

Dalbry gave the others a thin smile as they all headed back to the horses. "Squire Cullin is correct. Dragon slaying is an intense business that demands the utmost concentration. My squire and I require time alone in the forest for the three P's."

"Three P's?" King Norrimun asked.

"Prayer, pondering, and preparation."

Once they made their way to the horses and Pony, King Norrimun was glad to be far from the dragon's lair and perfectly content to let Sir Dalbry go through his usual pre-slaying routine.

"We'll be back before nightfall," said Cullin as he and the knight set off for some time alone in the forest. "Leave the dangerous work to us."

They soon lost themselves in the trees and headed straight for Reeger. He had moved his small camp closer to Old Snort and now stood waiting for them with hands on his hips. "All the pieces are in place—let's finish it up."

Dalbry took a seat on a stump. "We finally managed to get some elbow room from the duke and the king. Good work, Reeger. The dragon's lair looks very professional."

Reeger untied one of the larger sacks from the mule's saddle and dropped it to the ground. The beast brayed, but again no one could understand what it meant. "If you can convince the king and duke to let you slay the rustin' dragon yourself, it'll be much more convenient for all concerned."

He removed a battered reptilian head from the sack. It was large for a crocodile head, but small for a dragon's. Some of the stuffing had come loose, a few scales were flaking off, and one of the sanded-antler horns was wobbly. "It's our last one, and it's starting to look less than convincing."

"After we're done here, we'll go down to Rivermouth and get more from Ossio," Dalbry said.

Cullin added in a hopeful voice, "Maybe we'll even find Princess Affonyl down there."

Reeger rolled his eyes. "Dalbry, our lad is smitten. He needs to concentrate on more important things."

"Don't chastise the boy for having a soft heart. The princess was in a bad situation and solved it as best she could. Duke Kerrl manipulated the king, and I'm all too familiar with that situation. Some immoral nobles can steal more with the stroke of a goose-quill pen than a cutpurse can steal with a knife. Norrimun's a fool—no question about that—and he tried to save his kingdom by getting rid of his daughter, but I believe Duke Kerrl is far worse. Affonyl was out of good options."

"I don't trust the duke," Cullin said. "It makes me nervous just leaving him with the king."

"We can't watch him every minute, lad," the older knight said. "All we can do is finish our work here, take our reward, and move on."

King Norrimun didn't want to be alone in the forest, especially not so near a known dragon's lair, but he didn't like being stuck with his ambitious not-quite-son-in-law either.

Shortly after Sir Dalbry and his squire vanished into the forest to make their three P's, Kerrl sat on a rock and made a show of sharpening his sword. "I intend to have another look at that cave. Maybe I can find evidence of the princess. If the dragon did eat my fiancée, I feel obligated to avenge her."

King Norrimun was not overly pleased that the duke intended to abandon him in the sinister forest. "Shouldn't we leave it to the professionals?"

"Mere freelancers sniffing after an honorarium? If we can do the job in-house, we'll save on expenses—and I'm only thinking of the financial security of our dukingdom. Maybe just the two of us can handle this." The duke trudged away, flashing a glance over his shoulder. "Look at the silver lining. Even without Affonyl, the land will be in good hands with me, *Dad*. Don't you worry."

Norrimun had decidedly mixed feelings, but Kerrl set off with a determined glint in his eye. "I'll be back in a jiff."

And he was. Before King Norrimun had a chance to grow too nervous from all the usual terrifying forest sounds, the duke bounded back to camp. His eyes glittered, and he wore an urgent expression. "You have to come with me right away, Dad! I found something. I think your daughter is still alive, and *we* can save her . . . but only if we hurry. I saw a tatter of Princess Affonyl's clothing, just outside the dragon's lair, and another piece of torn cloth leading into the cave."

The king fiddled with his curly beard. The prospect of "hurrying" sounded problematic. "Oh—so has she been eaten?" If so, they wouldn't need to bother with the rescuing.

"No way to tell . . . but I thought I heard a woman's voice crying out for help. We may have very little time! We have to go there ourselves."

"But . . . but Sir Dalbry—"

"Sir Dalbry might not be back until nightfall. What if the dragon gets the munchies before then? We don't dare delay. Affonyl's probably anxious for some man to come and rescue her."

King Norrimun was torn, knowing he was expected to rescue

his daughter, but also worried about self-preservation. He would have liked to jot down a list of pros and cons, but there was no time. "All right, we'd better go—but remember, I'm not good at fighting dragons."

While Kerrl set off at a brisk pace, the king struggled to keep up. Although he wanted to stop and rest, he knew the dragon would be growing hungrier every second, and Norrimun knew how cranky he himself got when he grew peckish.

The king whispered, "What if the dragon sees us?"

"You heard Sir Dalbry—dragons are nocturnal. This one is probably sleeping. We'll be fine."

"But if it does come after us, we can't run faster than a dragon."

"I don't have to run faster than a dragon." The duke narrowed his eyes. "I just have to run faster than *you*."

King Norrimun stopped, not sure he had heard correctly. "That's . . . a poor joke."

"No joke at all, *Dad*. Just a tactless observation."

Steam seeped out of cracks in the ground, and the stench of brimstone curled out of the cave. Norrimun couldn't hear any beseeching cries from his daughter, and he wondered if she might be taking a nap along with the dragon.

Drawing his sword, Kerrl strode ahead of the king toward a large boulder beside the mouth of the cave. "Look, over here!" Bending down, he pulled up a tatter of bright blue cloth.

King Norrimun recognized one of Affonyl's lacy scarves. "Oh, I guess she's here after all."

Norrimun drew his sword as well, if only to maintain appearances.

The duke held up a hand. "Listen—that sounds like whimpering from deep inside the cave. Can you hear it?"

"I don't hear a thing."

The duke shaded his eyes and pointed into the dark passage. "Look, another scrap of her clothing. We'd better rescue her."

"I'm sure she'd appreciate that."

Placing a hand on King Norrimun's back, the duke nudged him forward. "Come, it's up to the two of us. We've got to find her and free her."

"Then can we let Sir Dalbry come back to do the actual slaying? I'd prefer that."

"Yes, that would be fine."

Together, they ventured into the steamy dimness. King Norrimun breathed heavily, and his skin was wet both from perspiration and from the sulfurous vapors. Squinting into the murk, he did make out another scrap of Affonyl's dress deeper inside the cave.

The king had never been so afraid, and he realized that given enough adrenaline, he just might be able to run faster than Duke Kerrl after all.

Deeper inside the cave, he heard a hissing, gurgling sound that surely must have been the dragon snoring, but he still couldn't hear Affonyl's voice. He turned to make sure the duke was close behind him.

Kerrl brought the pommel of his sword smashing onto the back of his head. The corpulent king collapsed to the cave floor with a crash loud enough to wake even a sleeping dragon.

Duke Kerrl froze at the unexpectedly loud sound, listening for movement. If the huge scaly thing came roaring after them, the monster would stumble upon a ready-made meal right there on its doorstep.

When no beast approached, though, Kerrl removed leather thongs he had stashed in his waistband and used them to lash the king's wrists and ankles together. Now Norrimun couldn't get away even after he woke, and the duke could take care of him later. He knew well enough not to count on a dragon to do the work for him.

Kerrl smiled. Now the dukingdom was all his.

CHAPTER TWENTY-ONE

AFTER REEGER SET off toward the cave's side entrance to make final preparations, Sir Dalbry gave his armor a freshening so that he looked like a proper dragon slayer, while Cullin made his own way back to Old Snort to reconnoiter. He arrived just in time to watch King Norrimun and Duke Kerrl vanish into the cave.

He found that especially peculiar. While *Cullin* knew there was no dragon inside, he couldn't believe the other two men would be so foolish . . . or brave? Either way, the current scheme had no room for additional would-be dragon slayers.

He crept forward, alert and suspicious. Outside the ominous lair, he spotted a scrap of blue fabric, a scarf he was sure he had seen on the floor of Princess Affonyl's chamber after the explosion. How had that gotten there? It seemed unlikely—

Suddenly, he realized that Duke Kerrl must be perpetrating a ruse of his own. Had he sneaked away with one of Affonyl's scarves so that he could use it to lure King Norrimun into the lair? Did he believe a dragon lurked inside?

Cullin hadn't trusted the ambitious duke (and not just because he was a suitor for the beautiful princess). Kerrl was surely up to no good.

He tiptoed up to the cave mouth, following the two men. Sir Dalbry would arrive momentarily to publicly challenge the dragon, but Cullin couldn't afford to wait.

Inside the dim passageway, he nearly ran into the duke, who was bending over King Norrimun's unconscious, corpulent form. The startled duke lurched to his feet, and Cullin accused, "You just attacked the king!"

Kerrl's white teeth flashed in the dimness, because his smile was so broad. "No, uh . . . he bumped his head. The dragon smacked him with its tail as it fled. He—"

How stupid did the duke think he was? He flicked his gaze to the unconscious king. "His hands and ankles are bound. Did the dragon do that, too?"

Cullin drew his practice sword and held it in front of him, looking intent and unwavering. He tried to imitate the intimidating poise of Sir Dalbry's Raven on Corpse stance. Cullin was extremely skilled—at bluffing, if not at sword fighting.

Duke Kerrl glared at him, also holding out his sword, but he seemed just as reluctant to fight. For a long, tense moment, the two engaged in a sharp-edged duel of bluffing.

Outside, he heard Sir Dalbry stride up in front of the mouth of the lair, playing his role. "Foul dragon! I have come to slay you and avenge Princess Affonyl."

Seeing no escape out the main entrance, Kerrl backed farther into the cave, and Cullin said, "Aren't you worried about the dragon?"

The duke said, "There is no dragon. After Affonyl disappeared, I had a long and painful talk with old Mother Singra—painful for *her*, though I rather enjoyed it. Eventually, she confessed to the game she and the princess were playing. But I don't know how you're involved in it."

Cullin yelled over his shoulder, "Dalbry, we're in here! Duke Kerrl attacked the king and tied him up. I, uh, could use a hand."

With a clank and jangle of chain mail and boots, Dalbry bounded into the cave. "I'm coming!"

Even if he believed the dragon was nonexistent, Duke Kerrl did not want to face two very real armed men with swords. He retreated deeper into the cave.

When Dalbry reached the unconscious Norrimun, Cullin sprang after Kerrl. "I'll make sure he doesn't get away."

Dalbry bent down. "And I shall save the king. It's my chivalrous duty." With a grunt, he started to drag the corpulent man out into the sunlight.

Running, Kerrl finally reached the central grotto, where thin rays of sunlight streamed through cracks in the ceiling. Warm mist thickened the air. When Cullin reached the chamber, he saw the hot spring pool that Reeger had described. The water bubbled and churned, belching out gasps of sulfur.

Cullin ran toward Kerrl, waving his sword in what was intended to be a threatening manner. Seeing that he had no place to go, the duke crouched. He looked around at the pool and the jagged walls just to make sure there was no dragon—sleeping, fire-breathing, or otherwise. "Where's the princess? Where are you hiding her?"

Cullin couldn't stop himself from making the obligatory explanations, even though he was not the story's villain. "Affonyl is gone. She faked her own death to escape from marrying you."

"That's fine with me, boy. I didn't want to marry her either. I got what I wanted. The king signed the paperwork. Our lands are now joined, and there's nothing anyone can do about it."

"If the king has you hanged, that would put an end to your inheritance."

"Then I'll have to finish the job—kill you, the fat king, and the old knight."

"Good luck with that," Cullin said.

"I've always been ambitious. Or instead, I could just expose your scam, and we'd see whose neck got stretched first. Or does this kingdom use the executioner's axe? I forget the local regulations."

Cullin remembered the corpse of the thief and rapist he had cut down from the tree. "It's hanging."

Duke Kerrl's voice took on a more solicitous tone. "Maybe we can reach some sort of accord? We both have plenty to gain. Think about it: With King Norrimun gone, I'll control the dukingdom's entire treasury. You and I can agree on a story: I'll say the dragon slew King Norrimun and Princess Affonyl, then we give Sir Dalbry credit for eliminating the monster. You'll receive a large reward—double his usual fee. We all benefit." He held out his hands. "Let's be reasonable."

Behind him, the hot spring began to bubble and stir, and more steam filled the chamber. Cullin had no idea how soon the geyser would erupt, but those symptoms made him uneasy. He didn't want to stay there any longer than was absolutely necessary.

Through the mist, he spotted Reeger slipping in from the side, working his way into the grotto. He saw Cullin standing there with his practice sword and the evil-looking duke in an evil-looking pose.

As the hot pool gurgled, Cullin said, "I never claimed there was no dragon. Haven't you seen the evidence? It's well known that dragons sleep submerged in hot pools. That's how they regenerate the fires in the gullet."

Duke Kerrl sneered. "Don't speak nonsense, boy! I know all

about dragons. No minstrel has ever talked about hot pools. And the water would extinguish its fire—you know nothing about science."

Reeger moved forward, unseen in the swirling fog.

Cullin stared at a fixed point behind the duke, widened his eyes. "Oh, no—there it is!" He raised his sword defensively and backed away. "We woke the dragon!"

Though he flinched, Duke Kerrl kept his gaze locked on his opponent even as the geyser bubbled and fumed behind him. "You don't fool me, boy. I know what you're trying to do."

Cullin stepped backward. "It's a dragon right behind you, Duke!"

Kerrl's sword wavered from side to side, but he refused to let himself be tricked.

Right next to him, Reeger yelled, "*Boo!*"

The duke practically jumped out of his fine clothing and dropped his sword. The loud clang startled him even more. His boots skittered on the slimy floor, caught on a rock, and Duke Kerrl plunged backward into the boiling hot spring.

Reeger grabbed Cullin's arm and pulled him out through the main passage. "*Move*, lad! The rustin' geyser's going to blow!"

The two bounced and ricocheted off the walls as they rushed toward the bright patch of daylight. Gasping for breath, they stumbled out into the blasted clearing, where Dalbry had deposited King Norrimun. The older knight was trying to rouse the corpulent king when Reeger and Cullin raced out, yelling a warning.

Dalbry propped up the groggy, half-conscious king just as the geyser erupted and sulfurous steam vomited out, drenching them with scalding moisture. They all tumbled off to the side, panting, exhausted, and terrified.

While the king remained stunned and disoriented, Dalbry jerked his chin at Reeger. "Better get out of sight—Cullin and I will make up a story."

"Rust! *I'm* the one who's best at making up stories."

"We'll do fine by ourselves." Cullin nudged his friend. "But you'll ruin everything if the king sees you."

Grumbling and dripping, Reeger trudged off into the trees.

When King Norrimun finally awoke, he groaned, complaining about his split skull. Sir Dalbry said, "You've had quite an adventure. You were injured in the dragon attack, Sire."

"Dragon attack?" The corpulent king struggled to get to his feet but managed no more than a sitting position before he clutched his head again. "What about Affonyl?"

"I'm afraid the princess is no more," Cullin said. "We dragged you to safety . . . but, alas, when Duke Kerrl faced the monster, he, too, was slain."

Norrimun groaned again, but not an entirely aggrieved groan, before he passed out again.

By the time they cleaned up the king and got him back to the horses, Cullin and Dalbry had concocted their story. According to their version of events, once Kerrl discovered that the princess had been eaten, the grief-stricken duke charged into the lair after the monster, while Dalbry and Cullin rescued the king. Norrimun awoke just in time to see the burst of fire, smoke, and steam as the duke battled the monster and was killed.

When reminded, Norrimun said he remembered every detail of that, including additional details that sounded right, due to his grogginess.

When the king fell unconscious again, Sir Dalbry had gone into the lair, dispatched the already-wounded dragon, and cut off its head. With somber gravity, Dalbry then revealed the patchy stuffed crocodile head, the last one from their supplies. "As you can see, Sire, the monster was bruised, battered, and damaged during its battle with me and Duke Kerrl."

Norrimun considered the reptilian trophy, not looking terribly disappointed. "So, my princess is gone, and now Duke Kerrl is gone. At least the monster paid for killing those innocent victims." He narrowed his eyes. "For the sake of history, though, I insist we say that *Duke Kerrl* is the one who slew the dragon. It's only right to honor him in that way."

Dalbry didn't seem pleased, but accepted the necessity. "I suppose that would be a nice gesture." Cullin agreed as well.

The king brightened. "And, thanks to the legal paperwork Duke Kerrl had me sign, the dukedom and the kingdom are merged. With the duke's death, *I* now acquire all of his lands and wealth. Everybody wins. Yay!"

They saddled up and rode back to King Norrimun's castle, having succeeded in their quest, albeit in a roundabout way. As they approached the castle, Sir Dalbry broached the important subject of remuneration. "Now that the monster is dead, might I request the promised honorarium, Your Majesty? The dragon would never have been slain without us."

King Norrimun frowned at the knight. "Promised honorarium? I intended to have Sir Phineal do all the work."

"But he did not, Majesty. That's not what really happened. And you did agree. . . ."

Norrimun sniffed. "Well, it seems to me that *Duke Kerrl* is the one who slew the dragon, and he's the one who paid the ultimate price."

Dalbry's expression grew dark. "Again, Sire, that is not what really happened."

Cullin pressed the matter. "Majesty, nobody wants two conflicting stories circulating among the minstrels. Sir Dalbry and I did participate in the heroic deed, and we are left with certain undeniable expenses. With your treasury so significantly increased by all of Kerrl's wealth, surely you can part with a token reward for our trouble. And our silence."

King Norrimun the Corpulent frowned. "Does your squire always speak so plainly for you, Sir Dalbry? Perhaps he needs a whipping."

"Squire Cullin always speaks for me in financial matters." Dalbry's voice was clipped. "A squire is supposed to do his knight's unpleasant work."

In the end, Norrimun let them keep the horse, Drizzle, and the pony, Pony, and grudgingly gave them a small sack of gold coins, provided they rode away as soon as possible.

In the Scabby Wench, Hob Nobbin petulantly sings his second encore of "The Goose and the Noose." At some point while I'm telling my story, Reeger slips to our table and delivers another "second" tankard of ale. For the evening, I too have lost my ability to count beyond the number two.

Prince Maurice seems dissatisfied with my tale. "Your stories are too cynical, Father—everyone is either foolish and gullible, or they're pulling off a scam."

So, he's starting to understand! "And that, my boy, is the way of the world—something you need to learn. Reality isn't as glamorous as stories. I'm afraid your father, the great dragon slayer king, has feet of clay."

"I've never looked at your feet," Maurice says.

"It's a metaphor. Or maybe a simile. I always get the two confused."

"A metaphor. I may not know the dragon business, but I do know my grammar."

The minstrel takes a break and flees the stage. Only the baker's girl and the candlemaker's daughter applaud. The rest of the patrons are distracted, rowdy, and unimpressed with the youthful singer who thinks much more of himself than his listeners do. Hob Nobbin doesn't have a bad voice, just a bad attitude.

"So there was no real dragon," Maurice continues. "What kind of story is that?"

"We had other adventures. I'll tell them to you—the night is young. We pulled the same con across the land, but each time it was new and fresh. First, we'd go to a tavern and—"

The boy sighs. "Is the story going to be like this again and again? You're disillusioning me."

"Trust me, it'll grow on you as I talk about the excitement, the danger, the romance, the narrow escapes, the piles of treasure."

"Can we just skip some of them and boil it down to the highlights?" Maurice asks.

I know I can get carried away sometimes, lost in my glory days. The queen often chides me about that. Even though it was less comfortable, that part of my life did have a certain charm before I settled down in a big castle, before I had a kingdom to manage, laws to enforce, taxes to collect . . . before I had a wife and son.

I know now that wanting a princess and winning a kingdom are quite different from actually *having* those things.

But I don't earn any sympathy if I complain too much. Aww, poor King Cullin with all his riches and his expansive lands . . .

Oddly, I realize that Prince Maurice is happy with his lot, his tutors, his duties. He seems a natural for this, but then he was born a prince, while I got it the dishonest way—the *resourceful* way. Still, I hope I can put a little spark in the boy's imagination.

"All right, I'll boil it down to just the interesting parts."

"Interesting parts to you, or to me?" he counters.

"Interesting in an objective sense—you'll see. I promise to leave out the boring stuff."

"I'll be the judge of that," Maurice says.

But at least he listens.

CHAPTER TWENTY-TWO

AFTER THE DISAPPOINTINGLY small honorarium they received from King Norrimun, Dalbry said he'd had enough of castles, banquets, courtly finery, and the attitudes of kings. "Cheated again . . . after we saved his kingdom, without even causing a scandal."

Reeger was particularly incensed as he led the mule along the rutted road. "Bloodrust! How am I ever going to afford my own tavern if our profits keep vanishing like turds down a sewer pipe?"

"You should've been a poet," Dalbry said. "You certainly have a way with words."

Cullin rode forward on his pony. "At least we got a horse for Sir Dalbry and Pony for me."

Reeger picked at his teeth, grimaced, then picked at a different tooth. "Along with all the accompanying expenses—stable fees, hay, blankets, tack. That rustin' reward will be gone before we know it."

"We have other expenses, too," Dalbry said. "Dragon business expenses. Since we're near Rivermouth, we have to buy materials to prepare for the next kingdom."

Reeger grumbled but looked ahead down the road that led to the port town. "Let's see if Ossio is in port. We're going to need what he's selling."

Reeger insisted that the best food, friendliest people, and most comfortable lodgings were to be found in Guttermouth—the section of the port city where thieves, cutthroats, and bandits liked to hang out. "We'll feel right at home."

The tavern's wooden sign showed a fish with a hook in its mouth. There were no words, because the tavern owner knew that most of his customers were illiterate, and he catered to his clientele. Inside, the inn was filled with a potpourri of body odors, fish odors, bad breath, bad gas, and spilled ale.

"They serve a special kind of fish pie here," Reeger said, "made with an imported fish cured with lye. It's said to be such a powerful preservative that it can last twenty winters without going bad."

Cullin and Dalbry were reluctant to pay the high price for such a luxury item, but Reeger insisted. The meal was not at all to Cullin's liking, with the strong taste of the lye and the enhanced reek of the fish. It was a good thing the preservative proved so effective, because given *any* food alternative, he would have let the lye-cured fish sit untouched for twenty winters or more.

Accustomed to eating foul things, Reeger smacked his lips and muttered his approval, while Sir Dalbry ate his fish pie with a stoic expression; he was a knight, and he knew how to endure.

A man dressed as a lumberjack from the highlands came in carrying a long, jagged-toothed saw; Cullin thought it odd for the lumberjack to bring his tools into the tavern, until the man sat on the hearth, propped the saw across his leg, and began to wring wailing music from it. He wasn't, after all, a woodcutter, but an avant-garde minstrel.

Much to Dalbry's annoyance, the lumberjack minstrel played a song about the sacrifice of brave Duke Kerrl, which had gone viral. In addition, Sir Phineal had made himself into a hero by forgoing the career-advancement opportunities of the dragon hunt so he could stay behind and nurse Sir Tremayne back to health. Cullin pointed out that in the wake of so much waterweed, cleaning Tremayne's chamber pot would've been a more frightening task than facing any dragon, so he didn't begrudge Phineal his glory.

True to form, Sir Dalbry gave a portion of the gold coins to the needy, and as soon as word got around, a great many of the "needy" appeared. Reeger grumbled about the knight's generosity, not understanding why he would waste good coins on other people, when he could just as well waste them on himself.

"Because I value my honor," Dalbry said. "The money I spend in this way earns me self-respect."

"Self-respect is overrated," Reeger said. "But it's your money; waste it if you like. I'll spend mine on another one of those lye-fish pies."

As they sat in the bustle of the tavern, Dalbry found a young scamp pestering the bar patrons. With his gaunt frame and sunken eyes, the boy was obviously an orphan; he looked hungry, hoping for scrapings of food from the plates. (Cullin offered him what was left of his lye-fish pie, but the orphan boy wouldn't take it.)

Dalbry held up a copper coin, catching the orphan's eye. "Run an errand for me, young man. Go to the marketplace and purchase as many dried apricots as this coin will buy, then bring them back here. When you're done, I'll give you a copper coin just like it for your trouble."

The boy snatched the coin and dashed away from the tavern. Dalbry sat back and explained. "My magic apricot sack is almost empty. I need to fill it again."

Though they remained in the tavern for the rest of the night, listening to songs played by the lumberjack minstrel with his musical saw, the orphan boy did not return. Apparently, he chose to bypass the effort of buying dried apricots and returning for his copper coin as a reward, when he could just keep the original coin in the first place. Sir Dalbry was saddened by the corruptness of human nature, but he resigned himself to go to the port market himself the next day and buy his own apricots.

Normally, preparing for the next scam, they would have told stories, dropped hints, and spread rumors to make the locals receptive to hiring a dragon slayer. It was a primary rule of marketing: create a need the customer isn't even aware of, then sell the solution to meet that need. But they were done with King Norrimun's kingdom and would soon set off for new territory.

Their travel plans were fluid, as always. Dalbry was content to wander wherever his boots—or Drizzle—took him. Reeger considered one kingdom as good as any other. Cullin went wherever his friends decided to travel.

He listened to stories shared by the tavern patrons, rumors they concocted all by themselves: horrific tales about a haunted castle inhabited by a hairy beast who howled at the moon. Others lived in terror of the local witch who had laid down a curse, declaring that fruit on apple trees would be infested with worms and that calves would be born with spots.

"Don't calves usually have spots?" Cullin asked.

"More spots than usual," said the frightened peasant. Cullin didn't point out that finding an apple without a worm was also a rarity.

Another patron told the tale of an enchanted piper hired to lure the rats out of a city; when that proved effective, the town elders paid him to play his pipe again and lure all the naughty children away.

"I don't suppose the same technique could be used to lure worms out of apples," Reeger said.

"And what about the spotted calves?" Cullin said. "Maybe we could whitewash them, call them cured, and be long gone with our fee before the spots reappeared."

With a sigh, Dalbry said, "So many opportunities, but there's only so much we can do. The greatest profit is in the dragon business."

CHAPTER TWENTY-THREE

THEY SHOPPED CAREFULLY for a budget-priced inn, one that claimed "we'll leave a candle on for you." Dalbry, Reeger, and Cullin shared a single room, which was meant to be an extravagance, although the tiny chamber seemed claustrophobic and more unpleasant than sleeping out in the open. The lumpy mattresses were as full of bedbugs as with straw.

The following day, they retrieved their livestock from the Guttermouth stable, where they were shocked by the hidden fees. Reeger occasionally stabled their mule during visits to towns, but now they had to board a horse and a pony as well. Oddly, Drizzle and Pony each cost more for upkeep than the nameless mule did. When Reeger demanded an explanation, the stablemaster shrugged. "Surcharges."

"What sort of rustin' surcharges?"

"The horse is a bigger animal, therefore it costs more."

"And what about the pony?"

"It's smaller, therefore more difficult to manage. Thus, the surcharge."

When the stablemaster showed them the fine print in the contract they had signed the night before, Reeger complained about the unfairness of the pricing, but they could do nothing about it. So they paid and left, stung by how they'd been cheated.

Dalbry insisted on stopping at the first dried-fruit vendor stand, so he could replenish his magic sack. "Next, we see if Ossio's in port." Fortunately, the piratical trader had an uncanny intuition for being at Rivermouth whenever the three comrades needed his goods.

At the docks, they moved among the bustle of trading ships, passenger vessels, fishing boats, even a piled-high guano barge loaded with rich fertilizer excavated from an offshore seagull rookery. The captain of the redolent barge stood with a shovel propped at his side and enticed any passersby to take home a load of his "gray gold."

Ossio's ship was at the same dock where they had done business with him before. The old bald pirate lounged on the deck, patting his potbelly. He recognized them as they came forward. "I'd know that mule anywhere!"

Cullin had seen him wear an eyepatch before, but that was just an affectation; last time, Ossio had worn the patch on his other eye. Now, he wore none at all, but a decorative iron ring dangled from the bald pirate's left ear. Although the iron did not gleam and had a tendency to get rusty, Ossio was of the opinion that gold was too valuable to be dangling from a man's earlobe.

"We're in need of your special wares," called Reeger. "Ready to trade?"

Ossio strode down the gangplank to meet them on the dock. "Trade implies that you have something to give me in return."

"We just got paid for a dragon slaying," Dalbry said.

"Oh, ho! From what I hear, it was Duke Kerrl who did all the dragon slaying."

Dalbry did not bother to hide his scowl. "Credit doesn't always go where credit is due."

"We can trade you a story for your goods," Cullin suggested. "Something you'll tell again and again in the dockside taverns."

Ossio frowned at the young man. "I've already got enough stories to bore every innkeeper up and down the coast."

"I'll bet you do," Reeger said.

Ossio swatted a fly away from his bald scalp. "As for payment, I was hoping for a few special items in trade . . . the kind you provided previously?"

"Rust! We've got enough to give you job security at any port you visit." Reeger dug in the mule's saddlebags, and the creature brayed mournfully. Drizzle and Pony didn't seem to know what to do with the beast, nor could they understand anything the other animal tried to communicate.

He withdrew a packet of unevenly round forest mushrooms, each the size of a dinner plate. They were the color of putrescent flesh and encrusted with lichen. Ossio ran his fingertips over the large mushrooms, ruffling the frills and releasing dusty spores. "Oh, ho—those are nice ones."

"Put them in a keg of vinegar before your next voyage," Reeger said. "They'll be well prepared by the time you reach port. No one can dispute that these are suckers from a monstrous kraken."

"I believe I see other suckers," Dalbry said.

Ossio and Reeger both found that funny, though the old knight didn't seem to be making a joke. The bald pirate gestured them toward the gangplank. "Come aboard to my cabin. You can tie your animals down there. I'll find a trustworthy orphan boy to watch over them."

Dalbry shook his head, still unhappy about his last experience with a trustworthy orphan boy. "We'd prefer to stay on the open deck, where we can watch the animals ourselves."

"Whatever." Ossio beckoned them to follow him up the gangplank. "Share a drink with me. I've got an awful-tasting beverage, but it's potent."

"Can't wait to try it." Reeger carried the pack of thick forest mushrooms, which would soon be converted into sea-monster remnants.

The piratical trader ducked into his cabin and emerged with a small cask and four gold-rimmed glasses that he had obtained at a nobleman's estate sale. He unbunged the cask and poured out an oily, milky-looking ooze that smoked as it entered the glasses. "Don't take more than a sip at a time—not if you value the enamel on your teeth."

Reeger, who had the least amount of tooth enamel in the group, gave a snort of disbelief, took a swig, then gagged.

"I get it from a local moonshine operation in Sewermouth," Ossio said. "Once I add a little bit of coloring, I'll market it as sea-serpent venom milked straight from the fangs of a creature that bit down on my deck. Plenty of apothecaries or potion-masters will pay well for genuine serpent venom."

"It's poison," Dalbry said after taking a tiny sip.

"No, just high-proof alcohol. It can cure many ills."

Cullin decided not to taste his drink.

Dalbry nudged. "I believe you have something for us?"

"Rust, we wasted the last of our trophies on King Norrimun the Corpulent—better known as King Norrimun the Stingy."

"Even so, we're still in the black," Dalbry said. "It's just a setback. We'll move on." He lifted his glass in a toast. The three older men each sipped the sea-serpent venom, competing for the worst grimace.

"Now, I'd say those kraken suckers are worth at least four dragon heads," Reeger said.

"Don't be ridiculous. A bargain should start with a realistic bid." Ossio looked down at the shriveled forest mushrooms with a deprecating expression. "I know what I can sell them for, no matter what story I tell. Do you know how hard it is to get dragon heads?"

"You mean, according to minstrels?" Sir Dalbry said. "Or the fake dragon heads that you provide?"

"Oh, ho, you think crocodiles are easy to kill? I have to spend a fat sheep or two to lure each one."

"Before we dicker any more, let's have a look at the rustin' dragon heads," Reeger said. "Go get them."

While Ossio went to his cabin to retrieve the items, the three companions whispered together, deciding on the price they were willing to pay.

The bald pirate came back out with four crocodile heads—though large, they were lightweight, dried and stuffed with sawdust and straw, their scaly leather cured. Each one had been painted with fearsome-looking spots or tiger stripes. "Put your own horns on them, unless you think they look monstrous enough already. I sell them as-is."

Cullin listened as the haggling began in earnest, and the voices grew louder with each sip of serpent venom. Reeger and Ossio were both masters of bargaining, while Cullin was out of his league, and Sir Dalbry considered the dickering beneath him.

It was a dance of indignation, cajoling, argument, and resistance, and finally they settled on trading the pack of kraken-sucker mushrooms and their last two gold durbins (from King Ashtok) for three stuffed dragon heads. Ossio kept one, which he would make into a convincing sea serpent head for his own scam.

When they left Ossio's ship, everyone acted as if they felt cheated and dissatisfied, but Cullin knew that both sides were happy with the bargain. Those fake relics would earn each of them a tidy profit.

CHAPTER TWENTY-FOUR

AFTER THE DISAPPOINTING dragon quest, Cullin was tired but awash with dreams of possibilities. He was entitled to his small share of the reward honorarium, although he knew it wouldn't last long.

After seeing Princess Affonyl, he thought more about finding a wife who was loving, beautiful, and interesting. He would even settle for two out of three. He had also heard stories, seen sketches, and imagined the wonders of the New Lands across the ocean. He wanted to go there, set up a homestead, make a new life.

But in order to do that, Cullin would have to give up everything and sail away, leave his friends behind, and never return. Or maybe Reeger and Dalbry would be willing to go with him. There must be opportunities for three resourceful, imaginative men on an entirely new, open continent.

Someday . . .

Cullin saw a vendor selling delicious-smelling, fresh-baked buns, accompanied by chunks of honeycomb from the famed town of Folly. Torn, he held the coins in his hand. He wanted to save his money, gather enough of a stake to buy a better life. If he squandered his coins on something that tasted sweet on his tongue and filled his belly, then he would never save enough.

But the smell of the hot buns was maddening, and the thought of real honey from Folly brought nostalgic drool to his mouth.

In the end, he spent his money on what he wanted most right at that moment, rather than what he wanted in the long run. The long run would always be there, and sooner or later he, Reeger, and Dalbry were bound to make a big score. Sooner or later . . .

He sat alone at the end of a vacant pier, watching the river empty into the sea. He also saw brown sludge come down from the gutters and canals in Sewermouth and dribble into the estuary. Nearby, a boy with a fishing pole caught fish after fish in the rich slurry of effluent, though Cullin doubted that any fish taken from such a location would taste good. Maybe that was where the lye-preserved fish came from.

Riverboats came down from the uplands of Norrimun's kingdom, trading their cargo with larger oceangoing vessels. With a pang in his heart, Cullin watched a three-masted carrack raise its sails and head out of the harbor, striking out to the open water where the horizon beckoned and the sunset called. That ship would be loaded with pilgrims, colonists, and supplies for the New Lands. He sighed.

How he longed to be among those people following their dreams and hopes, voyaging to an untamed continent where there were abandoned cities of gold, strange animals, and exotic plants that one could smoke (though it was not clear why anyone would want to do so). He watched the ship dwindle in the distance until it was gone over the horizon. He could have been aboard it. . . .

Cullin had also heard stories about a sheer precipice that awaited at the edge of the world, where the ocean drained like a waterfall into the universe. An unwary vessel could sail over the brink and plunge downward forever. But those were just stories. Cullin knew which ones to listen to, and which ones to ignore.

He left the dock, putting his dreams in his pocket for now. There would always be some other ship sailing for the New Lands, and the opportunity was always there if Cullin ever saved enough money. . . .

Still daydreaming as he wandered through the port market, he collided with a young woman in drab-looking clothes, a peasant's jerkin, breeches, and rough-cut blond hair. Since Dalbry had taught Cullin to be polite, regardless of whom he met (a lesson that was lost on Reeger), he bowed, excused himself, and looked up at the girl's face.

"I'd recognize you anywhere!" he blurted out. "You're Princess Affonyl."

During the feast of Saint Bartimund, Cullin had devoted much attention to staring at her beautiful features. Since she so studiously ignored him, he'd been able to keep gawking at her without feeling self-conscious.

She extricated herself from him and lifted her chin. "It's just Affonyl now. And you—oh, Sir Dalbry's squire! I remember your features."

"I thought you were ignoring me."

"A girl can look out of the corner of her eye."

He brightened. "Good news, I'm here to rescue you."

She raised her eyebrows and answered with a sarcastic tone. "Rescue me? I'm dead—devoured by a dragon, remember? Haven't you heard the stories?"

"I'm glad you recovered. That was a fine scheme, but Sir Dalbry and I figured it out right away."

Affonyl frowned. "What gave me away?"

Cullin was not about to explain all the clues she had left. "A dragon slayer knows what evidence to look for. We have specialized skills."

She turned to go, anxious to be away from a reminder of her past life. "Well, I'm doing just fine now, and I don't want to go back home. I was relieved to hear that the real dragon ate Duke Kerrl, though. Miracles do happen."

"So, you have nothing to worry about." Cullin was sure King Norrimun would give a more sizeable honorarium if they brought his daughter back safe and sound. "We could come up with a good story, say that you struck your head when the dragon stole you away. Ah, and then you managed to escape from the monster's foul, steaming lair and wandered through the forest for days, dazed. You lost your memory." He snapped his fingers. "But I found you here in Rivermouth. I'll bring you to your loving father, you'll have your inheritance back, we'll get a reward and . . ."

He stopped himself as an even better idea occurred to him. After performing such a worthy deed, maybe he could once again request the princess's hand in marriage, especially now that Duke Kerrl was no longer around. If only he had the nerve . . .

Affonyl looked as if she had just taken a gulp of sea-serpent venom. "Why would I want to go back there? A princess is a princess, but I'm a *person* now, an independent woman. I like being away from court intrigues. It's refreshing, and I've made a good living in the past few days."

Cullin was surprised. "At what?"

"I sell seashells by the seashore. It's one of the oldest professions."

Reeger came up to them with his cockeyed gait and his cockeyed gaze. "There you are, lad! There's work to do—I found a stable that offers a special Tuesday discount for boarding our animals, provided one of us sleeps there with them and mucks out the stable afterward. Dalbry and I chose you for the honor."

"Fine, I'll do it for the team." More concerned with his unexpected encounter, he turned to his friend with a gallant flourish. "Reeger, allow me to introduce Princess Affonyl."

"Just Affonyl," she repeated. "And I have to be on my way. It'll be low tide soon, and I need to collect seashells. A girl has to earn a living."

"Why don't you join us?" Cullin's eyes glinted as the idea sprang into his mind. "We're leaving your father's kingdom, off to find adventures and great riches. You'll see the world, have excitement every day."

Reeger scowled and spat. "Crotchrust, lad! Why would we want to take a girl with us—and a princess, no less?"

In the same breath, Affonyl said, "Why would I want to wander from land to land with a group of unwashed lowborn men?"

Cullin answered both questions at the same time. "Because we've got a lot in common . . . and it'll be fun."

Reeger remained unconvinced, and Affonyl appeared uninterested. Then, however, she reconsidered. "I suppose it wouldn't be a bad idea to go far from here, just in case somebody recognizes me. If I got dragged back to the castle, my father would start to make arrangements again ten minutes after he told me how happy he was to see me. I'm sure he could find somebody worse than Duke Kerrl if he looked hard enough." She nodded again, as if to convince herself. "I've always wanted to explore, see different landscapes."

Cullin turned to his skeptical friend. "She's a natural at it. You should've seen how she faked the dragon attack in her chambers. It was imaginative and masterful."

"Don't forget the explosion," Affonyl said. "That was the most impressive part of all." The former princess made up her mind that the option of adventuring was better than the option of remaining in Rivermouth, where the bottom was sure to fall out of the seashell market, sooner or later.

They hadn't expanded their small group since Cullin joined them years earlier. Reeger and Dalbry had worked well together, just the two of them wandering the countryside, but adding Cullin had broadened their horizons. Now he was certain Affonyl would do the same.

He continued to press. "We can increase our repertoire if we have a pretty girl on the team. Think of the opportunities."

Reeger chewed on the words. "She's pretty enough, I suppose."

"I'm not just pretty—I have a background in alchemy and the natural sciences. I've studied hard to get where I am now."

"Selling rustin' seashells? All right, maybe we could use a pretty girl at that—and explosions." Maintaining his surly tone, he held up one grimy finger. "But, even though we've been raised in a backward medieval feudal society, our group is still a democracy. Dalbry has to agree."

CHAPTER TWENTY-FIVE

ON HIS HONOR, Sir Dalbry was required to save any princess in distress—no matter what that distress might be—and the exact details of the "saving" were not well defined in the Knight's Manual. Without too much difficulty, Cullin convinced the old knight that having Affonyl run off with them was an unorthodox way of rescuing her.

She gathered her sack of necessary items and met them at the stables, where Reeger haggled to get their money back since they would be moving on after all. With the mule, Drizzle, and Pony, they made their way out of Rivermouth and headed toward the next kingdom.

Their time in King Norrimun's land had been sunny and warm, with soft salty breezes blowing in from the sea, but as soon as the group headed out of town and away from convenient shelter, gray clouds closed in like a strangler's grip, wringing moisture out of the sky in a constant cold rain.

Sir Dalbry pulled his dragonskin cape over his shoulders and a hood over his head, and simply endured the meteorological misery, since he was a true knight. Cullin tried to keep himself warm with a woolen camp blanket, but once soaked, it only managed to keep the cold and the wet even closer to him.

Attempting to be gallant, he suggested that Affonyl ride Pony while he trudged alongside. The former princess refused to be pampered, though, and insisted that she was as tough as any of them. "If you won't ride, then neither will I."

Reeger handed Cullin the mule's halter rope and swung into Pony's saddle. "I'll ride the rustin' pony, then—if only to prevent an argument."

The group traveled the coast road, which had become a river of sloppy mud, but at least traffic was light due to the storm. During a normal rush hour, oxcarts and horse-drawn wagons were bumper to bumper, slowing to a standstill for a mile outside of town. A second lane of the coast road had been under construction for years to alleviate the traffic jams, but there had been no noticeable progress in Princess Affonyl's lifetime.

Now she walked alongside Cullin, wet and bedraggled, shivering in the damp. He would have offered her his soaked blanket, but that would not have made matters better. Even in her wet and disheveled state, he still found her attractive, and now she seemed to be more in his league.

Hoping to strike up a conversation, he said, "So, what's your story, Princess?" He didn't really know how to talk to a girl, especially not one that he liked.

"*Former* princess," she corrected.

"But to me you still look like a princess, even without your braid and the fine clothes."

She gave him a sidelong look and rolled her eyes. "You're not very good at flirting, are you?"

"Why, it's the best I've ever done!"

"Prince Indico could give you some lessons . . . but, then, he was a liar. I'd rather be with an inept young man than a deceitful one."

He placed a hand on his heart. "I give you my word, Princess Affonyl, I will always be inept."

That drew a small laugh from her. "All right, I'll tell you my story. It's not the usual tale of princesses and castles. I lost my mother when I was very young."

Cullin remembered his own tragic circumstances, being orphaned when a bee swarm chased his father out the window of a mill. "How did she die?"

Affonyl bit her lip. "I'm not really sure. At first I was told that she died of a broken heart, because she had hoped for a baby boy. She didn't want to raise a girl."

"But girls make the best princesses," Cullin pointed out.

"Then I was told she died of a coughing fever, but I've since heard plenty of whispers around the court. I think the real explanation might be that she ran off with a circus, and the rest of the stories are just a cover-up because my father is embarrassed."

"Sorry to hear that," Cullin said, "but I suppose having your mother run off with a circus is better than dying from a coughing fever or from a broken heart."

The trees opened up on the coastal road, exposing them to wind gusts from the sea. The rain came down harder.

Affonyl continued, "I turned out to be more of a tomboy and scholar than a giggly lady at court. Our kingdom has engaged in a long-standing program to breed for vapidity. My father is disappointed that I'm a throwback."

"I prefer you this way." Cullin thought he might be getting better at flirting, but he couldn't tell if his compliment scored any points with her.

"When he heard that two neighboring kingdoms had court wizards, my father decided he needed one as well. So, he had the monks transcribe a classified ad to be distributed throughout the kingdom. Edgar, the candidate who answered the ad, was more of a natural scientist and alchemist than a wizard, but he did a good interview, and his résumé was impressive. He agreed to a starting salary lower than that of a fully licensed wizard, so my father hired him."

Wearing a wistful smile, she flung raindrops out of her eyes. "Edgar and I hit it off immediately. He had books and chemicals, charts of the elements, horoscopes, bottled animal entrails, toadstools and wolfsbane, sparkling smoke and explosive powder. Everything a curious girl could want. He taught me so much. He let me read his books, even when he wasn't there.

"One time, he said he was going to practice an invisibility potion and then disappeared from the castle for two weeks. I searched everywhere for him, even studied in his library to find an antidote to the spell. I was sure he had turned himself transparent and was unable to make a sound. When Wizard Edgar returned, though—coming to the front gates of the castle rather than through the dissipation of any kind of potion or spell—I learned that he had tricked me.

"Edgar hadn't wanted to hurt my feelings while he went off to a job interview with an evil wizard conglomerate. They hired him away, offered a higher salary and a better benefits package . . . and our kingdom lost a great wizard."

"Sorry to hear that." Cullin wanted to reach out and pat her on the shoulder, but decided he didn't dare.

"Edgar did give me all his books, his charts, his chemical library, his precious tomes, since the evil wizard conglomerate had their own extensive library that was made available to all employees. He had a soft spot for me, saw my potential.

"When Edgar left, I begged my father to hire a replacement so I could continue my studies, but by then personal wizards had fallen out of vogue. He spent his money on courtyard lily ponds instead." Affonyl sighed. "I kept reading anyway, and learning, and studying. Duke Kerrl thought literacy in a woman was overrated, and that's how I knew he would have made a reprehensible husband."

Trying to score points, Cullin said, "We've got a lot in common. I can read, too." He had never before realized what an advantage literacy might be in picking up girls.

They kept moving forward into the rain, hoping for the skies to clear and the drizzle to stop, but the clouds matched their pace exactly, drenching them all day long. Cullin managed to secure three fat squirrels for their lunch, though Reeger had a hard time building even a smoky, smoldering fire to cook them. Cullin shared his roast rodent with Affonyl, who decided she was more hungry than skeptical.

"Slayer of squirrels," she said to him. "You haven't quite made it to slayer of dragons yet."

"I'm working my way up. My part is just to play a squire."

"Squire? Squirrel, more like. I think I'll call you Squirrel."

"You can't just call me Cullin?"

Her brow furrowed. "What kind of endearment would that be?"

"Are you trying to find an endearing name for me?" He couldn't stop grinning.

The former princess just shook her head. "You really aren't very good at flirting, are you?"

As they moved on, Sir Dalbry seemed impervious to the rain, though his sword and chain mail would get rusty if he didn't take care of them. A brave yet rusty knight would never command a high price as a dragon slayer.

On their way along the headlands, they saw no prospect for shelter, not even a dragon cave. Cullin was so chilled to the bone that he would have loved to sit in the hot and steamy cave of Old Snort. The road crossed high cliffs with the sea below, though the gray drizzle leached the scenery out of the landscape.

Ahead, they heard a sudden rumbling roar—not a simulated dragon attack. It sounded more like a landslide. Reeger urged Pony forward, and Dalbry pushed Drizzle into a trot, leaving Cullin and Affonyl to pull the mule along. By the time they caught up, Dalbry and Reeger had both dismounted to stand at the edge of a sandstone bluff. Part of the sheer cliff looked fresh and white, where a section had dropped into the churning sea.

"These crumbly cliffs are sedimentary rock with line fractures," Affonyl said. "Given the rain, moisture probably seeped into the cracks, overloaded the porous structure, and allowed a segment to break away."

"So, it got wet and fell down." Dalbry glanced at her. "I agree with your analysis."

Cullin stepped to the edge, where the sea spray and the drop-off made his heart flutter, and was astonished to see what the landslide had revealed.

Embedded in the sandstone cliff was a huge reptilian skeleton, bones akimbo, and a fossilized skull as big as a wagon with yawning jaws full of teeth, powerful three-clawed back legs, and a long tail. The fossilized bones had been cemented inside the cliff for what might have been decades, even centuries! Cullin couldn't imagine a timespan longer than that. Now they were freshly exposed to the air.

"Those are some valuable bones!" Reeger said. "We better retrieve them."

Cullin was amazed. "It's a dragon—a dragon skeleton." He blinked. "That means dragons are real."

"*Were* real, lad," Reeger said. "Obviously, this one's been dead for some time."

Affonyl couldn't stop staring. "I've never seen anything like that in Wizard Edgar's books, and natural scientists have identified every single living creature on Earth—over four hundred of them! I'd like to have a closer look."

"Oh, you will, girl," Reeger said. "You're going to help us retrieve the bones. Get some rope. We'll lower you—it'll be just like when you climbed down from your castle tower."

"I'll bring a shovel," Cullin said.

The rope was slippery in the rain, but they tied it to a tree set back from the cliff edge. Dangling along the sheer bluff face, Cullin and Affonyl moved to the giant reptilian fossil and chopped away with their shovels. Thankfully, the rain had softened the sandstone, so they were able to wrench free some of the ancient bones and teeth. They tied the bones in a loose sack that Reeger and Dalbry could haul up.

Cullin and Affonyl dangled there, slipping on the wet rock face but trusting the not-very-trustworthy ropes. The princess lost her grip on one of the fossilized fangs she had chiseled away. She wobbled and spun as the fang tumbled down into the crashing surf. Cullin caught her as enthusiastically as possible, helping her keep her balance. The monstrous skull was much too huge to consider removing; besides, it would make their stuffed crocodile heads look laughably small.

"At least get some of the teeth," Reeger yelled down. "With those fangs and Dalbry's dragonskin cape, we can double our prices."

When they had harvested two sack loads of prize pieces, as much as Pony could bear, the two climbed back up, slipping and sliding on their ropes and the slick cliff.

"That was exciting," Affonyl said. She smiled at Cullin, and he found the smear of mud on her face to be charming. "Thanks for not letting me fall down that cliff, Squirrel."

"It was my chivalrous duty." He considered it a good start to their adventures.

CHAPTER TWENTY-SIX

ANOTHER DAY, ANOTHER kingdom—or in this case, a queendom.

The group set off into a warm, sunny day so bright and so pleasant it seemed to be nature's apology for the previous day's misery. But since their clothes were still damp and muddy, Cullin was not inclined to accept the apology.

"You're looking scruffy now, girl," Reeger said. "Just like one of us."

Cullin was ready to defend Affonyl by insisting that she was still a princess to him, but she didn't seem to take offense at Reeger's comment. "Good. I want to be like you—making my own way, earning a living. I'm tired of all the pampering and castles, the fine foods, fashionable clothes, minstrels, riches. It gets old after a while."

Reeger moved too late to cover his mouth as he belched. "Rust, I can see how someone would get tired of all that."

"A princess is a princess, but I want to be more than that. I want to see the world, wherever the dragon business takes us."

Neither Dalbry or Reeger could claim to know where they were going. Growing up as a feral orphan boy who aspired to be raised by a pack of wolves, Cullin had little familiarity with the geopolitical cartography of the land either.

Affonyl, however, did have a courtly education, and had recently memorized the boundaries of her father's kingdom when Duke Kerrl tried to redraw the borders to his own advantage. When the coast road swung inland, she studied the distant hills, noting a distinctive rock outcropping. She also seemed to be looking at the position of the moon and the sun in the sky. "We just crossed the border."

Cullin looked around, but didn't see any difference.

The former princess continued, "A few years ago my father wanted to hire a royal surveyor to paint a dotted line around his entire kingdom. In fact, one of Wizard Edgar's projects was to develop an indelible alchemical paint so that the borders of every kingdom, principality, dukedom, etcetera, could be recorded on the landscape itself. My father thought that would solve problems and end all wars, but Edgar never came up with the right formula for his paint." She shifted the bag of necessary items on her shoulder. "Ah, I miss Edgar—I took some of his most valuable books. I just wish they weren't so heavy."

"Who is the ruler of these parts?" Sir Dalbry asked as he rode on Drizzle, dressed as a knight despite the hard traveling. Since acquiring his iconic white steed (never mind the ash-gray and black speckles), he had become more absorbed in his role than ever before. "I need to prepare for when we appear in court."

"Old Queen Faria rules alone, a single mother. Her husband

died of a plague, or a jousting accident, or a wild boar attack—I forget which. It's usually one of those."

"A single mother?" Cullin asked. "So she has children then?"

Affonyl continued to explain. "The dowager queen is a hard but wise ruler, as cuddly as broken glass. And she's *ancient*. She imports barrels of powdered makeup for her face, attempting to cover her wrinkles. I saw Queen Faria once at a springtime ball my father hosted. She looked like a sugar-dusted pastry with all that powder. She even made overtures to marry my father, to join his kingdom and her queendom, but he rebuffed her." A dark expression shadowed her face. "He said marriage without love was a shameful thing. I guess he had different criteria for his own daughter."

Cullin tried to cheer her up. "Look how much better your circumstances are now!"

Affonyl snorted and continued. "Queen Faria is a single mother with one daughter, a princess, beautiful—as required. Princess Minima. Unmarried, with plenty of suitors. I am so glad to be away from that life."

In response, Reeger picked at something in his teeth and spat on the ground.

As they traveled, they discussed the strategies for their next scheme. (The horse, mule, and pony did not contribute much to the discussion.) At dusk they found a good wooded spot for a camp, and Cullin went out hunting for their dinner. He hoped to impress Affonyl by bagging a fat pheasant, but all he managed to kill was a scrawny, three-legged rabbit whose left hind foot must have been harvested as a good-luck charm. It made a decent enough dinner.

The following day, they set off into an even brighter, warmer, and sunnier day, as if the weather were growing more insistent in its apology. The queendom began to look more civilized, with cleared forests, planted fields, stone fences, clumps of peasant huts, all bucolic and serene. Birds chirped, wildflowers bloomed, and brooks babbled in the glens.

Until they ran into a family of haunted-looking peasants who were fleeing in the other direction. Their eyes were wide and panicked as they scurried down the road with all their worldly possessions, including bundles of sticks, rags that stretched the definition of clothing, a mangy dog on a leash, a mangy goat on a leash, and a flightless chicken (also on a leash).

They had three children so dirty as to be gender-neutral, and a bent crone so old that she had to be considered historical. They were all doing their best to run away.

High on his saddle, Sir Dalbry held up a gauntleted hand. "Ho, good people—where are you bound?"

The peasants stopped in the road, not wanting to show discourtesy to a brave knight. Clearly, though, they were in a hurry. "We're heading out of the queendom, sir," said the peasant father. "It's not safe here anymore."

The mother shifted the valuable bundle of sticks on her shoulders. "We have to protect our family, get out of here while we still can."

Dalbry put a hand on the pommel of his sword. "What is the danger? As a knight, I am honor-bound to protect the helpless and needy."

"Good luck," rasped the old crone. "We'll watch you from a distance, if it's all the same to you."

One of the children piped up. "A dragon burned everything!"

Reeger let out a loud laugh. "Rust, now I see what you're up to. Let me guess, the dragon torched your fields, burned your home. I'm surprised it didn't eat you for breakfast."

"It attacked at midday, sir, so it would have been lunch," said the father. "But you're right. Everything's destroyed, burned to the ground."

Reeger grinned at Cullin and Affonyl before he turned back to the anxious peasant family. "And I bet you saw dragon footprints all around?"

"Yes, sir—giant, three-toed prints!" said the mother. "And the monster will be back, mark my words. We need to flee."

Cullin joined Reeger in his chuckle, and Sir Dalbry could barely hide a smile. "Thank you for your concern, good folk, but we'll be fine. On your way."

One of the peasant children—a girl, Cullin finally realized—held up a twisted, anthropomorphic clump of tied rags and sawdust. "At least I rescued my doll."

Reeger whispered to Cullin, "A missed trick, that. The discarded doll would've added a dash of poignancy to the wreckage."

"Not everyone's as good as you are, Reeger," Cullin said.

Sir Dalbry raised his sword high for dramatic effect. "We will investigate this threat. You good folk be safe now."

The peasants scurried down the road, while the companions forged ahead. As soon as they were out of earshot, Cullin, Reeger, and Dalbry began to laugh out loud. Affonyl was still getting accustomed to the dragon business and didn't quite see the humor.

After the joke was over, Reeger grew surly. "I don't like someone stealing our techniques. We worked hard to develop those."

Dalbry nodded. "We should have asked the peasant family who paid them off."

Cresting a low hill, they saw a valley with a patchwork of cropland. The horse, mule, and pony grew nervous. At the top of the hill, Cullin stopped beside Affonyl to stare at what remained of a small peasant village.

Ahead lay a swath of fields burned to stubble as if a giant torch had ignited them. More than a dozen charred peasant hovels had collapsed.

They descended to study the area with a professional eye. Cullin was amazed by the scope of the scene. When they found seven skeletons sprawled among the burned hovels, even one out in the field with a now-melted sickle in a bony hand, Cullin thought the carnage looked far too real.

Reeger grumbled. “Somebody’s gone overboard.”

Sir Dalbry sat on Drizzle, his face tight. Affonyl leaned close to Cullin. “Is it always like this, Squirrel? Seems excessive.”

Cullin shook his head, feeling a chill as he noted three-toed tracks crushed into the ground, deeper than any tracks he or Reeger had left while wearing the wooden footprints.

“True,” he said. “This is well out of our league.”

CHAPTER TWENTY-SEVEN

DALBRY AND REEGER spent an hour at the charred village site, inspecting it for clues (according to the knight) or tips on how to stage a spectacular scene (according to Reeger).

The skeletons particularly troubled Cullin. He and Reeger had harvested enough bones from unmarked graves, and he knew the randomness of their own efforts. But these were whole skeletons, skin and sinew burned black. The scene looked almost . . . real.

Cullin wanted to shield the delicate former princess from such horrors, but Affonyl used a stick to poke at the rib cages, turn the skulls, and study the remnants of musculature. "This is fascinating—and you're sure it's a scam? I've never seen so many skeletons before. Wizard Edgar had only limited specimens for me to look at."

"Glad we could make your day, girl," Reeger said. "But if there's another con artist working the queendom—especially someone this ambitious—we're not going to be able to sell our services here. The market's already saturated."

Dalbry mused, "On the contrary, considering the magnitude of this setup, I might command an even higher price for my services. Queen Faria must be desperate to rid her queendom of a monster this destructive."

They left the devastation behind, continuing toward the queen's main castle in the central town. By late afternoon, they came upon more cropland and another peasant village half the size of Folly, but with a smaller population. *Much* smaller, in fact, since the entire village was abandoned. Everyone had packed up and left.

"Looks like our rival got here before we did," said Dalbry. "Somebody paid these peasants to skip town."

Reeger peered into the empty window of a rickety home. "It would have cost a rustin' fortune to bribe so many people. I wonder what sort of profit model he's using."

Affonyl frowned as she studied the silent hovels, walking from one structure to the next. "Maybe the town was already empty. This could be a tourist village—closed down for the season."

Cullin didn't consider that likely. "A tourist village would have souvenir shoppes and tour offices. I don't see any signs in the windows saying 'Closed for the Season' or 'See You Next Year.'"

Dalbry paced among the empty and silent buildings. "This makes no sense. Even if another alleged dragon slayer bought off the peasants and told them to run away, why would he leave the village intact? The last one was completely devastated—and very convincing. Maybe the frightened people just fled of their own accord."

Reeger yanked open the door of a quaint hut with a planter of geraniums out front. "Time to stop for the day anyway, and I'm not going to look a gift mule in the mouth. You all get to spend nights in castles with fancy outdoor plumbing, but I always sleep on the ground. Tonight, I'll take advantage of our good fortune and sleep with the bedbugs instead."

"Camping is still an adventure for me." Affonyl peered into one of the hovels and sneezed from the dust.

Cullin said, "Look in the cupboards. Maybe they left some food behind—bread, sardines, maybe some sweet pickles. I love pickles."

After tying the mounts to a post, they ransacked the abandoned hovels and found a barrel with a few mealy brown apples on the bottom, a partial block of gourmet headcheese, and a jar of pickles (but sour ones, not the sweet gherkins Cullin preferred). When added to the squirrel jerky in their packs and two dried apricots each, since Sir Dalbry had recently replenished his magic sack in Rivermouth, they had a satisfying meal as dusk settled in.

They built a campfire in the common area outside, and Affonyl took the time to unpack and organize her sack of necessary items. She set aside two natural history books from Wizard Edgar's library; they had been transcribed with very tiny letters for the paperback edition. She also had packets of chemicals and powders labeled with arcane symbols, as well as a sachet of dried flowers. When Cullin asked about the flowers, thinking they might be some sentimental keepsake from a former lover, she answered, "Deadly nightshade, in case I need to poison someone. You can never tell."

Cullin was curious about several sealed clay pots filled with chemical mixtures, which made him think of the apothecary in King Norrimun's castle with his various laxative and antidiarrheal potions. "A volatile explosive compound, Squirrel," Affonyl said, holding up a clay pot for Cullin. "I found the recipe in my books. How do you think I blasted through the wall in my castle chambers?"

With his face puckered from eating another of the sour pickles, Reeger gave a grudging nod. "I suggest you don't stand too close, lad, when that girl experiments with explosive compounds."

"I take precautions," Affonyl said. "In fact, my safety standards meet or exceed the wizardly guidelines. First, I always stir the explosive mixture with a stick. Second, I stand at least an arm's length away. See? Absolutely safe."

Since the village was entirely empty, they had a wide selection of abandoned hovels to choose from. Dalbry was satisfied with the first one he entered, Affonyl chose one that she called "charming," and Cullin made a point of sleeping in the hut next to hers. Reeger was pickier, moving from one to the next. "Rust! If I'm going to sleep inside a house, I want one with a master suite." He settled for a hovel with a largish main room and a wide cot.

Cullin had trouble sleeping. He was anxious to get to Queen Faria's capital and begin asking about local politics in the taverns. He especially looked forward to seeing what Affonyl could add to their effort. She had a sharp intelligence, a keen wit, and an excellent imagination, as demonstrated by her falsified dragon attack and abduction.

In the heart of the night the crickets chirped, the breezes blew. Cullin knew the former princess was just in the next hovel over, and he wondered if she was awake, thinking of him. He could hear Reeger snoring through the open window of the hut he had chosen.

Once again, Cullin's rest was interrupted when a reptilian roar shattered the darkness, louder than the snarl of a bear with an abscessed tooth. The crickets fell silent; Reeger stopped snoring. Everyone lunged out of their huts, fully awake. Dalbry carried his sword, looking around for an opponent.

The roar echoed again, accompanied by a fiery explosion louder than thunder. Affonyl gazed at the sky overhead. "Up there!"

A gigantic silhouette swooped across the starry sky: enormous bat wings, sinuous neck, triangular head, barbed tail. The monster's hinged jaws opened wide to paint the sky with orange fire.

"Bloodrust and battlerot!" Reeger yelped. "That thing's real!"

The dragon swooped low and belched flames to ignite a swath of wheat fields before it flapped its great wings and soared up into the sky again. The fire spread on the ground, snapping, crackling, and popping.

Dalbry held his sword up in the "Boy Picking Apple out of Reach" stance, but he could not fight such a creature from this distance.

Cullin ran to where the animals were tied; Drizzle, Pony, and the mule let out a loud, terrified racket. Affonyl dashed for her sack of necessary items and dropped to her knees by the embers of the campfire.

As the dragon reached the apex of its flight and began to swoop down toward them, Cullin got Pony untied and tossed the reins to Reeger before working to free the mule. Pony bolted toward the forest with Reeger on his back. Dalbry mounted Drizzle.

Cullin glanced toward Affonyl. "Come on, Princess—we have to go!"

But she grabbed one of her sealed clay pots and picked up a smoldering stick from the embers of the campfire. "Let me try an experiment first."

The monster's slitted eyes glowed yellow as it saw them. Its wings sounded like the canvas sails of a ship in a hurricane. The dragon dove like a hunting falcon toward the abandoned peasant huts, as if playing a target-practice game.

"Affonyl! Come on!"

She jammed the smoldering stick into a hole on the top of the pot. When a bright flame and white smoke curled out, Affonyl stepped back, cocked her arm, and like a female catapult threw the pot into the air.

As the dragon dove toward them, it turned its head closer to the thrown pot just as the clay grenade exploded. A flash of fire and a loud boom cracked the air, and the dragon looked as if someone had rudely slapped it in the face. The monster spun, more startled than injured, and pulled up into the sky. It let out an indignant shriek and soared away, becoming just a dark shape against the stars. No doubt it was flying off to find an alternative peasant settlement that it could destroy with less inconvenience.

Cullin stared at Affonyl, greatly impressed by what she had done. He wanted to throw his arms around her in a congratulatory hug, but thought she might not consider that appropriate.

Reeger finally got Pony back under control, wrestled his head around, and rode him back to the abandoned homes. Dalbry also returned on Drizzle, looking stunned. He said in a heavy voice, "We should rethink what we're doing. This is beyond our means." The dragon fire continued to spread through the fields.

Glowing with excitement, Affonyl repacked her items, shouldered her sack, and stood to join them. "Does that happen often, Squirrel? I can see why you like hunting dragons. What a rush!"

Reeger was exasperated. "Crotchrust! There aren't supposed to be real dragons, and we're certainly not real dragon slayers."

"But my experiment worked," Affonyl said.

Reeger gave a noncommittal grunt. "Change of plans: we head inland, find a different road and a different queendom. This one's got serious problems."

Dalbry watched the fire spread toward the hovels. "I agree."

They hurried off into the night-dark forest and away from the dragon's targeting zone.

CHAPTER TWENTY-EIGHT

IT WAS CULLIN'S turn to sit in Pony's saddle, while Reeger and Affonyl went on foot next to the overloaded mule. They made good time, heading away from the abandoned village in search of a connecting route out of the queendom. They did not expect to have trouble finding some other land where they could engage in the dragon business with less risk of encountering the real thing.

At midmorning, a group of knights came riding toward them. Even from a distance, Cullin could see their swords, shields, and flashing armor. Reeger immediately looked to the dense forest along the road. "You two can play knight and squire, but I shouldn't be seen with you."

He gestured for Affonyl to join him, but she wanted to stay with Cullin. "I'll say I'm a peasant girl keeping company with these traveling knights on my way to Queen Faria's palace, where I hope to find work as a muffin maiden."

Cullin tried to imagine the former princess as a muffin maiden in the castle kitchens. "You're getting the hang of making up stories."

"I've been paying attention, Squirrel."

"Suit yourself," Reeger said. "Just don't count on me to come rescuing you." He yanked the mule's rope and ducked into the underbrush.

Sir Dalbry reined Drizzle to a halt in the wide road so they could meet the five oncoming knights. The leader of the group wore dazzling armor and a spotless indigo-and-white cape. His white horse was unsullied by speckles of any color.

Dalbry lifted his bearded chin. "Sir Tremayne. I see you've recovered from the intestinal curse?"

"Fully recovered, Sir Dalbry." The knight looked grim. "I would have helped you slay the dragon that killed Duke Kerrl, but my unfortunate digestive problems made that impossible."

"Having diarrhea while wearing full plate must be difficult," Cullin said. "And impossible to clean. So much for shining armor."

The other four mounted knights blocked the road, swords drawn, as if intent on waylaying them. Affonyl tried to stay out of the way, and no one paid attention to her.

"We are honored to accept you into our chivalrous consortium, Sir Dalbry," Tremayne said. "This queendom needs our help—it is infested with dragons."

"*Infested?*" Cullin asked. "You mean there's more than one?"

"So far it is a singular infestation," said the burliest of the knights, a man with a ruddy complexion, dark eyebrows, and a dark beard. He introduced himself as Sir Hernon.

"Queen Faria requires our services," Tremayne said. "And now she requires yours as well. Normally, I would seek the glory of killing the monster myself, but after the incident with Duke Kerrl, I realized that dragon slaying requires a coordinated effort.

Therefore, we have formed this consortium of knights: myself and these four others, Sir Hernon, Sir Morgan, Sir Jems, and Sir Artimo."

As he introduced them, each knight lifted a visor, tipped a sword, or raised a banner. Tremayne added, "We all swear by the sacred words in the Knight's Manual."

"Revised edition," added Sir Morgan, an old bald knight with a missing front tooth.

Tremayne removed a fine leather-bound volume from his saddlebag, holding it as if it were a religious tome. "We studied every word and vowed to follow the expectations of knighthood."

Affonyl interrupted, "Has everyone in the land read the Knight's Manual? How does the public know what those expectations are?"

With a glance at Affonyl's drab clothes, shorn blond hair, and dusty face, Tremayne dismissed her as a worthless lowborn. He turned his attention to Sir Dalbry instead. "I know the expectations. We all live by the Manual."

"We all live by the Manual," said the other traveling knights in unison.

Tremayne continued. "The Knight's Manual even delineates the proper technique and requirements for an acceptable dragon slaying. That is one of the most important events of a knight's lifetime."

Dalbry's brow furrowed. "I'm afraid I've never read it. Is the Manual a new publication?"

Sir Tremayne raised his eyebrows in indignant surprise. "It is the most important chivalrous work ever written. I have spare copies in my saddlebag." He reached in, removed a tome identical to the first, and handed it to Dalbry, who reluctantly accepted it. "We are trying to put them in the nightstands of every guest room at every inn in the land."

Dalbry looked at the book for an awkward moment, but couldn't decide how to turn down the gift. "I haven't read the Manual yet, so I am at a disadvantage, but I look forward to studying it carefully."

Cullin leaned over from Pony to look, noting the name of the author imprinted on the leather. "It says Tremayne—did you write the Manual?"

The shining knight puffed with pride. "My father did, but I proofread it. This book standardizes knightly behavior, and all knights are implicitly bound by the rules." He turned his horse about. "Including you, Sir Dalbry. We are going to Queen Faria's Court. You will accompany us."

The older knight cleared his throat. "I'm afraid we're on a different quest. Now let us pass."

Trying to hide his alarm, Cullin piped up with what he hoped sounded like a good excuse. "We're headed to the barony next door where a cyclops has been kidnapping sheep and shearing them without the shepherd's permission."

"That can wait," said Sir Jems, frowning. "Killing dragons takes priority."

Sir Artimo said with a sniff, "It's in the Knight's Manual—Code of Honor, Section 12." He was the thinnest of the knights and carried the thinnest of swords.

Sir Dalbry pointed out, "You have five fully armed knights—the monster won't have a fighting chance. Queen Faria's dragon is all yours, gentlemen. I'll take care of the cyclops single-handedly, although I do intend to use both eyes."

Sir Tremayne had drawn his sword, and now the other knights drew their weapons, pushing closer. The mood grew dark. Tremayne said, "I fear we cannot accept nay for an answer." The five knights clustered around Pony and Drizzle. "You're coming with us. It's a matter of honor."

Sir Jems said in a surly voice, "Besides, we could always use your squire for bait."

Without giving Dalbry and Cullin a choice in the matter, the knights rode off toward Queen Faria's main city.

"Chivalry is serious business," said Sir Tremayne as they moved along the road. "If a knight's armor is tarnished, it's a sign that his honor is tarnished as well."

"Let's not paint with such a broad brush," said Sir Hernon in a deep voice, scratching his unruly black beard. "When you're living off the land on a vigorous quest, hygiene and suit maintenance aren't always easy."

Tremayne wasn't convinced. "And yet my armor is always spotless."

"We can't all be as perfect as you," said Sir Jems, whose favorite expression seemed to be a scowl.

"I wouldn't expect everyone to be." Tremayne flashed his white teeth. "But you can, of course, try." He rode onward.

Cullin felt trapped as the knights guided their mounts along. Affonyl hurried to keep up with them, but they made no concessions for the "peasant girl" following them on foot. She didn't complain, merely held her tongue and matched their pace. Though Cullin felt sorry for her, he knew she was a tough young woman. Still, she might have been better off running into the forest with Reeger and the mule.

When Sir Tremayne's white steed paused to munch on a clump of juicy weeds at the side of the road, Pony caught up with him.

"I take it your father was a famous knight, too, Sir Tremayne?" Cullin asked. "He must have been the greatest knight of all if he was the author of the Knight's Manual."

Tremayne glanced at the young man. "You might think my father was famed in story and song, but in truth he was just a knightophile, a collector fascinated by every aspect of chivalry and honor.

"He would buy dented or shattered shields after jousting tournaments. One entire hallway in our home was filled with pennants, and he collected trading cards of well-known knights. I grew up having to memorize coats of arms and heraldry sigils even before I learned how to read and write. Each night before I went to bed, he would tell me a story of some brave knight or other.

"As we learned tale after tale, we both realized that what we had assumed to be a mutually agreed-upon code of honor was not actually codified at all. Knights just blundered along, doing their best to behave in a knightly fashion, but they didn't have any standardized rule book."

He looked at Cullin, narrowing his eyes. "For instance, if a brave knight had to choose between retrieving his queen's favor from a mud hole or rescuing a young virgin from the clutches of a cannibal giant, which would he choose?"

Cullin was surprised, for the answer seemed obvious. "I'd save the virgin, of course. She's bound to be grateful."

"Ah, but if she were so grateful, then how much longer would she remain a virgin? Might it not be better to ensure that she remained pure, even if it meant the giant devoured her?"

"Better for whom?" Affonyl interjected, but the shining knight ignored her.

"I'd still say saving a girl is preferable to saving a queen's scarf from the mud," Cullin said.

"Again, the answer is not so clear—what if the virgin were a commoner? That would equalize the choice."

Affonyl gave a loud, annoyed cough, but somehow managed to prevent herself from making an unseemly outburst.

"My father spent years interviewing knights at festivals, jousting tournaments, even on the battlefield. One particularly well-known knight, Sir Eargon, had fought in a terrific battle against a goblin army. He slew a hundred of the creatures, but they had hacked off one of his arms and one of his legs. My father found Sir Eargon as he lay dying on the bloody ground and managed to conduct the very last interview. It was published in *Medieval Tymes*—maybe you saw it?"

"I'm afraid I don't read the newspaper regularly."

"Pity. He was very proud of that interview."

As they kept riding along at a slow pace, Tremayne withdrew his bound volume from the saddlebag, opened it, and flipped through the pages. "You can have your own copy, squire, once you become a full-fledged knight."

"That's all right. I'll have a look at Sir Dalbry's when he's finished."

Tremayne patted the fine leather cover. "When my father finished his opus, he went from monastery to monastery, but none of the monks would publish it. Limited interest, they said. They claimed that it needed *editing*." He snorted. "Who were the monks to tell my father that he needed editing? So we self-published the volume, and I've been distributing it widely ever since. Knights need to know how to behave. We have to abide by every letter of the rules."

Cullin knew what to say. "To promulgate the mystique of the knighthood?"

"Exactly! And he was so proud when I was dubbed Sir Tremayne after my unusual displays of bravery." He flushed, as if he didn't want to brag. "I left a copy of the book for Sir Phineal in King Norrimun's court. I hope he studies it carefully—that man has a lot of catching up to do. I was able to talk with him at great length while he nursed me back to health. I believe he's a changed man now."

Sir Artimo rode up to them. The wiry, beanpole knight grinned. "We all swear by the Manual. It's a good read, boy—a real page-turner. Sir Morgan even gave it a cover blurb."

Sir Hernon added, "Queen Faria will be impressed to see we have certain standards. She'll know exactly what to expect when our consortium of chivalrous knights arrives in her court."

CHAPTER TWENTY-NINE

HEADING TOWARD FARIA'S castle, Sir Tremayne led the group of knights along the rutted and muddy road known as the Queen's Superhighway. As Cullin got to know his new companions, he began to imagine how to tell this tale if it were ever told, what spin to use—a consortium of knights joining their swords even without a round table, a band of armored brothers traveling together to slay a horrific dragon.

"We should have a motto," said Sir Artimo. "A catchphrase the minstrels can use."

Artimo was a wiry whip of a man who flaunted a wiry whip of a sword. He had such finesse with his slender blade that he claimed he could pluck the eyelashes from his opponent during a duel. Cullin doubted that such an ability would be of use against the huge dragon that had attacked them at the abandoned peasant-tourist village, however . . . but who knew when such skills could come in handy? Perhaps Sir Artimo should have referred to himself as a dragon *tickler* rather than a dragon *slayer.*

He wore intensely bright fabrics: scarlet, emerald green, shocking pink—the better to catch the attention of the ladies, apparently, although not advantageous on a quest that required camouflage.

After pondering, Artimo suggested a motto: "How about 'All for one, and one for all'?"

"Sounds too sissy," said Sir Hernon. "How about 'Get on with it, or get out of the way'?"

Dour Sir Jems grunted, "How about 'Every man for himself'?"

Jems seemed happiest when he was unhappy, as fond of complaints as he was of his wineskin. He filled his outlook on the world with clouds, finding sunshine to be bothersome and bright. When Sir Jems squirted from his wineskin at a rest stop under an oak tree, the wine had turned to vinegar (possibly from proximity to the knight's mood). Rather than dumping it out, Jems relished having something else to complain about.

"Give the chivalrous consortium a chance," said Sir Tremayne. "We must provide a unified front when we make our pitch to dowager Queen Faria—and we are very lucky that Sir Dalbry has joined us. His credentials imbue our consortium with considerable gravitas."

"I daresay it would have even greater gravitas if my participation were *voluntary*," Dalbry muttered.

As the squire and apprentice dragon slayer, Cullin rode on Pony, while Affonyl hurried to keep up with them. At least she had good walking boots and comfortable clothes. For a formerly pampered princess, she was in terrific shape.

He was more concerned about being trapped among a group of serious knights who had an altogether different philosophy about the dragon business. Knowing the others could hear him,

Cullin commented, "We've slain so many dragons already, Sir Dalbry, we should give these brave men a chance."

"That defeats the purpose of a consortium," Sir Tremayne said. "Our aim is to promulgate the ideals of knighthood."

"Doesn't it negate those ideals if you kidnap us in order to accomplish your aim?" Cullin asked.

The shining knight with the improbably clean fabrics said, "Check the Knight's Manual. The bond of honor may seem restrictive to a young squire, but it provides a safety net for all brave knights."

"It feels like a net all right," said Dalbry.

Walking alongside Pony, Affonyl let out a disbelieving snort. The knights did not react at all, since dirty peasant girls were supposed to be neither seen nor heard.

They traveled along the Queen's Superhighway to the crowded city that had grown up around Faria's castle. Sir Morgan licked his fingertip and smoothed his eyebrows, which were the only remaining hair on his head. "Should we stop at an inn so we can freshen up and make ourselves more presentable for Queen Faria? I hear she's quite a looker."

Sir Morgan considered his loss of hair a blessing because otherwise it would have gone gray. He was missing a front tooth, which he claimed allowed him to stand out among the other smiling knights. He frequently talked about how handsome he had been as a young lordling, how women had fawned over him; he had lost count of the number of pretty scarves ladies had given him to win his favor. Morgan carried a small axe at his waist (he called it his "battle hatchet") and a sword with several notches on the blade.

"Each notch tells a story—would you like to hear them?" The other knights answered his question with a resounding "Maybe later."

Sir Hernon let out a deep growling sound. "Make ourselves presentable for what? We need to appear fierce and invincible—true dragon slayers." He plucked a beetle out of his voluminous beard. "That's what counts."

Hernon was big and gruff, with wiry black hair all over his head and face, as if he were preparing to infiltrate a group of recalcitrant bears. He wore a wolf-pelt cape, which to Cullin looked more like a dog skin. Because of his stocky, muscular build, Hernon had to have his armor and courtly clothes made by a specialist in larger sizes. Hearing about King Norrimun the Corpulent, Hernon had once asked for a recommendation to the big ruler's armorer and clothier.

"No time to stop at inns," Tremayne said. Despite their long, hard journey on the road, not a speck of dust had settled on him. "We have business with the queen."

Queen Faria's castle—which might more adequately be described as a palace—had a distinctive architectural style with an overabundance of arches, balconies, and crenellations, obviously more for aesthetics than for defensive purposes.

As the consortium of knights made their way to the front gates, Cullin gawked at the numerous statues and fountains, walls painted with frescos, flower boxes in every window filled with bright tulips that had been encouraged to bloom even out of season. Trellises were covered with morning glories; arbors were hung with grapevines.

Cullin admired the beauty. "I can see why the people don't want a dragon to destroy this particular city."

As the only squire among six knights, Cullin had the task of riding ahead with Pony so he could fill out the proper forms and get them an audience with the dowager queen. Affonyl accompanied Cullin, whispering protocol hints. With her help, they passed through the royal bureaucracy with no trouble at all.

But when Affonyl tried to accompany Cullin into the throne room, two guards frowned at her shaggy hair and dusty clothes. They barred her from entry. "Sorry, miss. We're not letting a dirty little peasant girl into the presence of the queen."

Affonyl's eyes flared. "I'm not—" Cullin flashed her a warning glance, and she bit her tongue, reassessed, and said, "I'm not *little*."

Cullin interceded. "She travels with the chivalrous consortium of knights as our personal assistant. While we go about our dragon-slaying business, would it be possible for her to stay at the castle, maybe find some work in the embroidery department? She has quite an interesting technique."

Even though the guards arranged for her to be whisked off to the castle kitchens, Affonyl did not thank Cullin for his gentlemanly consideration.

At court the merchants, trade ministers, decorative knights, and visiting aunts and uncles were fully aware of the dragon's horrific depredations. Peasants were evacuating the queendom, tourism was down, and everyone felt nervous.

When word got to the throne, the dowager queen was giddy at the prospect of so many brave and handsome knights coming to rescue her (particularly the "handsome" part). The six knights entered en masse, displaying their various suits of armor, banners, coats of arms. Cullin walked beside Sir Dalbry as he always did, but this time he felt awkward and unbalanced, not sure how to proceed. Normally, their scheme was well rehearsed.

Queen Faria's sergeant-at-arms introduced the brave knights by their brave names—Sir Tremayne first, who cut a dashing figure as if he had walked straight off the pages of an illustrated children's storybook, then Sir Morgan, Sir Jems, Sir Artimo, Sir Hernon, and Sir Dalbry. Cullin had intended for them to be introduced in alphabetical order, but the crier got the slips of paper mixed up. The knights rearranged themselves to step forward and take a knee before the old queen. Sir Morgan flashed his gap-toothed smile, trying to be flirtatious.

Queen Faria was as ancient and as powdered as Affonyl had suggested. The wrinkles on her prunish face were like troughs to hold white makeup powder. She had added dabs of rouge to her cheeks to imply a youthful blush. Faria beamed when she saw all the knights, and even giggled when Sir Morgan flirted, but she was most impressed when Sir Dalbry was announced.

The older knight stepped forward, cutting an excellent figure with his dragonskin cape, his sword, and his confidence. "We are here to save your queendom, Majesty." He bowed and then stepped back, for they had agreed to let Sir Tremayne do the talking.

Queen Faria had a breathy voice as she surveyed the knights. "My, my, so many legendary knights, right here in my throne room . . . although I can't say that I've heard your legends before."

"Trust me, Queen Faria," Sir Artimo said with a flourish of his chin as if it were a fighting blade, "we are indeed legendary."

"And *Sir Dalbry*—my, my!" The dowager queen grinned at him. "Everyone's heard your song. Minstrels sing it night after night, and here you are! Brave Sir Dalbry—right in my hallway."

She laughed at her own cleverness. Everyone in court laughed. The knights also showed polite amusement, although they were plainly unhappy to see the most reluctant member of their company receiving so much attention.

Sir Tremayne cleared his throat. "Majesty, a ferocious dragon is preying upon your queendom, and we are honor-bound to offer our services, according to the Knight's Manual. We will slay the dragon for you."

Knowing the unprofitable way that Tremayne conducted his business, Dalbry spoke up. "And in doing so, Majesty, we will incur certain expenses, yet we charge only a modest fee. As a profession, dragon slaying is highly skilled, but not lucrative. We can solve your dragon problem. We are ready to start the job today, provided we can work out the details of compensation."

The other knights fidgeted at Dalbry's boldness, but he remained firm. Queen Faria was not surprised by the negotiations and called in her court contracts advisor. "Are you suggesting I should hire *all six* of you to slay one dragon? It doesn't usually require such an effort."

"This is a dragon of substantial proportions, Majesty," Tremayne asserted, even though he had never seen the monster.

She smiled at Dalbry—flirtatiously, Cullin feared. "Maybe I should just have the famous dragon slayer Sir Dalbry do the job—not weighed down by a bunch of amateurs."

The other consortium knights were offended to be called amateurs. Appeasing them, Tremayne said to the queen, "Together, we can do a better job overall, Majesty."

"Well, if you insist . . . although I'm not convinced that dragon slaying by committee is necessarily more effective."

Having seen the real monster, Dalbry was hesitant. "The point of forming our chivalrous consortium, Majesty, was that this would be a team effort."

Tremayne stepped forward, holding the leather-bound Knight's Manual. "We will face the dragon one at a time, per the accepted rules of conduct, Majesty, but the others can provide support services in the meantime."

The queen brushed flaky white powder from her dress. "I understand the economic impact the dragon is having on my queendom, so the investment would be worthwhile. I can offer you a chest of gold coins for slaying the beast." She held up a gnarled finger. "That's one chest for the lot of you, mind—a fee for the job."

Tremayne and the other knights were uncomfortable even discussing financial matters. Dalbry got back to business. "When the dragon is duly slain, we will divide the reward according to the shares stipulated in our consortium's articles."

"But there's more to dragon slaying than mere money," Queen Faria said. "In order to make this endeavor more appropriate for the minstrel record of history, I will add a treasure more valuable than gold." She put her fingers to her lips and blew out a shrill whistle that could have shattered glass.

A young woman entered through a side door near the throne. She was slender to the point of waifishness, with brown hair, brown eyes, and a shy demeanor.

Queen Faria beamed. "Brave knights, this is my beautiful daughter, Princess Minima—my only child, my greatest treasure, and worth infinitely more than gems or gold. Whichever knight actually slays the dragon will have the hand of my daughter in marriage. Isn't that wonderful?"

In a dutiful knightly fashion, the would-be dragon slayers agreed that it was indeed wonderful. Princess Minima didn't seem overjoyed, though. "Thanks, Mom," she said without enthusiasm.

When the queen raised her eyebrows, flakes of white powder fell from her face onto her gown. "Only one knight can have the hand of the princess, naturally. Find some way to choose amongst yourselves when you actually fight the dragon."

The royal contracts advisor had already drawn up a document, based on a boilerplate from other dragon-slaying endeavors.

"If I could have each one of you sign?" He passed the document and a peacock feather around while his assistant carried an ink pot. Even Cullin was asked to affix his signature to the terms and conditions of the slaying.

When the paperwork was done, Tremayne bowed before the throne and seemed in a hurry to leave. "We'll figure something out, Majesty. We do this to promulgate the glory of knights everywhere, not for any personal gain."

Dalbry gave Cullin an unreadable glance. "Well, that does it. We have a dragon to slay."

By now, the hour is late, and most of the Scabby Wench's customers are either drunk, drowsy, or both.

Reeger says he can't afford an accurate clock, and the one he owns is permanently stuck at half-past midnight. Whenever he decides it's closing time—a combination of being sold out of Wendria's mysterious meat pies, running short in the ale keg, or just being tired of dealing with customers—he hauls out the stopped clock, points to the time, and announces "Last call!"

I know his tricks, but many patrons fall for it night after night.

The minstrel finishes his third and final set and plays yet another encore of "The Fart in the Park" in such a lackluster fashion that even the inebriated mercenaries don't demand more. Hob Nobbin claims it is past his bedtime and insists he needs sleep, thanks to his delicate artistic constitution. He takes his lute, waves farewell to the uninterested remainder of the audience, and leaves through the tavern door.

With shining eyes and silly grins, the baker's girl and the candlemaker's daughter flounce after him like two puppies hoping for a treat—thus reaffirming my long-held suspicion that women, especially lovestruck young girls, are incomprehensible to the rational mind. Maurice will learn that soon enough.

At least the prince isn't watching the vapid girls at the moment. In general, he is easily starstruck, but I take pride in seeing that he remains interested in my story. I pause in the telling to order another "second" tankard of ale as soon as Reeger shouts out his last call. Reality is thirsty work.

Maurice says, "I see where this is going—Princess Minima is Mother, right? Our kingdom used to belong to Queen Faria?"

I'm surprised he would even ask. "You really don't know much about your family history, do you, son?"

Maurice looks away. "I never thought it was interesting."

"Before tonight, you mean?"

The young man gives a noncommittal shrug. "We'll see. You didn't describe her much. Was Princess Minima pretty?"

I raise my eyebrows. "Was Princess Minima pretty, you ask? Well, pretty enough on the princess scale. It's a subjective measure."

The boy looks at Reeger's stopped clock. "Are we almost done with the story?"

"Getting there," I say. "You'll note that we're building toward the climax, bringing the plot threads together, reuniting the characters as the seeds I carefully planted earlier come to fruition."

"I am familiar with traditional story structure," Maurice says.

Reeger brings my last tankard of the evening. "Don't imagine that you know where the rustin' story's going, lad. This adventure is full of twists and turns, not to mention unexpected surprises."

"All surprises are unexpected, by definition," says the prince. "If they were expected, then they wouldn't be surprises."

I look at Reeger with a long-suffering "don't blame me, I didn't raise him this way" expression. Most of the remaining customers slurp down their tankards and upend them on the tables before leaving. "I'd prefer you settle up now, Sire, so I can close the till. How many tankards was it?"

"Two," I say in a firm voice.

Reeger snorts and gestures to the full tankard at the table. "I'd say at least four, counting that one."

Maurice surprises me by throwing in his support. "But you can't count beyond two, Reeger. You said so yourself several times tonight—so two it is."

Reeger grumbles, but knows when he's defeated. "All right, pay for two. And I'm charging you for two glasses of top-shelf cider."

I reach under the roughspun burlap robe for my purse of coins, only to come up empty. I pat my hip, then the other side, realizing that I was so excited to take Maurice to the tavern for his first real night on the town that I forgot to take spending money from the Royal Treasury. Or, just as likely, someone picked my pocket.

I frown. "Sorry, Reeger, old friend. I'm a little light at the moment. You know I'm good for it. Can you spot me a few coins?"

"Bloodrust, Cullin!" Reeger moves his lips as if he wants to spit on the floor, but Wendria holds up a scolding finger from behind the bar, so he restrains himself. "If I extend credit to you, then I have to extend credit to everyone."

"Really? I am your king."

"Anybody can be king. You proved that yourself."

"It is my face on the coins. My credit is good."

"Not a very good likeness—that could be anybody. I don't like this one bit." I feel highly embarrassed to have this happen, especially in front of my son, but Reeger gets a glint in his eye. "I can let the lad work it off. Wendria needs help scrubbing the pie pans, disinfecting the tankards, mopping the floors." He claps Maurice hard on the shoulder, and the boy flinches as if from a stunning blow. "And something special—mucking out the tavern's latrine, adding fresh corncobs and thistle leaves for the patrons."

The prince sounds shocked and offended. "The latrine?"

When Reeger grins, Maurice apparently finds his teeth disconcerting. "It's been newly refurbished, lad. You'll like it."

Now the boy turns to me, seeking rescue. "Do I have to?"

"I did promise you new experiences tonight. It'll build character. Think of it as enforced volunteerism."

"But—but what will Mother say when I come home with calluses?"

Reeger lets out a hearty laugh as he leads the uncertain boy back to the tavern's kitchen. "Calluses? Nonsense, lad! You have to get blisters before you can have calluses."

I snag my full tankard of ale and follow them to the back. "While you work, I'll entertain you with the rest of my story."

CHAPTER THIRTY

THE DRAGON-SLAYING CONSORTIUM set off into the wilds of the queendom.

The knights were full of tales, each one as imaginative as it was improbable. Cullin believed none of the stories, but he did file away the details for later use.

Sir Hernon puffed his broad chest and adjusted his wolf-skin cape. "Back in my own kingdom, I spotted a dragon flying overhead. I could tell it was intent on causing mischief, so I raised my fist, showed the monster my sword, and shouted to the sky. I threatened that dragon in no uncertain terms, explaining what would happen if it chose to challenge me and the land I was sworn to protect. So the terrified beast flew off, causing no harm." He crossed his arms over his chest in smug triumph.

Brave Sir Morgan snorted at the tale. "Maybe you scared off a large dragon, Hernon, but I once encountered a *huge* dragon. When it flew into my kingdom, it intended to cause *even more* terrifying damage than your dragon would have, but I was up to the task. So I issued even *harsher* threats than you used." The bald knight flushed. "I'm ashamed to recall some of my language, because it was definitely un-knightlike and not suitable for use in mixed company. I pulled my sword and my battle hatchet, threatening the monster with everything I had—and it flew away in terror."

As they rode along in the forest, Sir Jems took a long swig from his wineskin. "That's nothing. The dragon that came to *our* kingdom was indescribably gigantic, bigger than either of yours!"

By now, Cullin was getting tired of the one-upsmanship. So apparently was Sir Artimo. "Let's just stipulate that we've heard your story, Sir Jems, and move on to more interesting tales." The other companions applauded the idea.

Now that he had their attention, Artimo brushed his knuckles across his chest. "For my own part, I vanquished the dragon slug of Oglethorpe."

"Never heard of it," said Jems with crabbiness unbefitting a knight.

Artimo gave a lilting wave of his hand. "You've never heard of it because the locals considered it such a terrifying beast that they dared not repeat the story, although they whisper to their naughty children that if they don't behave, the dragon slug of Oglethorpe will crawl all over them in the dark and devour them."

Cullin asked because he knew everyone was wondering, "What's a dragon slug?"

"A hideous beast that defies description," Artimo quipped.

Sir Dalbry said, "Could you *try* to describe it? That would help the veracity of your tale."

"It's a monster, like a gigantic garden slug marked with black stripes, waving icky-looking antennae. And it has batlike wings, but the beast is so sluggish it can rarely get itself off the ground. Instead of breathing fire, like a normal dragon, the dragon slug breathes slime that can make a victim die from sheer disgust." His expression twisted. "The monster rolled over entire peasant villages, consuming whole fields. My squire and I followed it." Artimo heaved a shuddering breath. "Ah, my poor, brave squire. Ebbie, short for Ebberlin." He shook his head.

"We tracked the dragon slug, ready for battle. Since the creature moved at the pace of a slug, we could hunt it down. When we cornered the thing, it reared up on its soft, blubbery body and wiggled its icky antennae at me. But I, and my graceful sword"—for emphasis, Sir Artimo whipped out his thin blade and waved it in the air, like a boy wiggling a willow twig—"had speed and skill.

"As the dragon slug vomited slime at me, I circled and slashed its soft hide. I don't know that the creature felt pain as a person does, but it squirmed and tried to attack. I raced around to the other side, made another slash." He smiled. "I continued that way for more than an hour, as my squire Ebbie cheered me on—for that was his duty as squire, and no one did it better. I slashed and sliced; I danced around. I attacked; I withdrew. It was a death of a thousand cuts, but I was willing to make *two* thousand cuts, if necessary.

"Finally, I lopped off one of its antennae, leaving the monster half blind. And I knew it was time for our secret weapon." Artimo grinned at all of them. "I had consulted a natural-history guidebook, and I knew the only sure way to kill a rare but deadly dragon slug."

"And what was it?" asked Sir Tremayne, absorbed in the story. "So we can add it to our repertoire, in case any of us ever encounters a dragon slug?"

Sir Artimo held the pause for a long, masterful moment, then said in a low whisper, "*Salt.* Squire Ebbie had brought along two casks of sea salt, and he cracked open the lids as I harried the monster with my blade. When I was ready for the coup de grâce"—he swished his supple sword in the air again—"Ebbie tossed me one of the casks, and I ran behind the dragon slug and dumped the salt all over its back. It roared in agony, for salt is like acid to the creatures. Slime oozed in buckets from its pores. It thrashed and writhed.

"Next, I raced around in front of the monster. Ebbie gave me the second cask of salt, and I poured it onto the dragon slug's head, which made the thousand small gashes burn and sizzle. Its other icky antenna shriveled down. In its death throes, the creature oozed and shrank.

"But Ebbie, poor Ebbie. . ." Artimo heaved a deep breath. "He was too eager. He raced forward with his practice blade—like Squire Cullin's there— and tried to hack off the head of the dragon slug. Ebbie was my apprentice dragon slayer." He gave an appreciative nod to Cullin. "But now he lives only in my memory, rather than in the legends he had hoped to achieve.

"The dragon slug had one last surprise for us. In its last death convulsion, the monster vomited a wagonload of dying slime and inundated poor Ebbie. The slime itself was caustic and clingy, and I used my cape—my best cape, mind you—to try and save him, but before I could wipe the thick ooze from his head and face, Ebbie, alas, suffocated."

Sir Artimo hung his head in respect, and the other knights in the consortium did the same. "And that is why I have no squire."

Cullin was about to tell the story of why Sir Dalbry didn't have a horse, but that tale was no longer valid, since the older knight had Drizzle.

"I killed an even bigger dragon slug once," Sir Jems added, and the group rode on into the forest.

None of them knew exactly how to find a dragon. If this were part of their normal scam, Cullin, Dalbry, and Reeger would have set up a meeting place, planted clues, and arranged a rendezvous. Now that they had a real dragon and too many uninvited partners to contend with, neither Cullin nor Sir Dalbry knew how to plan.

They camped, told more stories, and set off again the next day for a popular nearby market town that drew travelers and merchants from miles around. The dowager queen's swap meet, flea market, and multifamily rummage sale was renowned throughout the land. The market town was also the site of a popular annual Renaissance Faire, but Cullin had never actually seen one of the futuristic festivals.

Sir Morgan thought he might check out a new set of armor or an improved shield; Sir Jems hoped to purchase a second wineskin "just in case"; Sirs Hernon and Artimo said they just wanted to look around. Dalbry and Tremayne maintained their focus, intending to interview travelers and merchants to learn if anyone had seen signs of the dragon. Tremayne said, "With so many travelers in attendance, we should get some clue to the monster's whereabouts." Cullin wished he could have gone there on a date with Affonyl, but maybe that was rushing things. . . .

When the group arrived at the flea-market site, however, they found more clues than they could possibly use.

The entire area was blackened and devastated. The air smelled of soot and burned flesh. The still-smoldering embers of wooden market stalls glowed here and there on the ground; part of a hand-painted sign from a lemonade stand lay charred in the wreckage.

Souvenir kiosks had been torn to pieces, colorful trinkets strewn about. Carts were overturned. Roasted and gnawed skeletons of horses and people lay scattered everywhere.

Cullin gazed nervously up into the sky, wary of the monster. This time they didn't have Affonyl to help out with her explosive mixtures if a dragon swooped down on them.

Stunned, Sir Dalbry and Cullin stood together by the large, deep impression of a three-toed footprint.

"We're going to need bigger swords," Cullin said.

CHAPTER THIRTY-ONE

GROWING UP IN her father's castle, Affonyl had always felt like an odd duck. Although she tried to empty her mind of challenging thoughts and focus her attention on giggles and gossip, she simply couldn't stand it.

The most intricate lacework couldn't hold a candle to dissecting frogs, testing various earthworm-and-chemical mixtures, studying alchemy texts, or spending far too much of King Norrimun's discretionary coinage on Wizard Edgar's experiments. To her delight, she had once succeeded in turning gold into lead (which, unfortunately, did not help her father's treasury).

But Wizard Edgar had left for a better job. Mother Singra offered a sympathetic shoulder to cry on, but much as she cared for Affonyl, the old woman was still invested in the traditional ways of the kingdom.

When Affonyl had decided flee her "princess is a princess" life to run off with the merchant prince Indico, he had merely been an excuse—her chemistry texts would have called him a *catalyst*.

Indico had given her a reason to escape the marriage with Duke Kerrl, run away from the castle, and strike out on her own. She realized she wasn't meant to be a princess. To her, being a person seemed far preferable.

In the court of old Queen Faria, however, Affonyl found few kindred spirits. She tried to make friends, but the serving girls, muffin maidens, and pot scrubbers were utterly lacking in curiosity, like most of her former ladies-in-waiting. The serving men, carpenters, bag haulers, masons, tinkers, chimney sweeps, torch-lighters, and candle-snuffers seemed unimaginative and rude. Their gossip was about a different sort of people, but it was gossip nevertheless. They brushed her aside, ordered her around, and treated her as an outsider, talking *about* her instead of *to* her.

She was assigned numerous chores, generally the jobs the management wenches least liked to do. Affonyl served as a chamber-pot emptier and polisher, flowerbed fertilizer distribution engineer (which went hand-in-hand with the job of chamber-pot emptier), trellis-vine detangler, and embroidery needle organizer. This was worse than selling seashells by the seashore.

One morning when she had to deliver Princess Minima's breakfast tray of tea and scones, she took time to observe the girl. Minima seemed nice enough, pretty enough, but barely sufficient otherwise. The princess was a princess and seemed to have no interest in becoming a person. Affonyl was reminded of what her father had wanted her to be: passive, unimaginative, and obedient, with plenty of possessions but no personality.

She really did enjoy the company of Dalbry and Reeger—and, of course, Cullin. *That* was where she fit in. Though she'd been terrified during the real dragon attack in the abandoned village, Affonyl was proud of herself for her quick thinking and innovative solution. Now that she understood the dragon business better, her life was just getting exciting.

While Cullin and Sir Dalbry went off on their adventures, Affonyl was not pleased to be left behind. Besides, when Reeger had ducked into the forest with the mule, he'd also taken her sack of necessary items, including her precious books and experimental chemicals.

She did not belong here. She had to get out.

The next morning, she roused herself at the crack of dawn, which she thought was early enough for her to slip out of the castle unseen while everyone else slept. When she did embark on her escape, though, Affonyl found that getting up at the crack of dawn was not particularly early for castle servants or kitchen crew. The kitchens were abustle with workers preparing breakfast, the ovens hot as they baked fresh bread. Stable boys prepared the horses for the day's horse business. Dismayed, Affonyl wondered if she had missed her chance.

When the head kitchen maid gave her a bowl of porridge topped with colorful sprinkles for the dowager queen, she took it with a meek smile. Instead of going up to the queen's chambers, though, she found a quiet corridor where she wolfed down the porridge herself, knowing she would need the energy.

She left the bowl on a windowsill, straightened her clothing, and walked out of the castle with a demeanor that told any observer she had important instructions from important people to do an important task.

She found Reeger out in the forest by sheer coincidence—which was a good thing, because otherwise she would have spent a long time looking for him.

The mule brayed, sounding like either a welcoming committee or an intruder alarm. Seeing her, Reeger raised his uneven eyebrows. "Bloodrust, girl! What took you so long? I've had to make plans with very little information. What's going on?"

When Affonyl explained Sir Tremayne's dragon-slaying plans and how the dowager queen had offered the knights a chest of gold coins as well as the hand of Princess Minima, Reeger wasn't impressed. "What are we going to do with a princess? They're useless—why would anybody want one?" After Affonyl gave an indignant sniff, Reeger remembered who she was. "Present company excepted."

He didn't seem surprised by her story, however, and when she pressed him he admitted that he had spent the last several days snooping around town, haunting the taverns (for informational purposes only), and gathering most of the story himself. "I could use a hand for the next phase. I usually have to do everything myself, but you may as well give me a reason to keep you around."

"Oh, really? Didn't I drive away a dragon that would have killed us all?"

"That's why I'll admit that you might be useful. With all those other knights in the game, and a real dragon in the mix, this is going to be more complicated than usual. I wish we could have started fresh in some other queendom, but that ship has sailed—and sunk. Now we have to find a way to finish this in a satisfactory fashion . . . by which I mean the dragon is dead, we're all alive, and we win the treasure."

"And another princess, for what that's worth," Affonyl said.

"Let's just focus on figuring out how to kill a dragon and stay alive."

Reeger was uncouth, unwashed, ill mannered, and rough around the edges. But he was quite skilled at finding dragon lairs. By the end of the afternoon, he had tracked down where the monster slumbered between depredations.

The cave was nestled in the rugged hills, surrounded by dark pines that made rushing sounds in the breezes. Reeger led her to the edge of the trees near a befouled rocky clearing, where a deep black opening resembled the yawning mouth of a dead man. Sounds of growling and snoring came from within, echoing in the deep cave.

The dragon had uprooted trees around the mouth of the lair, then set them on fire in a sort of landscaping that played to reptilian sensibilities. A few charred remains lay strewn about.

"Rust, this looks better than anything I could set up," Reeger whispered. "It's got a real sense of primal evil about it. Imagine the appetite of that thing."

"I'd rather imagine it from out here, thank you," Affonyl said. "Now that we've found the place, what do we do about it? What's our plan?"

"Unless you want to kill the dragon yourself, girl, I'd say we leave it to the professionals."

"Like Sir Dalbry, you mean? Or Cullin?"

Reeger shook his head. "They're smart enough to let the others try first. Five puffed-up knights ready to show their testosterone—maybe one of those heroes wants Princess Minima enough to fight a dragon for her."

Affonyl didn't add her opinion of Princess Minima. In fact, she thought the dowager queen had made an error in letting the consortium of knights see the uninspiring girl as an incentive.

"Dalbry has to keep up appearances, though," Reeger said. "As the senior dragon slayer among them, he's supposed to know how to track down the monster. That's where I'll need your help."

"How?" she asked.

Reeger led her away from the ominous cave, keeping his voice low so they didn't disturb the slumbering creature. "Sneak in to wherever the knights are camping see if you can catch Cullin while he's doing one of his squirely tasks and tell him how to find the lair. He can slip clues to Dalbry, so he leads that group of knights right to the dragon's doorstep."

Affonyl nodded. "I can do that, but I don't know that I'm doing them any favors."

CHAPTER THIRTY-TWO

THE MASSACRE SITE at the queen's flea market shook the brave knights to the core. In their minds, the quest had now changed from a theoretical job to something that might well kill them all.

The knights looked to Sir Dalbry to bolster their confidence, since he portrayed himself as a brave warrior with many successful kills, but the devastation they had witnessed in the marketplace beggared his ability to cope. In reality, Dalbry did not have much experience battling powerful foes, reptilian or otherwise.

When the knights asked him for tales of his exploits, Cullin noted that Dalbry told stories about his father's various crusades, rather than concocting his own victories. "After a lifetime of adventures and triumphs, my father wanted nothing more than a comfortable home, a wife who was fond of him, and an apricot orchard to tend."

Sir Tremayne cited a chapter in the Manual that allowed such an end to a knight's life, provided that dying in battle or on a quest was not a viable option.

Feeling generous, Dalbry reached into his magic sack and offered dried apricots to everyone in the company, including Cullin, asking only that they return the apricot pits to him when they were finished. Dalbry didn't admit that mercenary knights had chased him out of his own fief, and he had not dared to fight them.

The consortium members headed toward the hills, because that was where they decided a dragon was likely to live. As a matter of fact (though he couldn't admit it aloud, as Sir Dalbry's handpicked "apprentice dragon slayer"), Cullin wasn't eager to find the monster's lair. He was also skeptical about Tremayne, Jems, Hernon, Artimo, and Morgan, all of whom were expert at telling stories, although the young man was not quite sure he could believe them.

For Cullin, being youthful and energetic had its disadvantages. The knights in the chivalrous consortium had no problem making the token squire keep watch during the longest, loneliest hours of the night. Sir Tremayne insisted that the real knights needed their dragon-slaying sleep so they could be refreshed to fight the monster with full vigor.

During his late-night watch, Cullin sat in the dark of the camp listening to insects and hoping not to hear the horrible hissing shriek that had awakened them in the abandoned tourist village. Unless somebody stopped the monster, it would devastate the land and move to the next kingdom and the next. Sir Dalbry's dragon-slaying services would be in more demand than ever—and it might be time for him to choose a different career.

Cullin stirred the embers of their campfire, eliciting a small flame. He had let the blaze die down so as not to attract any prowling dragons. Beyond the perimeter of their camp, he heard the crack of a twig, a rustle of leaves, and he came instantly alert. Rising to his feet, he put a hand to his small, dull practice sword.

He considered shouting "Who goes there?" to rouse the knights and send them scrambling to defend against nighttime marauders. Fortunately, before he could sound an alarm, he saw Affonyl's shadowy form slip out from between the trees; she put a finger to her lips.

Cullin hurried over to Affonyl, bending close. "What are you doing here? Shouldn't you be in Queen Faria's castle making muffins?"

"I'd rather be part of the dragon business, so I ran away and found Reeger." Her lips curved in a smile. "I miss your squirrel cooking."

Sir Dalbry cracked an eye open, then silently rose from his camp blanket and crept over to join their conversation. "We are honor bound to do this deed. All six knights accepted the quest from Queen Faria." He put a hand on Cullin's shoulder. "As did my apprentice dragon slayer."

Affonyl frowned. "I understand about the treasure, but what does Cullin want with a princess?"

"I do want a princess," he said, "but I had my sights set on a different one."

Dalbry glanced back toward the camp, afraid their conversation would wake the other knights. Sir Artimo fidgeted and rolled over, but Hernon snored so loudly that the noise covered the distraction.

Affonyl quickly gave Cullin and Dalbry directions to the dragon's lair. "You can't miss the place—a giant cave with a bad stink and bones scattered all around."

Dalbry nodded. "Thank you. If you and Reeger find any additional information, come here at the dead of night with your report. I'll make sure Cullin stands the late watch from now on."

The young man groaned. His eyes were already scratchy and bloodshot, and now his situation wouldn't improve. "I'm not going to get a good night's sleep until that dragon is dead."

Affonyl flashed a quick smile toward Cullin before she slipped away into the forest.

After a day of wandering through the forests and looking for signs, Cullin and Sir Dalbry led the band into the rugged foothills. When they reached an area where the rock outcroppings stood taller and the stunted black pines bent over, the older knight nodded and nudged Drizzle forward. "We're close. This type of terrain is a dragon's natural habitat."

They wound their way up a gorge, climbed a steep hillside, and tethered the horses so they could proceed on foot. The knights insisted on wearing their armor for protection, though Cullin supposed that so much metal would do more cooking than protecting in the presence of a real fire-breathing dragon. Also, the plate mail, boots, shields, and swords made an unstealthy clanking sound as the six men tried to creep forward.

According to Affonyl's directions, they were almost upon the lair. By now, the sun had set and long shadows draped the gorge. The pine forests grew more ominous, and the whispering boughs produced an evil snicker instead of a shushing lullaby.

The air smelled of cooked flesh, brimstone, and something especially pungent. The other knights wrinkled their noses. Dalbry grimaced. "Dragon feces—the stink is unmistakable."

Cullin was not eager to keep going in the gathering dusk, though he wouldn't have been eager in broad daylight, either. The six knights fell silent as they pushed past the last line of trees and saw the ominous cave overhang. The gnawed and burned bones looked more realistic than any scene Reeger had ever staged.

Straight-backed, Sir Tremayne emerged from the trees and stood exposed. Sir Artimo and Sir Morgan backed away; burly Sir Hernon stepped forward to get a better look, and Sir Jems hid behind Sir Hernon, while Dalbry and Cullin pulled Sir Tremayne back out of sight. "We don't want the dragon to spot us."

They heard a stirring inside the cave, a rattle of rocks, and a phlegmy huffing sound like a blacksmith's bellows half full of swamp water. In the last light of the gloaming, they saw the enormous angular shape of a hideous primeval monster. A long head emerged from the cave, shaped like a spearpoint with blazing eyes and several rows of teeth. It crawled forward, its wings tucked against its body until it was free of the cave opening. The dragon spread its wings, let out a horrifying shriek, and spat fire into the sky.

Cullin ducked, sure they would be seen, but the dragon turned its head skyward. With a thrust of its muscular legs, the dragon launched itself into the air. The giant wings beat downward, and the heavy monster rose above the trees, flapping into the starlit night and leaving its lair behind.

Cullin stared in awe. He and Sir Dalbry had seen the creature before, and this second encounter was as terrifying as the first. The other five knights were speechless, eyes wide, mouths open.

Sir Jems had brought his wineskin with him, and now he drained the entire thing. "Maybe we should reconsider. Princess Minima isn't all *that* pretty."

Sir Tremayne rounded on him. "How dare you! You are a knight. You swore an oath. You read the Manual. The reputation of all knights rests on our shoulders—it's up to us to promulgate the mystique."

Dalbry took Tremayne's side. "If knights have no honor, then no one does. You saw the bodies in the flea market. This beast will kill again. Do you want minstrels to sing about the group of knights who accepted a sacred quest, took one look at a dragon, and fled?"

Sir Morgan nodded slowly. "We should find a safe and sheltered place far enough from the lair that we can build a camp and discuss strategy. It will serve as our base of operations."

CHAPTER THIRTY-THREE

IN THE DARK, they set up camp in a sheltered place next to a rock outcropping with a clearing for an eventual cook fire, trees for tying the horses to, and a nearby stream, everything a group of dragon slayers could want for a nice vacation spot—or military camp. Cullin retrieved all the mounts while the consortium of knights hunkered down in the dark, without risking a fire. They discussed their plans in edgy voices.

"We should declare war on the beast," said Sir Artimo. "Leave a formal document on the doorstep of that cave with an official seal from Queen Faria. Then we can all fight together, like an army."

"Document? Can dragons read?" Cullin asked.

"No matter. It is a question of honor," Tremayne said. "We have to follow the rules of the Knight's Handbook in regards to the slaying of dragons. One brave knight at a time goes to face the beast." He retrieved the leather-bound tome from his saddlebag. Although it was too dark to read, he recited for his comrades. "For a proper challenge against a dragon, a knight must go to the lair, call out the monster, and fight it alone. Ideally, the conflict ends with him slaying the beast."

"Ideally," Sir Jems said with a twinge of sarcasm.

Tremayne squinted at the pages in the moonlight, flipping back and forth, but could not find what he was looking for. "Unfortunately, the Manual is unclear in the circumstance where there's more than one dragon slayer available, but the traditional rules say that it's a solo job."

Sir Hernon snorted. "We need to be pragmatic. Only one of us can have the princess anyway. Who gets chosen as the lucky one?"

Tremayne looked around at them. "Does anyone want the princess enough to go first?"

They had all seen the bland Princess Minima. Apparently, her attributes were insufficient to inspire any of the knights.

Sir Dalbry thought a moment and came up with a solution, as Cullin had known he would. He collected a handful of dried grass stalks, choosing the six best ones. "We'll draw straws." He trimmed them with his dagger so that each straw looked identical. "It's the fairest way." With a raised eyebrow, he looked at Sir Tremayne. "Does that fit the terms of the Manual?"

"I believe my father would approve. We'll include that in the revised edition."

The bright moon was high in the sky, and the gathered knights could see that the straws were all the same. Dalbry cut one in half and discarded the other end. "Six straws. The short one is somebody's ticket to a dragon slaying."

"Oh, boy," said Sir Jems.

Dalbry extended the handful of straws toward the dour knight. "Would you like to draw first?"

"Not really."

"Someone has to."

"I'll do it." Sir Morgan plucked the first straw out of Dalbry's hand. A long straw.

Realizing that his odds would get worse with each selection, Sir Jems quickly drew a straw of his own. Another long one.

Sir Tremayne drew the third long straw. Dalbry's handful was getting smaller.

Sir Hernon reached forward. "Give me one of those." He grabbed without looking—and stared at the short straw. The shaggy knight looked confused, then resigned.

Sir Artimo applauded. "Bravo! Good work, Hernon."

Sir Tremayne lifted his chin. "We're proud of you, Sir Hernon. Now go and make all knights proud."

"You got lucky," said Dalbry.

"I have luck all right." Hernon scratched his bushy black beard. "Bad luck."

"Don't be like that," said Sir Morgan. "Princess Minima is attractive enough. You could certainly do worse. Why, back in my day—"

Hernon cut him off. "We know the dragon's out prowling right now, but it'll sleep during the daytime. I'm going to take a nap. You others keep quiet so I can get some rest." He trudged to a pile of dry leaves, fluffed them into a bed, and used a rock for a pillow. Within minutes he was snoring.

Cullin tried to doze off, but the tension in the camp was palpable, and he couldn't find a comfortable position on the lumpy ground. The rest of the knights were nervous.

With a whoosh of displaced air and a reptilian shriek, the dragon returned to its lair in the dark hour before dawn, but Sir Hernon slept in. He kept snoring long past sunrise.

Sir Jems nudged him awake. "Shouldn't you be out slaying that dragon, so the rest of us can go home?"

With a grunt, Hernon lifted his head from the rock. "I'm giving the monster time to fall into a deep sleep. With any luck, it ate a whole herd of sheep last night."

"And with bad luck," said Dalbry, "it ate a peasant village."

"Don't fret, I'll take care of the beast today. It's on my list of things to do." Hernon rolled over and snoozed for another half hour before rising with a stretch. He shook leaves out of his matted hair and beard, and asked for breakfast. Cullin was able to produce some old squirrel jerky, and Dalbry offered two dried apricots. "Not much for a last meal, I'm afraid."

Hernon grunted. "It's not my last meal—just my last meal as a virgin dragon slayer." He chuckled at his joke, and the other knights were amused out of politeness.

The shaggy knight gathered his armor, and Cullin—being the only squire around—helped him with the chest plate and helmet. Hernon tucked his long hair back from his visor so he could see.

"Good luck, brave Sir Hernon," said Tremayne.

"Say it like you mean it!" said Hernon. "Or are you after that princess yourself?"

Tremayne was taken aback. "Not really."

All the knights gave him their enthusiastic endorsement, still not quite sure what they had gotten themselves into. Sir Jems added, "I speak for all of us when I say we wish you every success . . . so we won't have to make the attempt."

Dalbry shook Hernon's gauntleted hand. The big knight hiked up his broadsword, dusted off his shield, and turned his back on the camp. He headed off for his appointment at the dragon's lair.

The rest of the knights sat in camp, sullen and anxious. Cullin took care of the horses, giving Sir Hernon's mount a special encouraging pat. They waited.

Sir Morgan started telling about a beautiful plump countess he had once bedded, and how her husband had caught them together. "He punched me right in the mouth for the affront. The count's signet ring was responsible for my missing front tooth." He fingered the gap, slurring the words around his finger. "I think he left a chip of amethyst in there, and I got to bed the duchess. So . . . a good trade all around!"

Cullin finally stood up. As the squire and apprentice dragon slayer, the unpleasant work fell to him. "I'm going to see. Maybe Sir Hernon has already cut off the dragon's head and needs help hauling it back."

He glanced at Sir Dalbry, who gave him a nod. Cullin sprinted away from camp, his heart pounding. He hoped that his preposterous idea was correct, that Hernon simply needed assistance. The head of that dragon was the size of a handcart, far larger than the stuffed and preserved crocodile heads they had used for their scams. Now that he'd seen a real dragon, Cullin couldn't believe that even the most gullible king had ever been convinced.

He crept through the forest, approaching the dark cave. He half expected to hear a shouted challenge, the clang of steel against scales. When the lair came into view, he did hear a growling snort, saw something heavy stir in the depths of the darkness. A loud roar and an explosion blasted from the cave mouth, followed by a tongue of fire.

Cullin ducked, holding his breath.

After another commotion in the deep shadows, a dented armor breastplate tumbled out onto the barren area in front of the lair. It landed among the other bones there. The armor was punctured by fangs, its edges half melted. Shortly thereafter, a few chewed and cracked bones were also tossed out onto the ground, after which came Sir Hernon's battered shield.

With a heavy heart, Cullin plodded back to the knights' camp, trying to decide how to tell the story of brave Sir Hernon—the epic battle of the shaggy knight and the beast, and how Hernon had never backed down, never showed fear.

But Cullin didn't have the fortitude to make up such a tale. When he arrived at camp, the remaining knights turned toward him in hopeful anticipation.

They learned all they needed to know from his expression. Instead of the story he had wanted to concoct in honor of Hernon's memory, Cullin managed only, "We're going to need to draw straws again."

CHAPTER THIRTY-FOUR

AFFONYL LURKED ABOUT the knights' camp, hiding in the bushes, waiting for the opportunity to speak with Cullin. When he went to the nearby stream to fetch water and try to catch fish, she saw her chance.

As he hunched over the stream, the young man was obviously troubled by the fate of brave Sir Hernon. He glanced up when he saw her coming. She usually saw a flirtatious, shy glint in the young man's eyes, but right now he seemed exhausted, tense, and wary—and rightly so.

"They drew straws again," he explained. "Sir Morgan will be the next one."

"Those knights don't waste any time," Affonyl said. "Do they have a better plan than just having a man stand there and face the dragon?"

"Not really. They spent an hour this morning studying the Knight's Manual, looking at the fine points, trying to figure out what options we have. They even read the appendices."

Affonyl pointed out the obvious. "Nobody reads appendices."

"That shows how serious the situation is. They've convinced themselves that Sir Hernon must have wounded the monster after putting up a terrific fight. Sir Morgan intends to finish off the beast single-handedly, according to the strictest interpretation of the Manual."

Affonyl frowned. "When will he go out?"

"He's preparing himself, limbering up, sharpening his sword. He plans to make his move late in the afternoon, before the dragon goes out for its nightly hunt."

Affonyl knelt beside him at the stream bank, cupped her hands in the cold running water, and splashed her face. "Won't the dragon be at its most fearsome after a good rest?"

Cullin plunged his hands into the brook and tried to grab a trout that obliviously swam too close; he made an impressive splash, but missed the fish. "Are *you* at your best and most alert the moment you wake up?"

"I suppose not."

Cullin sat back on a tuft of grass, shaking water from his hands. "I don't know what I'll do if Sir Dalbry draws the short straw next—assuming Sir Morgan doesn't kill the dragon, of course."

They were both convinced that Morgan would not, in fact, kill the dragon.

"This is more than you counted on, Squirrel. If that happens, you and Dalbry should just slip away from here and not risk facing the beast at all. I'd rather have you . . . intact. The dragon business is supposed to be fun, not fatal."

"Dalbry won't do that," Cullin said. "He's made a career out of misleading gullible people, but his honor is real. He wouldn't have accepted this quest if he knew the true danger, but the burden was placed upon him. Now he and the entire consortium of knights will finish their quest—or die trying."

"One at a time really doesn't sound like the best method. Why don't they all attack the monster together? They'd have a better chance of killing it."

"That's what the Manual says." Cullin shrugged. "Besides, there's only one princess."

"It would be a lot more sensible if they drew straws for her *after* they kill the dragon."

"Honor isn't all it's cracked up to be. Sometimes it just makes grown men stupid." He let out a long sigh, clearly afraid for Dalbry.

Affonyl touched Cullin's shoulder to reassure him. "Well, *we* don't have to be stupid. Facing a dragon all alone, armed only with a brave face and a sword, isn't the smartest approach. I've got an idea for a secret weapon. I'll send Reeger into town with a shopping list." She smiled. "There's more than one way to skin a dragon."

As the sun dropped into the western hills, Sir Morgan left the camp, accompanied by a flurry of well wishes, comradely pats on the back, and congratulatory grins from his rival knights (although their expressions fell into deep concern as soon as Morgan's back was turned).

The bald knight carried his portable battle hatchet, which looked most useful for chopping wood, and his notched sword. Every one of those notches had a story, and Cullin now regretted that he had never encouraged Morgan to tell the tales. The knights granted him privacy to go kill the dragon, which would also leave him free to embellish the story however he liked, should he succeed. There would be no witnesses to contradict him.

But Affonyl needed to get a better grasp of what they were up against. She found a rock outcropping with a good view of the lair and the bone-strewn clearing and settled in to watch Sir Morgan's challenge. Her stomach was knotted, her throat dry. Such stories were supposed to be uplifting, and the minstrels would sing about the brave knight's exploits, but Affonyl had a bad feeling about Sir Morgan's chances.

King Norrimun had often held jousting festivals, and she had seen Sir Phineal demonstrate his "Phineal squirm" more than once. Princess Affonyl usually sat in a fine dress underneath a silken awning, bored but pretending to watch. She wasn't much of a sports fan, and saw jousting as nothing more than a way for grown men to prove their foolishness by charging at full speed toward each other while carrying long pointy sticks. For fun.

Now, crouched among boulders and twisted trunks, Affonyl had a good seat for the dragon-slaying—definitely *not* a silly sporting event—but she wasn't looking forward to it.

As Sir Morgan approached the cave, he looked from right to left, as if to make sure no one was watching. Then he unfastened his crotch plate and urinated on the ground, like a dog marking his territory. More likely, the old knight was just so nervous he had to pee. It took him a long time to get the flow started, but it finally came out in a rush. He finished, refastened the crotch plate, adjusted his armor, and then stepped right up to the mouth of the dark and noisome cave. He held his trusty battle hatchet in his left hand, his notched sword in his right. He shouted as if reciting from the Knight's Manual, "Bloodthirsty monster, I challenge you! Come forth and meet your fate."

He waited, standing firm . . . and when nothing happened, he shuffled his boots. "Dragon, come forth, I say! I don't have all day."

The dragon lunged out, jaws wide. It belched a brief burst of flame that consumed Sir Morgan. Before the knight could scream in agony, the fanged jaws crunched down on him, and the monster dragged its still-cooking meal down into its lair.

The knights would have to draw straws again.

Affonyl bit her lip to keep herself from crying out. A lump formed in her throat. She had seen knights get injured or killed during jousting tournaments. It had angered her then, because the tournaments were entertainment, the deaths unnecessary.

Now she was angry because Sir Morgan had been trying to save lives, trapped by chivalrous obligations. A book of pointless rules had gotten him killed. But Affonyl was a *person* now, and she didn't have to play by the old rules. She had work to do.

CHAPTER THIRTY-FIVE

AGAIN, DALBRY HELD his handful of straws—three long, one short.

When it was his turn, brave Sir Artimo casually drew the short straw and looked at its length. He tossed the straw over his shoulder in a flippant gesture. "Ah! Exactly as I planned."

Artimo straightened his bright yellow tunic and looked around for his stylish armor. "This is the perfect part of the quest, the sweet spot. The dragon has been tested by two great warriors, so therefore it will be sorely bruised and weary, yet not entirely beaten down. What would be the honor in slaying a beast that posed no challenge? Ha!"

He swished his thin sword and looked at Sir Jems, trying to change the sour knight's disposition through force of will, but it didn't work. He gave a formal nod to Sirs Tremayne and Dalbry before flashing a final smile toward Cullin. "Cook me a fat squirrel, lad—I'll be back in time for breakfast."

Artimo flounced out of the camp, extending his long thin

sword as if one of the trees might attack him. The blade wobbled most unthreateningly, but he went off to his destiny, head held high.

Cullin caught a squirrel, skinned it, and cooked it in the stewpot. They waited past breakfast. Then lunch. At dinnertime, the three surviving knights and the squire ate a fine meal of overcooked squirrel stew.

Dalbry used fresh straws each time. He trimmed and clipped three stalks of grass, snipped one in half, and held out his palm for Jems and Tremayne to see.

"Properly done, according to code," said Tremayne. "The hand of fate will guide us in our choice."

Jems said, "I'd like to have another look at that Manual. Didn't you say your father was just a knightophile, not even a real knight? Why should we feel bound by what some fan wrote in a made-up rule book?"

Tremayne recoiled, taking offense. "A fan? My father was the world's authority on the subject. He didn't make up the rules, merely codified them."

"We know the way it's done," Dalbry said. "Already established." He closed his hand, evened the straws, and extended the choice to Tremayne first. The shining knight drew a long straw, as he had three times before.

Sir Jems scowled at the choices left to him—one long straw, one short. "How do I know you're not cheating?" He seemed to be stalling rather than accusing.

"How could I cheat?" Dalbry's extended hand remained steady. "You're the one who makes the choice."

Tremayne, already safe, grew stormy with anger. "Sir Jems, you do Sir Dalbry a grave disservice by questioning his honor. His heart is pure, his faith and loyalty unshakable. He would never speak a falsehood and would never cheat another man."

Dalbry didn't flinch or flush upon hearing the statement. "Would *you* like to hold the straws, Sir Jems?"

"Yes . . . no."

Cullin blurted out, "*I'll* hold them. No one would ever accuse me of cheating, right?"

For some unknown reason, Jems found that to be an acceptable solution. Cullin took the two remaining straws, mixed them up, hid them, and extended his hand. "Which of you picks first?"

"I will," said Jems. "I won't let Dalbry leave me with the short straw." He reached forward and plucked the short straw all by himself. "Figures." He exhaled a put-upon sigh. "I suppose it's better than spending another night in this godforsaken camp."

"You're such a cheerful person, Sir Jems," Dalbry pointed out.

"I keep an open mind. If you look hard enough, you can always find something to complain about. Now I'm going to give that dragon something to complain about."

Without waiting for a farewell or encouragement from his dwindling number of companions, brave Sir Jems set out to confront the monster.

The only thing he gave the dragon to complain about was indigestion.

Reeger had been gone for a long time with the shopping list Affonyl gave him. While she waited for him to return, Affonyl sorted through the packets of chemicals from her sack of necessary items and flipped through Wizard Edgar's alchemy textbooks to make sure she hadn't forgotten any ingredients. If she had to send Reeger back into town, he would not be cheerful.

Finally, late in the afternoon, the mule plodded back through the forest, led by Reeger. "Bloodrust, what do you need all these supplies for? I didn't realize purified guano with a high saltpeter content was so hard to find—or so rustin' expensive. I had to go to three different shoppes." He shook his head, unloading the packs from the mule's saddle. "And empty casks, bits of rope, charcoal. I spent two days at the mall, and I don't even like shopping."

Affonyl helped him sort the supplies. "It's what we need. I've used the recipe before." She inspected the stout, empty casks and opened the waterproof sack of powdered saltpeter, wincing at the pungent whiff of ammonia.

Reeger continued to grumble. "And why do they charge so much for powdered charcoal! They should be happy I took some of it off their hands."

"Looks like you got plenty of it *on* your hands," she said. Reeger looked at his black-dusted fingers, then wiped his face, which distributed the black stain more evenly.

She pulled out the smaller packets of esoteric chemicals, checking them off on her mental list. Reeger watched, still skeptical, but she said, "Any time now, Cullin or Dalbry will be forced to face that dragon. We have to put a stop to this nonsense." She started pouring powders from the chemical pouches, then removed other packets from her sack of necessary items. She inspected the labels, doled out proper amounts.

Reeger picked at his teeth. "It looks complicated."

Affonyl poured her completed mixture into one of the empty casks. She had already cut the narrow rope into fuse-length segments. "If it was easy, everybody would be blowing things up—and then the land would be in a sorry state." She sealed the first cask after inserting the fuse. "Make sure this doesn't get close to the fire, or you'll be sorry."

"Rust! I wouldn't want it to get close to the *dragon*—not until we're ready."

Affonyl agreed, hoping they would be finished before Dalbry drew the short straw. She filled another cask with her explosive mixture.

That night Cullin lay awake, feeling the oppressive gloom closing in. The dragon business had once been a lucrative and exciting scam—good, clean fun, with many satisfied customers—since the kings believed the dragons were slain, what was there to be unhappy about? Each one even had a stuffed crocodile head as a trophy for their throne room walls. Cullin knew there weren't supposed to be real dragons . . . and even if there *were,* brave knights were supposed to defeat them, not be digested by them.

He heard a rustle of underbrush as Affonyl crept to the camp. Cullin crawled away from the two slumbering knights so he and the former princess could talk in hushed tones. "Time to change tactics, Squirrel. You don't have many dragon slayers left."

"I know. This plan of 'dragon slaying by attrition' isn't working well for us. I think the Knight's Manual needs to be rewritten." Cullin felt dismayed. "Dalbry's digging in his heels, insisting on honor. He intends to finish this, regardless."

"Stall if you can. Reeger and I are working on a way to kill the dragon that isn't so sword-dependent." Affonyl started to leave, then turned back. "It's almost ready. I miss you back at our camp. If Sir Dalbry wins the hand of Princess Minima, then you and I can go off on adventures of our own."

Afterward, Cullin was even less inclined to sleep, but his dreams were filled with much more pleasant fantasies. . . .

The following morning, as Sir Dalbry prepared two fresh straws for himself and Tremayne, Cullin tended to the fine mounts that had belonged to Hernon, Morgan, Artimo, and Jems, along with Drizzle and Pony. "There was a time when I wished we had even one horse," Cullin said sadly. "Now we have four spares."

Sir Tremayne said, "When a knight falls in battle, his worldly goods go to his comrades. As we formed our consortium of dragon-slaying knights, the Articles of Incorporation specified an equal division of spoils among the survivors."

"But I was never part of your original consortium," Dalbry pointed out.

Tremayne was unconcerned. "We added you in a legally binding addendum, which was ratified by all original members."

Dalbry sat down on a stump and looked at the two straws in his hand. "I'm less concerned about worldly goods than about slaying the dragon. No reason to procrastinate—let's get on with it." He handed the two straws to Cullin. "Squire, if you would do the honors."

Cullin closed the straws in his fist so that only the tips poked out from his knuckles. He gave Dalbry first choice, and the older knight plucked the long straw. Apologetically, Cullin opened his hand and extended the short straw to the other knight. "It's your turn to promulgate the mystique, Sir Tremayne."

The shining knight looked like honor incarnate in his thin, flexible armor. The prospect of facing the dragon seemed to fill him with stoic energy.

Dalbry, though, was troubled. He looked at the obsidian chips in his sword hilt. "Maybe we should learn from what has transpired before. Attacking this dragon one knight at a time has been ineffective. Let us act together as partners and kill the monster. I'll even let you have the princess."

Tremayne's face was unreadable. "I'm afraid not, Sir Dalbry. That isn't how it's done—there's a princess at stake, not just a treasure, and I'm trying to save lives. I intend to do the honorable thing. I've been waiting for this all my life, and my father would be so proud. I won't let you diminish my victory."

"Or your martyrdom," Cullin muttered. "Would it be so bad to split the glory if it means that both of you can survive?"

"And go against the Knight's Manual? Never!"

"He's right, lad. We can't change now," Dalbry agreed. "This is the way it's done."

Tremayne adjusted his white-and-indigo cape and used a corner of the fabric to brush an imagined smudge from his gleaming breastplate. A flicker of apprehension crossed his face, and he looked long and hard at Dalbry and his apprentice dragon slayer. "I've heard accounts about killing these monsters, but I don't know how reliable they are. You've faced and killed numerous dragons already—I'd appreciate any advice you might have."

"I wish I could give you pointers, but there's no easy way to kill a dragon. Each one is different." Then Dalbry swallowed hard and made a confession that moved even Cullin. "For years I've had a low impression of knights and nobles. When I had my own fief with my own homey castle, I thought honor was enough . . . until a group of knights cheated me out of everything. You, sir, seem to have more honor and nobility than all those others combined."

Tremayne bowed. "I thank you for that, Sir Dalbry. And now I must do my duty as a knight." As he left the camp, he called back, "Fear not. I have a plan. I will slay the dragon in my own way."

CHAPTER THIRTY-SIX

AFFONYL'S PLAN WITH the explosive kegs was about ready, but Sir Tremayne seemed intent on stalking off to face the dragon by himself. She didn't think she could convince him to wait on the sidelines and let them blow up the monster from a distance.

With her skulking skills well practiced from sneaking in and out of the knights' camp, Affonyl was confident she could follow Tremayne without him noticing her. The proud holder of the short straw strode off to meet his destiny.

She crept along, easily following Tremayne's white cape and his improbably shiny armor as he worked his way through the trees, never looking back. But he set off into thicker trees, heading away from the lair, which puzzled Affonyl.

The forest grew dark, tangled with shadows and deadfall. Thick underbrush made travel difficult, but Tremayne moved quickly nevertheless. Affonyl tried to keep up with him, hindered by having to move stealthily.

She lost track of the knight. She hurried to where she had last seen him, but Sir Tremayne was gone. What was he doing? She wondered if he intended to slip away and let everyone else assume the dragon had eaten him, while he made his escape, slipped out of the queendom, and kept a low profile. She realized it was a good scheme—who would ever know? She found the idea troubling, though. If Hernon, Morgan, Artimo, and Jems had found the courage to face the monster, she never expected Sir Tremayne to become a coward.

She still didn't see him. Flustered, Affonyl decided to head back to Cullin and Dalbry at the camp, so they could discuss what to do next. She turned around—and nearly ran into Sir Tremayne. "Oh!"

"Ah!" the shining knight replied, with an uncharacteristic sinister edge to his voice. With a supple gauntleted hand, he seized Affonyl by the cropped blond hair, twisting his fingers and yanking her head back. "Just what I needed."

She struggled, beating at his hand, but only bruised her knuckles on his armor. Adept in fighting, Tremayne caught her arms and wrenched one up behind her back. She bent over with a gasp of pain.

"That's enough struggling from you." He forced her to turn around. "I've had a long, hard week, and I don't need any further inconvenience."

She thrashed, but he lashed her wrists behind her back, then tied a rope around her neck so that he could lead her like a dog on a leash. He yanked, forcing her to follow.

"You're an important part of my dragon-slaying plans." He paused before adding, "Princess Affonyl."

That startled her, and she stumbled. "You know who I am?"

He snorted. "I recognized you from the moment my knights came upon you in the road. Oh, you had cut your hair, covered yourself with dirt, and dressed in rags. I grant you it's a good disguise, but an honorable knight can sense nobility. A princess is a princess . . . though I was surprised to find you alive. I heard the explosion in King Norrimun's castle and the old woman's story. I saw the torn-open wall, the claw marks, and the dragon scales with my own eyes." He nudged her hard, forcing her to keep walking. "I don't know how you managed it. Were you secretly in league with the dragon that killed Duke Kerrl? Did the two of you come up with some twisted plot?"

"There was no dragon, just a trick that I staged myself."

He pursed his lips. "I could probably have seen that for myself, but I was indisposed with a bit of indigestion."

"More than a bit, from what I heard," Affonyl said. Tremayne made her move along. When she didn't trudge fast enough, he yanked on the rope and jerked her head around. "What do you intend to do with me?"

"Thanks to you, I'll be able to slay the dragon. My four comrades failed because they were missing a key element in the scenario."

"And what is that?"

"Everyone knows the best way to lure a dragon is to give it a virgin sacrifice."

A chill shivered down her spine, and she stumbled on a root, but Tremayne yanked her back to her feet and pushed her toward the ominous lair.

"How do you know I'm a virgin?" she demanded in a haughty voice.

Tremayne didn't seem to care. "If I can't tell, then the dragon won't be able to either." He gave her a condescending look of villainous apology. "Everybody already believes you were killed by a dragon. I'm just helping the facts catch up with the story. When minstrels write songs about brave Sir Tremayne, no one will know the difference."

"*I'll* know the difference!"

"Ah, but you'll be dead, dear princess."

"Then I'll come back as a ghost and haunt you."

He chortled. "I highly doubt that. I can believe in dragons, but only fools believe in ghosts."

They finally reached the bone-strewn clearing in front of the cave mouth. One spindly, barren tree stood like a gibbet in full view of the lair. Tremayne yanked Affonyl to the tree and used the rope to lash her up against the trunk. She kicked at him, but he grabbed her feet and bound them against the base of the tree.

"I'll scream," she said, struggling without success at the bonds.

"Go right ahead. I'm almost finished. Remember, the louder you shout, the sooner you'll bring out the dragon."

Affonyl fell silent.

Tremayne smiled at her. "Take heart, Princess. While the dragon is busy eating your tender flesh, I'll sneak up from behind and strike it dead."

"Could you maybe do that *before* it eats me?"

"That wouldn't fit with the plan."

"I still think we ought to go help Sir Tremayne," Cullin said to Dalbry. "Or at least cheer him on."

The older knight remained firm. "He asked us not to. We must honor his request." He had pulled up a handful of dried grass stalks and was plucking the leaves, as if he needed spare straws just in case.

Cullin paced the camp. "Well, I'm going to go see. If nothing else, I can bring back news about what happened to him." Feeling short on time, he left the camp and hurried up the narrowing gorge, dodging trees as he made his way along the slope until he reached the dragon's lair.

There he saw Affonyl tied to a tree, struggling against the ropes.

Every knight's dream is to find a damsel in distress, and Cullin was already smitten with the former princess, but he was ill-prepared for a dragon slaying. He only had his practice sword, which was unadorned and nothing to brag about, but at least it was hard and halfway sharp. He also had a dagger, which he used for skinning game more often than for knife fights.

"Affonyl!" His voice cracked as he ran forward. "I'll save you!"

Her eyes were wide with fear, and she shook her head. In a stage whisper, she said, "Quiet, Squirrel! The dragon will hear you."

He dropped his voice, saying, "Sorry," then repeated in a hush, "I'll save you." At such low volume, however, his words carried little dramatic impact.

He pulled out his knife and was about to cut the ropes when he heard an angry sound. Sir Tremayne charged toward him from his hiding place in the trees. "Leave her there, boy! You'll ruin my plan."

"Your plan?" Cullin said. "*This* is a plan?"

"He means to use me as a virgin sacrifice to lure the dragon," Affonyl explained, then rolled her eyes at the absurdity of the suggestion.

"That's not a good plan," Cullin said. "Nor an honorable one."

"It works." Tremayne drew his sword. "I suppose I'll have to tie you both to the tree now. Young squires make good dragon bait as well."

Even though Cullin had not managed to cut the ropes binding Affonyl, he had to take care of Tremayne first, since the knight's sword was more of a threat. He thrust the knife back into its sheath and drew his practice sword instead.

"Don't be an idiot, boy," Tremayne said. "I'm a knight in shining armor, and you're just an apprentice. You can't possibly defeat me."

Cullin flailed with his blade, banging it against Tremayne's sword. The knight easily parried his blow and swung at Cullin. The young man lifted his sword to block it, and steel crashed together with a loud clang.

Cullin hoped to confuse Tremayne, for whatever advantage it might gain him. "I'm not even a real apprentice, and Sir Dalbry's not a real dragon slayer. In fact, there aren't supposed to be any real dragons either." He swung his sword in an attempt to hit something, anything at all.

Tremayne blocked the blow with his shield, and Cullin battered again and again with his ever duller blade, succeeding only in chipping some of the paint on the shield. Tremayne's polished flexible metal armor gleamed in the sunlight.

"What do you mean? I've heard the songs about brave Sir Dalbry. His reputation is unassailable."

"It's a scam. We made it all up. The part that went wrong, though"—Cullin clenched his teeth and drove in with a harder blow, since Tremayne was not taking the attacks seriously—"is that this dragon doesn't know it's supposed to be a myth."

Affonyl struggled to break free of her bonds. She clearly wanted to cheer Cullin on, but the two were already making altogether too much noise, which was sure to rouse the dragon.

The knight clipped Cullin on the head with his shield, hard enough to stun him. As the young man reeled away, Tremayne laughed. "You lack skill and finesse. Dalbry is indeed no true knight if he's the one who taught you how to fight."

Not giving up, Cullin staggered toward Tremayne. "Sir Dalbry taught me how to fight with honor." He wove as if nearly passing out, panting hard, and took a step closer. "And my friend Reeger taught me how to fight *dirty*."

He swung his left foot upward with all the might he could muster. His hard boot slammed into the center of Sir Tremayne's crotch plate.

While the gleaming armor made the shining knight an impressive figure out of a storybook, such dazzling armor plate was necessarily thin and supple. When Cullin's boot struck the crotch plate, it buckled inward and clenched Tremayne's testicles in a death grip.

The shining knight collapsed to his knees and let out a sick groan in a most unnoble manner.

Cullin whacked Tremayne on the back of his helmet with the flat of his practice sword. The blow rang like a church bell falling out of its steeple and striking the flagstones below. The knight fell forward, unconscious, into the dirt.

Cullin stared in amazement at what he had done. Feeling his heart pound, his blood rush through his circulatory system, a slow smile grew on his face. He felt alive, victorious!

Affonyl cried, "Don't just stand there, Squirrel—can't you hear it? You woke the dragon. It's coming!"

He did hear snarls, explosive breaths, and scraping movement. Flickers of orange flame lit the inside of the grotto. Cullin raced back to Affonyl with his knife and sawed through the ropes binding her hands before working on the cords around her ankles. Affonyl squirmed and strained to break them.

"Hold still!" he said.

"Really? There's a dragon coming."

Cullin snapped the last rope. He grabbed Affonyl by the hand and dragged her to the trees just as the dragon emerged. Its head quested from side to side, nostrils leaking smoke. When its eyes caught the shining form of Sir Tremayne sprawled on the ground, the dragon seized him in its jaws, tearing the pristine fabric of his white-and-indigo cape.

As Cullin and Affonyl watched in horror, mixed with some small amount of satisfaction, the dragon pulled Tremayne into the cave to finish its meal.

CHAPTER THIRTY-SEVEN

THOUGH SCUFFED AND worse for the wear—not to mention rattled by Sir Tremayne's unexpected dishonorable turnaround—Cullin was exhilarated. As he and Affonyl hurried from the dragon's lair, even the disconcerting sound of crunching bones and bending armor did not dampen his mood.

After all the stories he had told and the scams he had pulled, now he could honestly say he had fought a knight in shining armor and rescued a princess!

Affonyl was also overjoyed. Escaping a horrible death was enough in itself to make her happy.

Bursting with news, they rushed back to Sir Dalbry. As they approached the camp, they heard the indecipherable bray of their mule and discovered that Reeger had rejoined them. He sat on a broken stump, chewing on the grass blades that Dalbry had peeled in preparation for a straw-drawing that was no longer necessary. Reeger picked his teeth with one of the stalks and tossed the crumpled weed away. "Rust, Dalbry—we have to get out of here, no two ways around it."

"I won't abandon the quest, Reeger. It's a matter of honor."

Reeger snorted. "Have you seen the mortality rate of knights who set out on this quest? You're being as stubborn as my mule." The mule brayed, but whether to agree or disagree, no one could tell.

The older knight said, "If you don't understand, then I can't explain it."

Cullin was panting with excitement and exhaustion as he ran up. "We survived the dragon! We got away."

Dalbry's brow furrowed. "You weren't supposed to go close to the lair."

The former princess still rubbed her rope-burned wrists. "We survived betrayal, too. Sir Tremayne tried to sacrifice me to the dragon."

Dalbry rose to his feet. Of all the stories he had told and heard, this one seemed incomprehensible. "It's not possible. Sir Tremayne—a coward?"

"Among other things," Cullin said. "Right now, he's primarily dragon food. I defeated him in a sword battle."

Reeger snorted in disbelief, but Affonyl came to his defense. "He did! Squirrel protected me. Saved my life."

Dalbry frowned at his apprentice dragon slayer. "And how did you defeat a well-trained knight in shining armor?"

"Kicked him in the crotch plate so hard I left a crater. After that, the rest was easy." Taking turns, Cullin and Affonyl told the entire story.

Dalbry looked grim and saddened. "Sir Tremayne is such a disappointment."

Reeger piped up, "Now will you listen to reason? Our only alternative is to pack up and leave. This isn't what we signed up for." He glanced at the mounts still tied to their trees, running calculations in his head. "We've got all these horses now, practically a herd. If we sell them, we'll have enough coins to last a long time."

Cullin perked up. "We could buy passage on a ship leaving out of Rivermouth—sail to the New Lands, make a fresh start."

Affonyl added her vote. "We can slip out of the queendom without being seen. No one will know what happened. Couldn't be simpler."

His face darkening, Dalbry shook his head. "And let the dragon keep preying on the people of this fair land? *I gave my word!*"

Cullin had seen the dragon—much too close—and had no desire to face it, but if he and his companions fled, the queendom would be without so much as an amateur protector. "I guess pretend dragon slayers are better than no dragon slayers at all."

Reeger, however, thought along more practical lines. "Rust, Dalbry! This isn't our game, and it isn't our problem. Forget the treasure—we can always earn more, but we can't spend it if we're being digested in a dragon's stomach. Forget the princess. You're not the marrying type anyway."

Dalbry looked disappointed in him. "You are free to leave, but I won't flee from our responsibilities. That would be dishonest."

Cullin blinked in surprise. "When has dishonesty ever bothered you, Dalbry?" Brave knights might have a restrictive sense of honor, but con men and scam artists had no such code.

Cullin had learned a lot by watching the chivalrous consortium of knights. Although his opinions about the men varied, he couldn't deny that they were bound by an invisible network of honor and expectations. It was something the young man had never been brought up with.

"It's *always* bothered me, but I got over it." Dalbry opened his magic sack and withdrew the last dried apricots out of habit, not because he was hungry. "Now, it's different."

The knight slid the pits from the apricots into his other sack, but kept one out, holding it between his thumb and forefinger. "Do you know why I keep these? Because they symbolize hope. Each apricot pit contains a seed. It doesn't look like much—it's hard, and most likely won't germinate . . . but there's a chance.

"After all I've been through, my own sense of honor is a hard, dark pit, but I won't throw it away. Someday I'll find fertile ground where I can plant it and tend it, and hope I'll have a strong tree again."

Cullin nodded gravely, because Dalbry's words seemed to carry great import. Then he shook his head. "Is that a metaphor? What's it supposed to mean?"

"If I have to explain, then the metaphor wasn't as effective as I thought." Sir Dalbry seemed to be talking himself into greater and greater determination. "Even though Sir Tremayne had no honor in the end, I need to get my own back. It's my turn to promulgate the myth of knighthood. Tremayne made me remember who I really should be."

Affonyl sniffed. "Tremayne kidnapped me and tied me to a post as dragon bait!"

The old knight was implacable. "All the more reason. I swore, and now I am honor bound. My promise surrounds me, just as my armor does. I must go alone to face the dragon as the last of our band of knights, and hope I fare better than those others."

"That's a stupid idea," Affonyl said. "Reeger and I have a better plan. We've made explosives. If we survey the lair and plant the casks in the proper places, we can blow—"

Dalbry shook his head, refusing to listen. "That is not how it's done." He adjusted his armor and took his sword. "If I fail, make sure Nightingale Bob adds a poignant final verse to my song."

Though frustrated, Reeger knew he couldn't change his long-time friend's mind. Cullin looked at Affonyl, who seemed distraught and helpless. The young squire rose to his feet as Sir Dalbry fastened his dragonskin cape on his shoulders. "I shall go and face that horrible dragon—and only one of us will survive." He turned to go.

Cullin raised his apprentice sword, just as he had done when facing Sir Tremayne. He wished he could be more gentle, but knew he dared not. He struck Sir Dalbry on the back of the head with the flat of his blade. The older knight grunted in surprise and collapsed, unconscious.

"Sometimes common sense trumps honor," he said.

Reeger got to his feet and wiped his hands on his trousers. "Bloodrust and battlerot, now we can do this the sensible way—with big explosions. By the time Dalbry wakes up, we'll have this dragon business all wrapped up."

CHAPTER THIRTY-EIGHT

TEAMWORK—THAT WAS THE key. For all their grandiose attitudes, the independent legendary knights had not played well with others. By insisting on all the glory, they had ended up as individual, memorable failures rather than sharing the reward.

Cullin, Affonyl, and Reeger worked well together, though. While Dalbry lay unconscious, for his own good, they planned the fastest way to eliminate the monster.

Affonyl couldn't wait to try out her explosive casks. If just one powder-filled clay pot had blown a hole through the solid stone wall of King Norrimun's castle tower, then three whole casks filled with the mixture should be enough to turn the dragon into reptilian sausage meat.

"There may not be much of a trophy left to hang on a castle wall," Cullin pointed out. Dalbry would have considered that the largest flaw in their plan.

"Doesn't matter," Reeger said. "We still have the spare crocodile heads we bought from Captain Ossio. One of them will convince Queen Faria."

After Affonyl made long powder-dusted fuses for her casks of explosives, the three prepared to set off for the lair, leaving Sir Dalbry on the ground near the horses. With a twinge of remorse, Cullin adjusted the unconscious knight, gave him a lump of firewood for a pillow, and straightened his dragonskin cape.

Cullin felt guilty about knocking out his old friend, but it soothed his conscience to know that he was saving Dalbry's life. In fact, he had reason to be upbeat. He had already rescued a damsel in distress, and would soon be a genuine dragon slayer (or at least a participant in a group dragon-slaying event). Maybe he could apply for a certificate.

He ran to catch up with Reeger and Affonyl, who were leading the mule away. The beast seemed uneasy, questioning the wisdom of these humans and their schemes.

When they arrived at the ominous lair, Reeger, Cullin, and Affonyl listened intently to the phlegmy rumble from inside. The dragon seemed to be sleeping but restless, perhaps suffering from indigestion because of the traitorous knight he had just eaten.

Reeger flicked his eyes from side to side. "That rustin' thing in there already killed five brave knights, not to mention all the sheep, cattle, and peasants it devoured over the past week or so. It's a menace to society."

"That means it can't still be hungry," Affonyl said. "Right?"

The skittish mule flared its nostrils, but it was wise enough not to bray or call attention to itself.

Cullin and Affonyl each took one of the explosive casks from the pack saddle and tiptoed among the bones and ash. The debris of knightly victims lay all around: the dented shield of

Sir Tremayne, part of Sir Hernon's helmet, the remnants of Sir Artimo's long and delicate blade (now drooping from a blast of heat), Sir Morgan's miniature battle hatchet, and a frowning skull that bore the indisputable likeness of Sir Jems.

Loud snoring from within the cave indicated that the dragon was not inclined to lunge out at them.

Cullin and Affonyl crept to the side of the lair and positioned the first cask, then set a second one on the opposite side. Without even a whisper to each other, they rolled the fuse rope out behind them.

Cullin retrieved the third cask from the mule and picked his way up the rocks to the overhang above the mouth of the cave. He wedged it between two large boulders and tossed down the fuse rope. Affonyl caught it and scampered away to join it with the other fuses.

For his own part, Reeger tugged on the mule's rope and dragged it forward. The stubborn animal did not like the change of scenery: the burned bones and half-devoured carcasses strewn on the ground provided ample evidence that this was no fit place for human or beast. The more Reeger tugged on the rope, the more the mule dug in its hooves and drew back its lips to show square teeth.

Reeger went behind the creature to smack it on the buttocks. Indignant, the mule stumbled forward enough that Reeger was able to wrap the rope around the sturdy pine trunk where Affonyl had been bound. The mule realized the trick and pulled against the rope, letting out a loud bray of terror. Startled by the noise, Reeger dashed to shelter in the forest and turned back to watch. Affonyl joined him, pulling the fuses along with her.

The mule stood in full view of the dragon's grotto. "I'm fairly sure that mule is a virgin, so it'll make an appropriate sacrifice," Reeger said. "If not, it's still good, fresh meat. How can a dragon resist?"

The mule let out an even more extravagant braying that sounded like a rusty hinge, then regretted the loud sound it had made.

With all the noise and commotion outside, the dragon let out an explosive roar of its own. Awake and alert, it began to move.

Pain rumbled like thunder in the back of his head, and Sir Dalbry groaned and sat up. His skull throbbed worse than his hangover after the one and only time he had tried to beat Reeger in a drinking game (and lost). But he was a knight, and he had a quest. He would never let a mere splitting headache divert him from it.

He didn't remember how he'd gotten on the ground, and wondered if he'd been attacked. Maybe an ogre had smashed him on the head with a spiked club . . . but he looked around the empty camp and saw no ogres. Nor did he see Reeger, Cullin, or Affonyl. He was alone.

They had abandoned him—or maybe they'd been kidnapped by a goblin force! No, that didn't sound right. His ears were ringing. His vision blurred, doubled, then focused again. He had trouble differentiating between memories and fictitious stories. It was hard to think.

Ah! Now he remembered the dragon and the other brave knights who had fallen. Yes, Sir Dalbry was the last surviving member of the chivalrous consortium. He looked down and saw broken, half-chewed straws on the ground. Yes, that was it. The responsibility fell to him.

The dragon was his to slay. He had the duty and the glory.

After he swayed to his feet, he caught his balance on a tree, looked at all the horses and Pony tied nearby. The animals had foraged the fresh greenery within reach of their ropes and seemed to be wondering where their owners' priorities lay.

Brave Drizzle stared at him with questions in his large eyes, but Dalbry didn't think his horse was right. He was supposed to have a white stallion, not this speckled gelding. *Lightning* . . . yes! That had been his real horse's name! A valiant steed that had died defending him during another dragon attack.

He adjusted the scaly cloak on his shoulders. Yes . . . dragonskin. He had killed the monsters before, and he would do so again. Dalbry gripped the hilt of his sword, saw the gleaming black chips of hardened dragon blood that reminded him of his prior conquests.

He walked out of camp, stumbling through the underbrush, but kept his balance. It was hard to focus. When he realized he was heading in the wrong direction, he turned about and trudged off again. The knights had been at their camp for so long they'd actually worn a footpath to the monster's lair.

Dalbry drew a deep breath, stilled his nerves, and went to face the dragon.

Before the dragon could come after them, Affonyl tried to light the three joined fuses using a flint and steel. She made ten attempts, but couldn't make the spark catch. As a former princess, she didn't have much practice starting her own fires.

Reeger snatched the implements from her and lit the fuse. The flame began to burn along the rope, then separated among the three strands. The three sparks raced toward the trio of explosive casks.

Tied to the tree, the braying mule let out a racket loud enough to wake the dead, or at least wake a slumbering dragon. Deep within the shadows of the bone-strewn cave, bright reptilian eyes shone, and a flicker of flame snorted out as the monster worked its way forward to its next meal.

The fuses continued to burn toward the casks. Cullin scrambled down the rocks at the side of the cave to rejoin the others. Affonyl held her breath. Reeger was grinning.

The mule was not at all happy.

Suddenly another figure lurched out of the forest—Sir Dalbry in his armor with his sword raised, the reptilian cape flapping behind his shoulders. "Dragon, you have met your match!"

Dalbry went to the tree, swung his sword, and slashed the animal's rope. Freed from the tether, the mule didn't stop to thank the old knight, but galloped away into the forest, avoiding Reeger and Affonyl altogether.

With uncertain balance, Dalbry wove toward the open cave, sword held high. "Face me, monster, and I will cut off your head."

Cullin waved his arms from the other side of the clearing. "Dalbry, get out of there!"

Simultaneously, Affonyl yelled, "Run—the fuse is almost to the kegs. *Run*!"

From within the cave, the dragon roared and thrust its head out.

The knight looked up at them in surprise, then turned toward the dragon, ignoring his noisy companions.

"Crotchrust! *Somebody* has to move." Reeger ran faster than seemed possible with his cockeyed gait. He slammed into Sir Dalbry and drove the old knight away from the cave opening just as all three casks detonated. Smoke, fire, shrapnel, and broken rocks flew in all directions.

The explosion caught Dalbry and Reeger and flung them away. The two lay on the ground among the skeletal fragments, looking like the poignant discarded rag dolls Reeger often placed in his staged scenarios.

CHAPTER THIRTY-NINE

THINKING NOTHING OF their own safety, Cullin and Affonyl scrambled out of the shelter of the trees to where the men sprawled unmoving. Reeger and Dalbry had been thrown by the blast and now lay singed and bruised among the broken skeletons of the dragon's other victims.

From where it had bolted, the rescued mule let out a loud bray, either to taunt them for their treachery or to reassure Cullin that it did not need further saving.

Tangled as if in some medieval dragon-slayer wrestling match, Dalbry and Reeger both groaned. While Affonyl bent over the two to check their injuries, Cullin cast an anxious glance at the dark overhang of the dragon's lair.

The explosions had driven the beast back into its cave, but Cullin could hear the huge creature stirring, claws and scales scraping on stone as it moved. Maybe it was injured. Maybe it was angry. Maybe it was hungry. Too many maybes.

"We have to move them," he said. "Right now!"

Affonyl said, "In my bag of necessary items, I have salves, unguents, and assorted good drugs we can use. Maybe the mule will help us get them to camp."

From the shelter of the forest, the mule brayed to indicate that there was little chance of that happening.

Cullin got his hands under Reeger's arms and tried to lift him. "You take Sir Dalbry. I'll drag Reeger."

As Cullin hauled his friend across the rough ground, Reeger thrashed in pain. The young man tried to reassure him. "There's a first-aid kit back at camp—fresh leeches and everything—but you'll have to endure for the time being. Sorry."

Reeger woke enough to sway to his feet and pull away from Cullin. "Bloodrust and battlerot, my arm's broken! Pulling on it doesn't help."

Affonyl managed to get Sir Dalbry to his feet, and they made their way through the trees, weaving, crashing, staggering—away from the dragon.

They finally arrived back in camp without any mishap other than the mishaps they had already encountered. While a groaning Reeger sat on a tree stump and nursed his arm, Cullin and Affonyl worked to remove Sir Dalbry's armor. He had been closest to the blast, and the former princess clucked her tongue when she saw his skin: some parts were blackened, others covered with red blisters. The older knight grunted, but endured the pain.

"I still don't know what happened—it's a blur," Dalbry mumbled. "I appear to have been burned and blasted. Did the dragon get me?"

"No, it was an explosion of my own making," Affonyl said. "Part of our plan to kill the dragon."

"But that plan didn't turn out as planned," Cullin said.

"Plans usually don't." Dalbry touched his tender burned skin. "That's going to leave a scar. I wish I could claim it came from dragon fire." The beard on one side of his face had been singed away, and his cheeks looked an angry red.

"You can *say* that," Cullin said, trying to be helpful. "It's closer to the truth than a lot of our stories."

Affonyl rummaged among her necessary items, pulled out several packets. "These will help, Sir Dalbry."

Reeger grumbled, "Rust! What about my arm? I think Cullin dislocated it when he dragged me."

"On the contrary, he set the broken bone. You should be thankful."

"It still hurts."

She handed one of her packets to Reeger. "Take this—one of my best potions."

Reeger held the packet with his good hand, sniffed it. "Isn't a potion supposed to be in liquid form?"

"This is the extra-strength version, just for you."

Beyond arguing, he dumped the powder into his mouth, grimaced, and swallowed. "Tastes like bone dust."

Cullin wondered whether Reeger had ever consumed bone dust before and decided he didn't want to know.

"Bone dust is one of the ingredients," Affonyl said. "And the highest quality guano, plus a good dose of poppy milk."

"Ah." Reeger seemed content—more content by the minute, in fact, as the drugs began to work. Affonyl mixed a second batch of the powder and gave it to Sir Dalbry, who at first resisted but relented when she continued to poke and prod his burned skin.

Affonyl mixed salves to treat the burns, and Cullin assisted by watching as intently as possible. As she slathered creams on the reddest patches, he asked, "Where did you get your medical training?"

She didn't look up from her work. "I read my natural history books and dissected a few frogs. From that solid foundation, it was simple extrapolation to a medical degree."

Cullin grew more impressed with Affonyl the more he got to know her.

Reeger began to giggle, sounding loopy. He held up his broken arm as Affonyl bound it with trimmed sticks, tightening the rags so that the makeshift cast and sling held the broken bone in place.

Reeger found his splinted forearm amusing. "Rust! Now Cullin's going to have to do the grave harvesting and latrine refurbishing by himself."

Cullin humored him. "By the time that arm heals, I'll be even better than you."

Reeger snorted and spat. "Nobody's better at latrines than I am."

Reassured that his friends were not mortally wounded—although out of commission—Cullin began to feel more troubled. The tension had been building for some time as each knight faced his duty and went out on an unsuccessful dragon-slaying attempt.

Cullin had gotten to know each member of the consortium of knights, knew their different personalities, and realized that not one of them had ever questioned the need to kill the monster. Even Tremayne, who had turned treacherous, never lost sight of what he was required to do. A quest was a quest. The knights had varying tactics, but a fundamental underpinning of honor, just as Sir Dalbry said.

Apart from any sensible reason, with all of his comrades killed and very little chance of success—or even survival—Sir Dalbry had still dragged himself out to slay the dragon or die trying.

Cullin couldn't understand it. He had spent so much of his life as an outcast, amused by scams, feeling superior, using people's gullibility against them. But he had seen something strange on Dalbry's face as he strode out to almost certain death. Even Reeger had done an unexpected brave thing, rushing into danger in the face of the imminent explosion—and right in front of the dragon's lair.

Cullin looked at Reeger now, who seemed blissfully happy after his painkilling potion. When it wore off, he would probably question what he had done—or at least he'd say so out loud. But Reeger had instinctively known when he needed to be brave and selfless.

The consortium of chivalrous knights had come to Faria's queendom and offered their services—not as a scam, but as a sincere gesture. When going to face the dragon, Sir Hernon had been brave, but—being first—he might have underestimated the danger. Not so for Sir Morgan, Sir Artimo, or Sir Jems. Despite knowing the murderous ferocity of the dragon, they had tried to do their duty.

Faria's chest of treasure would have been a substantial reward, but Cullin didn't think gold mattered much to those knights. And the prospect of winning a moderately beautiful princess couldn't explain it either.

Those brave people had dared so much. Sir Dalbry and even Reeger were in no condition for further dragon-slaying attempts—and the monster was still in need of slaying.

Cullin realized with a heavy heart and a queasy stomach that the duty fell to him now. He had to finish the job, become a real dragon slayer, instead of just a would-be apprentice.

When the burned knight was resting comfortably and Reeger sat grinning and humming to himself, Cullin picked up Sir Dalbry's famed sword with its obsidian-decorated hilt. "My turn," he said, and avoided looking at Affonyl. "After all it's been through, the dragon should be slayable by now."

She stared at him, wide-eyed. "Squirrel, what are you talking about?"

"I have a duty to do, for honor."

She rolled her eyes. "You've listened to too many stories. Don't be a fool."

"I'll be a *knight*—there's a difference. Somebody has to promulgate the mystique of knighthood. Our reputation is at stake. Besides, there's a fairly substantial reward."

"Reward? You mean Queen Faria's daughter? You're willing to risk your life to marry Princess Minima?"

"Not exactly the princess I wanted, but that's the luck of the draw." For this brave deed, Cullin wanted to be as prepared as possible. He had already traded his practice sword in favor of Dalbry's more impressive blade. Next, he picked up the older knight's chain mail. "Will you help me don this?"

"No." He thought Affonyl was just being petulant, but she added, "All that metal covering your body won't protect you if the dragon blasts you with flame. The armor will only slow you down. Better that you stay unencumbered and nimble."

Cullin realized that made sense. "Thanks. Any other advice?"

"Don't go face the dragon in the first place."

"All right. Any *useful* advice?"

She went back to her sack to remove more packets of chemicals and herbs, which she mixed in a large pot; when it smelled right to her, she added mud and water to create an oozing mess. After letting it cool, she dipped her hands into the goop and slathered it over Cullin. "This salve is flame resistant. It won't protect you from full-fledged incineration, but it might stop a blister or two. I wouldn't want you to ruin your pretty face."

He felt himself grinning. "You think my face is pretty?"

"I think it'll be less pretty if it's burned." He couldn't argue with that. She heaved an angry sigh. "If you're going to insist on this foolishness, then I want you to have the best chance possible."

Cullin searched among Sir Dalbry's possessions in Drizzle's saddlebags and withdrew a small item that was unlikely to be effective, but might serve as a talisman. "I'm taking the magic beans as well."

"It can't hurt." Then she leaned close and gave him a quick kiss. Cullin felt giddy, but before he could respond, she hurried to tend to Reeger, who began chuckling in delirious shock. Affonyl wouldn't look back at him.

Cullin set off, thinking more about the former princess than about the monstrous dragon he was about to face.

CHAPTER FORTY

CULLIN QUICKLY CONCLUDED that his brave and honorable decision was not, in fact, a good idea after all. But it was too late to change his mind.

The dark lair was surrounded by the shadowy forest, and he heard suspicious sounds everywhere. He feared the dragon might spring out and grab him from behind a tree (although the monster was far too large for that). Dalbry's sword felt heavy and unwieldy in his hand, and he had a hard time gripping the hilt because his palms were sweaty. Cullin had not practiced with this weapon at all. In fact, he was barely proficient with his own smaller blade.

He took a circuitous route, convincing himself that he did so for reasons of stealth rather than procrastination. Since they had already blown up Affonyl's three explosive casks, he wanted to plan his strategy, develop a worthy new scheme that used his wits and finesse to slay the dragon, instead of brute force and naked steel (which had not previously proved effective).

Nevertheless, he hoped for the best. Maybe the dragon had been injured in the explosion and would be considerate enough to heave itself forward and die without causing further trouble. Yes, and maybe a fairy queen would swoop down to rescue Cullin and take him to a fine palace on the moon. . . .

Since the area in front of the dragon's lair was already devastated, the exploding casks had simply rearranged the debris. He spotted Sir Morgan's scorched battle hatchet lying on the ground and wondered if that might be a more viable weapon than Dalbry's heavy sword . . . but a sword was more true to form, and he decided to keep up appearances.

Swallowing hard, Cullin swiped the back of his hand across his forehead, smearing the anti-flame cream Affonyl had slathered on him. Once he gathered his nerve, he emerged from the trees and stepped forward in full view of the cave.

By now he was sure the dragon must be tired of all the interruptions, but Cullin did not feel guilty about bothering it yet again. He intended to kill the monster. He didn't need a virgin sacrifice or a tasty mule as bait.

He grasped the sword in both hands, held it straight up, and shouted his challenge, but he was so nervous that his voice came out as a dry squeak. So he cleared his throat and called again. "Dragon, I command you to come out and face me like a man!"

By now the dragon knew what to do, and it stirred deep within the dark cave.

Cullin held his ground, though he felt sweat prickling under the drying fire-protection salve. "Come out and pay for all the blood you have on your claws and fangs!" His voice was husky, and the words were little more than a whisper, not ferocious enough to frighten a giant reptile.

The dragon's eyes blazed bright as it emerged from the shadows with a sound like a cauldron boiling over. The creature was huge, titanic, mammoth, colossal, enormous, gargantuan, and every other adjective used to convey great size.

Cullin braced himself, and the hideous monster lunged toward him.

"Let me tell you a thing about dragons, Maurice," I say. "Something of a natural history lesson." I crack my knuckles, warming up for the climax.

The prince has washed the dishes to Wendria's satisfaction, stacking pie pans on the sideboard. Inside the common room of the Scabby Wench, Reeger finishes rousing and chasing off the last customers, while his wife prepares for the next day's crowd.

The prince turns to me with wide eyes. "You're interrupting the story *now?* I don't want a science lesson! What happened?"

I am pleased to see him finally engrossed in the story. He's even forgotten about the sloppy, unprincely labor he is performing. "It's necessary, so you can put everything in context."

"But . . . but the dragon's attacking! How did you escape?"

"Patience, boy." I am unable to stifle my grin. He is wrapped around my little finger. "There's something you need to know first. Dragons are solitary creatures. Once a dragon has an adequate lair, it rarely comes out of its cave.

"Under normal circumstances, the monster will gorge itself on some cattle, maybe a stray peasant or two, then lie low for a while. Such large reptiles have very sluggish digestive systems. You must have heard stories about giant pythons from the jungles? Once they consume a large meal, they can barely move until they finish digesting it."

"But what does that have to do with the story?" Maurice asks. "The dragon—how did you get away?"

"Now, son, don't get so caught up in the tale that you forget all the careful foreshadowing I've laid. In addition to the normal terrorizing and devouring this particular dragon had done, it had also devoured five full-grown knights, one after another, all in a matter of days. That might have seemed a feast at first, then gluttony . . . then just an unpleasant duty."

Prince Maurice wipes his hands on the apron Wendria loaned him. "Ah, now I think I see."

He grins, and I grin along with him. "But there's still another twist or turn in the story."

The gigantic dragon tried to lunge, but it was so gorged and fat that it could barely move. The monster was nearly catatonic after being harassed, knight after chivalrous knight, when all it wanted to do was sleep off its meal.

The lethargic creature snorted a challenge that sounded more like a groan of complaint than actual fury. Its scales were stretched so tight they squeaked as it walked, and the dragon's belly scraped on the ground.

It was obviously uninterested in devouring yet another knight, but the beast let out a tired growl and prepared to do what it had to do.

Affonyl yelled from the overhang above the cave. "I've got it, Squirrel!" She threw her weight into a branch she had shoved under a large boulder, which the earlier explosions had loosened. With a great heave, she pried the rock free. It toppled over the edge and crashed onto the fat dragon's head, stunning the monster before it could even burp out a small flame toward Cullin.

He stood holding Dalbry's sword in amazement. The dragon collapsed, groaning, in front of him. Affonyl yelled, "What are you waiting for, Squirrel? Hurry, while it's still dazed!"

The dragon snorted greenish black smoke. With a cry of vengeance, he ran forward and swung Sir Dalbry's sword with all his might down on the dragon's scaly neck. "For Sir Hernon!" He struck again, chipping several scales. "For Sir Morgan!" Another blow knocked a few scales loose. "For Sir Artimo!" At last, his blade struck sensitive flesh, and the dazed dragon flinched. But Cullin focused on his gradual slaying of the monster. "For Sir Jems!" His arms and wrists ached from the repeated blows. "For Sir Tremayne!"

"Not so much for Sir Tremayne," Affonyl called down.

The dragon had begun to recover enough to snort and lift its head. When it turned toward Cullin, his heart nearly stopped. But he had to finish the job, so he backed up, closed his eyes, and charged forward, sword pointed straight ahead. He thrust the blade in all the way to the hilt in the exposed flesh where he had laboriously dislodged the scales.

Too fat to retreat into the cave in its death throes, the dragon shuddered outside the lair and collapsed.

"Now you're a real dragon slayer." Affonyl sprang down from the rocks and bounded across the bones, gravel, and cinders in front of the lair. "Aren't you supposed to cut off its head?"

"I think so, but I might need some help." With Sir Dalbry's unwieldy sword, he struck a mighty blow against the dragon's neck, but did little damage. This was going to be harder work than he had expected.

Affonyl retrieved Sir Morgan's battle hatchet and joined him in the task. "We'll take turns and get this done, but I'll let you have all the official recognition when you tell Queen Faria."

Dazed and disbelieving, Cullin stood over the fallen monster. "But you and I did this together. Why would you give *me* the credit?"

She snorted. "So you can get that princess you want so much."

CHAPTER FORTY-ONE

BEHEADING THE DEAD dragon was a more arduous task than slaying the beast had been in the first place (not to mention messy and inglorious). Cullin ruined Sir Dalbry's sword by hacking through the scales, the still-smoking meat, and the vertebrae. The obsidian-adorned hilt looked fine, and he supposed the older knight could make up an exaggerated tale to explain the notched, bent blade.

Concerned for their friends, although too injured to do any dragon slaying of their own, Reeger and Dalbry made their way back to the lair, where they were relieved to see the task already done. "Rust, Cullin! You killed that dragon all by yourself."

Affonyl sniffed. "Excuse me? He couldn't have done it without my help."

"She's right." Cullin chuckled. "Affonyl's my new apprentice dragon slayer." Both of them were covered with reptilian blood and several varieties of slime that had oozed out while they took their trophy. Exhausted, Cullin turned to Reeger and the old knight. "We could use some help hauling that dragon head. We're a team, right—all in this together?"

With an unconvincing apologetic expression, Reeger lifted his splinted arm in its sling. "Sorry, my arm is broken, but I'll help by keeping a careful watch for other dragons in the vicinity."

"A wise precaution," said Dalbry. "No telling how many of those monsters are at large. As for me helping—this is your triumph, young Cullin. I wouldn't feel right taking any part of the experience from you."

Reeger did return to camp to retrieve Pony and the still indignant mule. Stubborn but not stupid, the mule realized that it was being led back toward the dragon's lair, and it did not wish to repeat the previous ordeal. Its eyes went wide and wild, and froth formed at its mouth. But when it saw the beheaded dragon, it decided it had no objection to the changed situation, and placidly snuffled at the ground in search of fresh weeds.

Bringing the reluctant mule had left Reeger spent. He looked gray and ill as the ache of his broken arm got stronger again. "Crotchrust! I hope you have more of that pain medicine, Affonyl."

"I'll need to make a new batch. I have more purified guano and bone dust," she said, "but not much milk of the poppy."

Reeger winced as he tried to shrug his cockeyed shoulders. "That'll be fine. It's probably not an active ingredient anyway."

The dragon's head lay with its eyes closed and its black forked tongue lolling out. Even dead, it looked fearsome. The head was as large as Pony.

Dalbry looked at Cullin with paternal pride. "You are now a true dragon slayer—which is more than I can say for myself. You have the monster's head to prove your victory, and it's not a stuffed crocodile head either." The young man felt a warm flush of pride come to his cheeks.

Affonyl added, "This is it, Squirrel—what you always wanted." But her voice had an edge of disappointment. She turned away from him, looking incomprehensibly stung.

Cullin was disappointed that she couldn't feel triumphant for him. "Of course, it's what I wanted, and minstrels will sing about me. It might be one of Nightingale Bob's greatest hits. Aren't you happy for me?"

Affonyl sniffed. "I am. Totally delighted."

Cullin looked at her: blond hair hacked short and sticking out in all directions, dried dragon blood smearing her face and clothes. She was a far cry from the gorgeous princess who had so flirtatiously ignored him in King Norrimun's court. She was also a far cry from Princess Minima, who wasn't exactly drab, but not what Cullin was looking for. Nevertheless, Minima was the princess he had won.

Confused by Affonyl's attitude, he took ropes from Pony's saddle and fashioned a makeshift harness, tying cords around the dragon's pointed ears, looping the fearsome horns, securing another rope around its formerly ferocious jaws. He cinched the knots tight, tugging on the cords to make sure they were secure.

He looked up at Dalbry and Reeger, who were both burned and scruffy. Even though neither one was remotely presentable at Queen Faria's court, Cullin didn't want to go alone. "Will you accompany me? We can get our story straight by the time we reach the palace."

Dalbry shook his head. "No, Cullin, this is your victory and, as we have oft repeated, we can't split a princess. You'll be settling down now. The palace, the queendom, and Princess Minima—all yours. Henceforth, that will be your lot in life, the dragon-slayer knight and the beautiful princess he claimed as his prize." The old knight nodded to himself. "Nightingale Bob should be able to work with that."

Reeger picked at his teeth. "Since you'll have all the riches of a queendom, you won't really need the chest of treasure the queen promised. You could share that with your old comrades, cover some of our expenses. Meanwhile, we'll sell those spare horses, and the tack, see if we can find collectors for the genuine knight memorabilia we don't need. That should give us enough spending money to make it to Outer Innermiddle."

"Is . . . is that where you're going next?"

Dalbry said, "I've always wanted to see Outer Innermiddle. But one place is as good as another. You know how it is. We're just drawing out the dragon business."

Cullin felt a lump in his throat as he realized how much his life was going to change. As a feral orphaned boy growing up outside a village best known for its killer bees and the honey they made, he'd never dreamed he would marry a princess and rule an entire land (or at least co-rule, depending on how much involvement Princess Minima wanted). A lump formed in his throat.

Dalbry clapped him on the shoulder. "We have enjoyed your company over the years, Cullin. You've been a useful part of our business. I'll miss having a good squire to accompany me into court and brag about my deeds. Fortunately, we now have Affonyl, so we'll get by just fine."

Reeger chuckled. "We'll concoct some good stories for her, too. That girl's got talent."

"And imagination," Affonyl added. "And experience in alchemy, natural sciences, medicine." She frowned again, glanced at Cullin, then away. "I doubt we'll miss you at all, Squirrel."

Now that Cullin thought about it, he wasn't sure he wanted to settle down. The theoretical goal of killing the dragon, winning the treasure and the princess, had seemed so far-fetched that he hadn't thought it through. Now he was stuck.

"Maybe we could just leave the dragon's head here," he said. "Send a note to Queen Faria informing her that the menace has been taken care of, but that no reward is necessary. We could say that as dragon slayers we've been intending to take on more pro bono cases."

Dalbry crossed his arms over his chest. "That would not be the honorable course, Cullin. All those other knights died trying to win what you want to throw away. You qualify as a knight in your own right now. You must accept both the pedestal and the shackles of honor."

Affonyl took the ropes that formed a makeshift harness for the dragon's head, tied them to the mule's saddle, and gave the knot a hard yank. "Ready to go."

"What about you, Affonyl?" Cullin said. "Maybe you could come along and—"

"No, I'll go back to camp, and tend to my two patients. Reeger and Dalbry are seriously injured and need time to heal. But brave Sir Squirrel emerged without a scratch." She made it sound like an accusation.

Cullin climbed onto Pony's saddle and took the mule's leading rope. Reeger said, "Once the mule gets up some speed, it'll be able to drag that monster's head through the underbrush."

Dalbry added, "Better go straight to the castle now. Don't dawdle."

"Yes," Affonyl said, "go claim your treasure and your princess." She made no further sound, but her sniff of displeasure was implied. She turned back to her two new comrades as Cullin rode into the forest, dragging and bouncing the giant reptilian head behind him.

CHAPTER FORTY-TWO

When Cullin reached the court of Queen Faria, he saw that for once the minstrels were not exaggerating. Being a hero was magnificent. Riding proudly through the streets on Pony and leading the mule, he cut a dashing figure.

Too late, Cullin realized that he really should have taken one of the white stallions left posthumously to their band. That would have been more in line with the expected image. A pony might be appropriate for an apprentice dragon slayer, but a victorious knight deserved a full-fledged horse. But Cullin made do. He liked Pony, and when he rode the small beast, his own stature was increased, relatively speaking.

The mule plodded along, dragging the monster's head behind it. On their way through the countryside, a rope in the makeshift harness had snapped, and Cullin made quick repairs before anyone saw him in town.

The dragon's iridescent blue-green scales protected the trophy from the relentless bouncing, bashing, and battering, but even so, by the time he arrived in town the ferocious monster looked well pummeled, and several of its fangs had been knocked out. Cullin explained the wear and tear by claiming that he had given the monster a good beating during the slaying process.

As he rode down the paved streets toward Queen Faria's terraced and well-decorated castle, awed crowds came out to cheer and laugh and applaud the brave knight. Children danced in the streets, singing "Ding-dong, the dragon's dead!" Unfortunately, none of them could remember Cullin's name offhand, since on his previous visit, he had been overshadowed by the more impressive knights in Sir Tremayne's chivalrous consortium.

Cullin sat erect in the saddle, keeping his gaze on Queen Faria's palace. Pony snorted and also lifted his head high, although the mule maintained a sedate pace as if wondering what all the fuss was about, and then wondering when someone would get rid of this bothersome reptilian burden that it had been dragging along for miles.

Carrying lavender pennants, the queen's guard rode down from the gates on matching chestnut horses. They offered their services as escort, which impressed Cullin, as he had never before used an escort service. The people continued to cheer, and colorful flags were raised from the castle towers.

One of the guards leaned close and whispered, "What was your name again, so the criers can make a proper announcement when we get to the castle? Queen Faria wants to welcome her most impressive and dear friend by name." After Cullin answered, the guard broke away from the group, wheeled his mount, and trotted back to the gates.

A persistent monk scurried alongside Pony and the mule. Holding a quill pen and a torn section of scroll, he asked Cullin a succession of questions about the time and date of the dragon's demise, the full names of the other knights who had died, the complete scoop on what had happened. "It's for the queendom's newspaper. My fellow monks will transcribe it and put out an Extra edition. This is real stop-the-presses stuff! We'll have it distributed within the month. Now, is that Cullin spelled with one or two els?"

"Before I give interviews, I feel obligated to inform Queen Faria first. Sorry."

Cullin hoped the dowager queen wasn't too overwhelmed; if the old woman collapsed from heart failure, that would put Princess Minima on the throne too soon, and the princess might not consider herself bound by the previous agreement for treasure and matrimony.

On the other hand, maybe that would be for the best. Cullin still felt conflicted, even depressed about the whole settling-down-in-a-castle situation. But he was obligated. The Knight's Manual was clear about what he had to do.

Pets and horses were not allowed inside the palace except for service animals, and Cullin's arrival caused some consternation: he obviously had to deliver the enormous dragon's head to Queen Faria's throne, but the large scaly trophy required a mule to drag it. After a quick discussion, the queendom's protocol ministers wrote up a temporary exemption for the mule.

Pony, though, had to remain tied up outside. Cullin dismounted and gave his trusty half-sized steed a consoling pat. Pony's obvious disappointment changed to contented acceptance when handlers gave him a trough of sparkling spring water and a bucket of oats to snack on. The mule gave Pony a look of sheer envy as the escort service guided them into the queen's court.

The sergeant at arms bellowed at the top of his voice, "Brave Sir Cullin, dragon slayer!" Although he was standing right next to the throne, the sergeant at arms had to yell because the ancient queen was hard of hearing.

By now, the severed end of the dead dragon's neck had stopped leaking, but it still left an ugly zigzag smear across the marble tiles. Cullin shuddered to think what King Ashtok would have done upon seeing such a mark on his coveted parquet floor. A guard cut the makeshift rope harness so the dragon head could be deposited in place.

Old Faria's vulture-like eyes were bright, and she grinned so broadly that a full teaspoon of white facial powder was displaced from her cheek wrinkles to fall like dandruff on the front of her dress. Her enthusiastic applause dislodged more white powder.

Cullin bowed. "As you can see, Majesty, your dragon is slain, and I've come to claim my reward."

To add its commentary, probably referring to the part where it had been tied to a tree as dragon bait, the mule defecated on the throne room floor. This caused a flurry of dismay among the protocol officers, who sent for a scribe to draw up an order revoking the exemption that had granted this specific mule a one-day pass into Queen Faria's throne room. Handlers shooed the mule out, while the queen's court pooper-scooper took care of the mess.

The dowager queen leaned forward, squinting. "I am surprised to see you, Sir Cullin. Were you not just a squire when you visited us last?"

"I was, Majesty, but I've since earned an honorary knighthood. Of our consortium of chivalrous knights, only I remain."

"Oh, dear." The dowager queen fluttered her hands in front of her face. "Whatever happened to brave Sir Tremayne?"

"Dead, Majesty. Devoured by the fire-breathing dragon."

"And brave Sir Morgan? He was quite handsome."

"Likewise dead, Majesty. Devoured by the dragon."

"And Sir Artimo, with his strangely effeminate sword?"

"Dragon food as well."

"I see a trend here." She folded her gnarled hands on the quilt that covered her lap. "But those are just peripheral story lines, I suppose. You are obviously the main character in this tale—sometimes it's difficult to tell." She heaved a deep breath. "Regardless, my queendom is saved. Hooray!"

She clapped her hands in command rather than applause. "Bring forth the designated treasure chest." The dowager queen adjusted the quilt. "And bring forth the lovely Princess Minima. We've got a wedding to plan."

Two royal assistants staggered in with a wooden chest, which they set next to the dragon head. They opened the lid to display a mound of sparkling gold coins and an assortment of precious gems.

Next, Princess Minima entered, carrying a hoop with stretched white fabric on which she was painstakingly embroidering a tangled pattern. Cullin recognized one of Princess Affonyl's modern abstract designs, which were sweeping the land. Since Affonyl had never signed her work, the patterns were attributed to "the artist formerly known as Princess."

"Sorry to interrupt you at your embroidery, my dear, but I thought you'd like to meet your husband-to-be," said the queen. "It's all been arranged."

Minima looked at Cullin as if she were assessing a cow in the marketplace, deciding whether or not to purchase it. She studied the dragon head, then the chest of treasure, then Cullin. "Of all those knights, you're not the one I expected. You're adequate, I suppose. Certainly better than some of the matches my mother has proposed over the past year."

"It was the luck of the draw, Princess. And I am proud to be your betrothed." He bowed.

The queen gave another commanding clap of her hands, and royal helpers came forward to slam shut the chest of treasure. "Since you're going to be my daughter's husband, we'll hold this gold here for safekeeping." She raised her eyes expectantly. "Now, young man, suitors after the hand of Princess Minima generally offer a special gift to woo her. What did you bring to show her your undying love?"

Cullin's mind raced. "But . . . I brought the head of the foul dragon terrorizing your queendom. Isn't that enough?"

Queen Faria gave a dismissive gesture with her hand. "Dear boy, don't be silly. Killing the dragon was a gift to *me*. And while it's always wise to stay in the good graces of your mother-in-law, you should be thinking of your own wife-to-be."

Cullin felt dizzy. He was just a poor imitation squire who now claimed to be an honorary knight. The few coins he had been saving for passage to the New Lands would barely buy Princess Minima a cup of gourmet coffee. Even the finest imported beans wouldn't be enough to get him out of this fix.

Then he remembered. He struggled to hide his relieved grin as he gave a deep respectful bow. "Of course, Majesty." He dug into the pouch at his belt and withdrew three small, hard objects. "These are *magic beans*, unlike any you've ever beheld, reputed to have powerful protective properties. Of all the brave knights who tried their hand at slaying the dragon, only I survived—in no small part because of these beans."

He held out his palm, and the queen gestured for her chamberlain to take the three beans. The man touched them as if they were precious diamonds before presenting them to Queen Faria, who then gave them to her daughter.

Princess Minima inspected the beans. "We could have them set into a wedding ring."

Beans. Cullin gave another smile. "I can think of no more appropriate way to symbolize our marriage."

Prince Maurice helps Wendria prepare pie pans for the next day's baking. The Scabby Wench's Sunday brunch is known throughout the kingdom and gets very good reviews.

By now it's late, and we are ready to go back to the castle. The prince's mother will already be worried about him, afraid that I'll undo all of her careful mothering. Given my own questionable background, the queen believes I will lead our son down a path of juvenile delinquency. I'm not convinced that spending a year abroad being raised as a feral child among a pack of wolves would be altogether bad for Maurice. He needs toughening up, but I'll never convince my dear wife of the idea. Nobody is that good of a con man.

Maurice removes his apron and hangs it on a peg. He has been enthralled with my tale at times, but now looks disappointed again. "I expected something a little more romantic—fireworks, maybe, or love at first sight? You're talking about my heritage here, Father."

Wendria puts a stack of dishes away. "Life is full of disillusionment, young man. Those silly romantic stories are a con job foisted on people by minstrels. Reeger here thought he'd have a glamorous life as a tavern owner."

Reeger has been dozing in a chair, bored by my story since he's heard many variations of it over the years. Now he stirs. "And a beautiful wife." Wendria shoots him a sharp glance, and he quickly adds, "I came close enough, though."

"Don't give up hope yet," I tell the prince. "I'm not quite finished with the tale."

CHAPTER FORTY-THREE

PREPARATIONS FOR THE wedding of Sir Cullin and Princess Minima proceeded with as much spectacle, regimentation, and expense as the queendom's last war. The happy couple were feted with feasts, jousting tournaments, juggling performances, acrobatics, even puppet shows, which the dowager queen enjoyed more than anyone else.

Cullin sat beside the princess while she smiled at the crowds and waved. Minima moved her hand in a well-practiced gesture that showed just the right mix of fondness for the people and the haughtiness of nobility.

A protocol minister spent an hour working with Cullin on how to wave properly. Again and again, the young man raised his hand, while the minister held his wrist and directed him to move it from side to side in a languid gesture. Despite the vigorous training, Cullin had a difficult time getting the hang of it, and the protocol minister grew exasperated. "Come on, Sir—you're to be a *prince*. Show the public you really mean it!" Cullin practiced and practiced waving, trying to get just the right amount of suppleness in his wrist.

Whenever Princess Minima sat beside Cullin during court functions, she treated him like a piece of furniture. Each time he tried to strike up a conversation, Minima rolled her eyes or glanced at him with disapproval and then looked away again. This was far different from the flirtatious way Affonyl had ignored him during the feast of St. Bartimund. "You have much to learn about courtly manners, Sir Cullin. It is inappropriate for a man and his fiancée to speak to each other."

He was crestfallen, but tried to hide it. "I just wanted to get acquainted with the princess I'm about to marry. I hardly know you. With all these spectacular wedding preparations, we don't have time to talk." He gave her a hopeful smile. "Still, I suppose we'll have many years of wedded bliss to catch up on conversation."

Minima eyed him with continued displeasure. "Why ever would a husband and wife want to do that?"

Done with talking, she folded her hands in her lap and turned to watch the continued escapades of the royal pie-throwing contest, which Queen Faria had staged in celebration of the wedding. The best pastry bakers in the queendom displayed their prowess by destroying one another's wares. The entertainment was unlike anything Cullin had ever seen.

Meanwhile, Queen Faria had assigned the best taxidermist in the queendom to stuff, preserve, restore, and polish the dragon head. The royal taxidermist mounted two red glass spheres in the eye sockets, then painted them with an evil-looking reptilian slit. Replacement fangs for the missing teeth came from a dead Saint Bernard, a beloved old family pet. The canine teeth didn't match the dragon's missing fangs in either size or shape, but they were the best the taxidermist could do, unless Sir Cullin felt like killing a second dragon for spare parts. Cullin declined. The taxidermist folded the scaly lips down over the affected area and hoped no one would notice.

As the days went by, Cullin began to have more doubts. When he'd first glimpsed Affonyl in King Norrimun's court, he had been smitten with her, and even after she discarded her royal trappings, the attraction remained undiminished. Affonyl was the standard by which he judged all princesses, and Cullin was sorry to admit that Minima fell far short of the mark.

Still, caught up in the constant and exhausting wedding preparations, Cullin tried to put those regrets aside, but his heart weighed heavy within him. It wasn't because of some puppy-love mooning for Affonyl, nor was it merely that he saw how lacking Princess Minima was in conversation, sense of humor, common interests with him, and other regards. He also missed his footloose life on the road, seeing the world, going from kingdom to kingdom. He missed his friends.

At court, he often thought of all the lessons Dalbry had taught him. He regretted that the old knight now had only an unadorned practice sword, because Cullin had brought the damaged fancier blade to bolster his dragon-slaying story (it wasn't seemly for a knight to kill a bloodthirsty monster with what amounted to little more than a toy sword). He should have seen to it that Dalbry got a new sword for his trouble.

And Reeger . . . rust! The man had a broken arm. How was he supposed to harvest graves for usable skeletal components? Cullin supposed Affonyl was their helper now, but he couldn't let the girl do all of his former duties. No matter how she dressed now, Affonyl was still a former princess, with all the inherent delicateness that implied.

For his own part, Cullin didn't know anything about being a

prince. It was all he could do to pretend to be a squire, and then an honorary knight. Now that he had an insider's glimpse of what the real job of a prince entailed, he couldn't rely on what he had heard in stories. He studied how Queen Faria went through her days and met her responsibilities. It came as a shock to Cullin when he realized that the old dowager didn't even *like* ruling the queendom—and Princess Minima wasn't looking forward to taking her place either.

And what did that mean for him? He was only prince by proxy and under somewhat false pretenses. . . .

On the night before the gala wedding celebration, when the church bells rang so loudly and so constantly that no one in the queendom would be able to sleep, Cullin went to the royal stables. He wanted to spend time with Pony and the mule, his only remaining links with his fond past.

While the squire/knight/prince felt restless with his new situation, the two animals were quite content to have a comfortable stable, straw to lie in, and all the oats they could eat. "At least somebody's happy," Cullin said. The mule snorted.

He barely had ten minutes of peace before a court pageboy found him in the stables. The boy looked flushed and flustered, as if he feared a spanking. "Queen Faria sent all of us to find you, Sir Cullin! You must come back to court for the rehearsal."

"Another rehearsal? We've already done thirteen."

"Yes, sir, but thirteen is an unlucky number, so the queen wants to do it again just to be sure. And the protocol minister has scheduled another hour with you to practice your wave."

With a groan, Cullin patted Pony's head. "Stay here and be content, my friend. Some of us have duties to do."

The relieved pageboy said, "I have an entire written list of what's expected of you this evening. Would you like to see it?"

"Not really."

The page was taken aback. "I can read it aloud to you then."

"No, I'd just like a quiet walk back to the castle."

The boy didn't know what to do. He couldn't resist chattering. "I'm entitled to extra dessert tonight because I found you. All the other pages will have to go to bed without supper." He grinned. "I'm going to get a plum pudding—with a cherry on top."

"I've heard that's delicious."

Back at the castle, they went through the wedding rehearsal twice more for good measure. Princess Minima said her lines to perfection, batted her eyes, and smiled as a princess was supposed to, but her smiles were not directed toward Cullin. He worked hard not to fumble his lines. He wanted his performance to be perfect, because he didn't wish to endure another rehearsal.

After another hour of successful hand-waving practice in the conservatory, Cullin retired to his room for a good night's rest before the wedding day. He wished Reeger, Dalbry, and even Affonyl could attend the ceremony, for moral support if nothing else. But by now he was sure they had moved on to Outer Innermiddle, or wherever the roads had taken them.

When he entered his chambers, he was startled to find the royal tailor standing there with bolts of stiff but colorful fabric, paper patterns, stickpins, measuring tape, and scissors. "There you are, Prince! Hurry, we have a dozen outfits to try on. I'll be doing alterations all night."

Cullin allowed himself to be stripped of the already formal clothes he wore around court. He had considered them fancy enough to get married in, but the dowager queen would not hear of it.

In a wardrobe in the corner of his private bachelor suite he kept his old patched dragon-business clothes, laundered to remove the stains of reptilian blood. But they had only sentimental value now. Princess Minima and her mother would never let him be seen around court in those old rags.

Wearing his perpetual frown, the tailor tugged a doublet onto him and stepped back to inspect it. Then he had Cullin pull on a pair of tight lavender hose, offering his assistance and fumbling with the fabric around Cullin's thighs, though the young man did not need or want the help.

"It's a little tight." Cullin adjusted the waistband and fiddled with the doublet's hem. The garment rubbed under his arms, and the collar felt confining around his neck.

"A little tight?" the tailor said. "I'll make adjustments then. It must be *extremely* tight, or I'll lose my reputation."

"Then I'd barely be able to walk," Cullin said.

"That's the point. You must sit straight and rigid, the better to look regal. Once I have your measurements, I can make an entire wardrobe of fine-looking and extremely uncomfortable clothes. You'll wear them every single day."

"Why would I want to wear uncomfortable clothes?"

"Because that is the fashion, my good sir knight. The more uncomfortable, the better. Enduring unpleasantness is a sign of regal character."

Cullin didn't think he was going to like this—not one bit. The royal tailor grunted with the effort as he cinched the waistband tight. Cullin lost his breath. "Good, that's the way to do it! Exhale deeply, so I can tighten it further."

Black spots of suffocation hovered in front of his eyes before the tailor let go of the measuring tape. Muttering to himself, he used a lead pencil to jot down numbers. "I have all I need to complete the final alterations. You'll look so fine, I guarantee the princess will have no further regrets about marrying you."

"That's just what I wanted to hear," Cullin said.

The tailor left in a flurry of threads and fabric, leaving Cullin blessedly alone at last. But his thoughts continued to whirl.

He liked being with his friends. He enjoyed traveling and camping. If he stayed here—princess, castle, and all—he would never have a chance to see the New Lands. Even though he was legitimate now, a true dragon slayer, was a brave knight expected to retire after only one impressive victory? That didn't seem right.

After he married his princess, every day would be like this. Circumstances confined and suffocated him even more than the uncomfortable clothes did. The tailor was the last straw, but Cullin had been collecting straws for a long time, reason after reason why he should change his mind.

He waited until late at night when the castle was asleep (despite the ringing of too many church bells). He changed out of his stiff everyday court clothing, which the queen and the courtiers considered casual wear, and put on his old clothes again. Comfortable and familiar clothes. He closed his eyes and drew a long, wistful breath.

He had slain the dragon and earned his reward, but since the dowager queen kept the chest of gold and gems locked in the treasury for safekeeping, he would never be able to sneak it away. He would have to leave it here. Without regret, he decided to leave Princess Minima behind for safekeeping, too.

Cullin felt a pang of guilt at having to ruin the extensive and expensive wedding plans, but he realized that the dowager queen was more excited about the planning and the pageantry than she was about having a real son-in-law. Sooner or later, Queen Faria would find someone else to be her daughter's husband. This way, she would get to enjoy the wedding preparations all over again.

Taking one last look around his room, not regretting a bit what he was leaving behind, Cullin rigged a rope and swung himself out the window of the tower room. He dropped down into the courtyard and sprinted away into the darkness, leaving the queendom and his princess behind.

Prince Maurice is shocked when I end the story. "Now wait a minute—that's not how it's supposed to be!"

After we leave the Scabby Wench, I keep trying to hurry him through the streets back home. I nudge him to keep up the pace as I talk. It is long past midnight, and the streets are empty, the whole town sleeping—as we should be by now. We're both going to catch it from the queen for staying out so late.

I give him an innocent look. "What do you mean? That's how it really happened."

"I thought you were telling me how you married Mother and got your kingdom!"

"I didn't say that—you just assumed. It was artful misdirection, the type of thing we learned how to do in the dragon business. I never claimed I married *that* particular princess, or that my kingdom once belonged to Queen Faria. You really should know your own mother's name, and a bit more about your family history."

As we walk through the chilly night air, we pull our black burlap cloaks tighter. We no longer need the disguise, just the warmth. "That wasn't the end of our adventures, you know."

Maurice follows me, deep in thought. During his days in the castle, he spends far too much time reading poetry about fairy princes, but tonight I engaged his attention with my tales. I consider that progress.

"But I feel dissatisfied," he finally says. "The story's not finished."

"It seemed like a good stopping point."

"But did you find your friends? At least tell me that part."

"Ah, you mean the epilogue? Of course. Just let me catch my breath as we go up the steep path to the castle."

Fortunately, Cullin knew that his friends intended to make their way to Outer Innermiddle. During the days of tedious wedding preparations, he had studied charts of the queendom and the surrounding lands, so he knew the general direction Dalbry, Reeger, and Affonyl would be heading.

Now, Cullin crept through the darkness toward the royal stables. A sign that hung on the door said "Closed. Will Return at—" A flat clock face had the hands pointing down toward "Dawn."

He had no trouble jimmying open the lock and slipping inside. Pony saw him and nickered a greeting. The mule saw him and snorted, unimpressed. Both animals endured Cullin's efforts to saddle them up and prepare them for a journey.

The mule let out a low groan, as if it had not expected this life of luxury to last long, while Pony seemed willing to be off to further adventures. Maybe being kept in the pampered stables had made him afraid that another kindly family with far too many rambunctious children would adopt him. Given the choices, Pony would much rather be on the road with a group of faux dragon slayers.

Cullin led the two mounts out of the stables and closed the door behind him. Then he rode away from the palace through the city's darkened streets and off along the Queen's Superhighway. Before dawn, he left the queendom behind, though he never saw any painted boundary lines across the landscape.

Now that he was back in his familiar traveling clothes, no one would recognize him as the dashing knight who had been betrothed to Princess Minima; few people would confuse him with a real dragon slayer at first glance.

Cullin traveled from town to town, stopping at inns and keeping his ears open for rumors. On the third night away, news about the missing prince-to-be caught up with his travels. The story was that a dragon had broken into Cullin's tower chambers and stolen him away. He smiled.

Then, when he began to hear stories about alleged dragon depredations, he knew he was getting closer. The next night, he entered a cozy inn with a broad hearth, the smell of baking bread, the sounds of intent conversation.

He heard Reeger's distinctive voice rise above the din. "It's true, I tell you! Jaws wide enough to swallow a cow whole, neck like a serpent, green scales like armor." He lifted his splinted arm. "I barely got out alive."

Unable to contain his excitement, Cullin burst in. "He speaks the truth! I saw it with my own eyes—the monster breathed fire, destroyed an entire peasant village. All that remained were ashes and bones." He sniffed. "And a little rag doll."

Reeger's grin was so broad that Cullin saw several more brown teeth he'd never noted before. From another table, he heard a delighted cry and found Affonyl rushing toward him. She wore a drab peasant girl's dress now, and her hair was starting to grow longer. Cullin thought she still looked beautiful.

"You're safe, Squirrel! We thought you were married by now." The girl flung her arms around him and, in order to be gentlemanly, Cullin had no choice but to embrace her as well. It was a requirement of chivalrous behavior. He picked her up and swung her around. "Yes, I escaped, but I was almost devoured by . . . my circumstances." He smiled at her. "Now I'm back."

Sir Dalbry, wearing his reptilian cape, rose to his feet at a table of his own. "That dragon has caused enough pain and death. Someone has to slay it."

The people at the inn murmured uneasily, turning gazes filled with hope and worry toward the knight. Cullin raised his voice, "We're lucky to have brave Sir Dalbry, renowned dragon slayer, right here in this village."

"You're Sir Dalbry—like the one in the song?" said a tavern wench, almost dropping the tankards of ale she carried.

"Yes, that would be me, ma'am."

"He will save us all," Affonyl added.

Obviously overjoyed but trying to hide it, Dalbry went over to Cullin, slipped his arm around the young man's shoulders, and gave him a brief, paternal hug. "We'll all go together, lad." He looked around at the customers and the obviously frightened innkeeper. "Tomorrow, we will offer our dragon-slaying services at the castle."

The innkeeper poured them each a tankard of ale on the house. "Do you have experience slaying dragons, then?"

Cullin lifted his tankard and clanked it against Dalbry's, Reeger's, and Affonyl's in a toast. "Absolutely," he said. "And we've never had a disappointed customer."

As we approach the castle gates, I clap a hand on my son's shoulders. "We caused a lot more trouble, had more fun—and satisfaction—before I was forced to . . . er, I mean, *decided to* settle down. In these parts there are as many princesses as there are dragons."

"But why didn't you just skip to the end if you were trying to explain what happened?"

I chuckle. "Because if I told you everything, I would never get you to come with me to the Scabby Wench again. I've still got plenty of tales to entertain you for many more happy visits."

I enjoyed this special evening with my boy, and I can count on doing it again and again. There needs to be a father/son bond, but it doesn't happen automatically. Later on, if we are still enjoying ourselves as I near the end of my real adventures, well, I can always make up more.

"If we go to the tavern again," Maurice suggests, "do I have to wash dishes?"

"Depends on how much of a story you want." I feel warmth in my chest, pleased by his reaction. "I could help with some of the pots, I suppose. Reeger's made me do far worse."

We cross the moat and head through the gates of my castle—*King Cullin's* castle in *King Cullin's* kingdom, won by a little bit of prowess as a dragon slayer, a little bit of luck, and a lot of fast talking and sleight of hand.

Prince Maurice stares up at the impressive stone structure with a new interest in his eyes, as if he sees something he's never noticed before. I am pleased—this is what I had hoped for. It's a good start. He might turn out to be a decent king after all, and I won't have to worry about him being scammed by some clever rogue . . . like me.

Spotting a single candle burning bright in one of the windows, I point it out to the prince. He smiles. The queen has left a light on for us.

ABOUT THE AUTHOR

Photo by Author Services Inc. 2010

KEVIN J. ANDERSON is the author of 120 books, fifty-one of which appeared on bestseller lists; he has twenty-three million copies in print in thirty languages. Kevin recently launched a hilarious new series featuring Dan Shamble, Zombie PI. He also coauthored thirteen *Dune* novels with Brian Herbert, as well as their original Hellhole trilogy. He followed his epic Saga of Seven Suns series with his Terra Incognita fantasy trilogy, and wrote the novel *Clockwork Angels* based on the new Rush album. In addition to numerous *Star Wars* projects, he wrote three *X-Files* novels and collaborated with Dean Koontz on *Frankenstein: Prodigal Son*. He is the publisher of WordFire Press.

THIS BOOK WAS originally released in Episodes as a Kindle Serial. Kindle Serials launched in 2012 as a new way to experience serialized books. Kindle Serials allow readers to enjoy the story as the author creates it, purchasing once and receiving all existing Episodes immediately, followed by future Episodes as they are published. To find out more about Kindle Serials and to see the current selection of Serials titles, visit www.amazon.com/kindleserials.